EverFall

Joe Hart

ISBN:0615812155
ISBN-13:9780615812151

EVERFALL

DEDICATION

For my family—I would go anywhere to find you.

.

SPECIAL THANKS

I just want to say thanks to a few people who helped make this one possible. First off, my editor, Neal Hock. Thanks for helping me become better at the craft; your insights and suggestions make a world of difference and I can't tell you how much I appreciate it. My interior artist, Wil Lee. Your drawings helped EverFall come to life, their depth and insight to the story is phenomenal. My wife, you are the world to me and you always make sure I have time to write—for this I am forever grateful. And you, Reader. You brighten my day to no end just by giving my words some of your time—I thank you.

CHAPTER ONE

THE STORM

The night my family was taken from me I'd had too much to drink. Storms did that to me. For as long as I could remember, clouds, thunder, lightning—any of them started the feeling inside. The itching feeling of something with too many legs crawling, first, in the base of my stomach, and then up into my chest, where it sat and prodded my heart into a staccato rhythm. I'd start sweating and shaking, and before I knew it, I'd reach for a bottle. It was worse when I was younger and wasn't allowed to partake in liquid courage. I'd huddle in my room until the storm passed, after which I felt like I'd just escaped something that had been looking for me, hunting me. My parents did what they could, assuring me it was an entirely normal fear that many people dealt with, but hearing that others go through the same thing as you do doesn't make it any better. When they couldn't calm me and my terrors got worse, they took me to a therapist who talked in a quiet voice and asked me so many questions I found it hard to follow where he was going half the time. I guess my parents thought the therapy helped, since I was always fairly relaxed when I came out of that little room with two chairs and a single fountain between them, the water trickling over a few rocks and never failing to make you want to pee. Problem was, there were never any storms raging overhead when I went to see the good doctor. It's easier to talk about something you're afraid of when it's not there staring you in the face.

So the years went on like that. I'd get up every morning and check the weather for the day. I came to know which weathermen knew their stuff and which were just shooting from the hip. Some days, when I knew a storm was imminent, I'd sneak back home after heading off to school and sit in the basement of our house, the quietest part I could find, and just wait it out. The muffled rumbles and strobes of the lightning still reached me there, but it wasn't near as bad as having a panic attack in the middle of a history lesson with thirty other sets of eyes on you. No, for a fifteen-year-old kid there isn't much worse than that.

I found out that drinking helped when I was a senior in high school. My best friend, Bobby Anderson, snuck me a half-empty bottle of Malibu in the empty locker hall between fifth and sixth hours.

"Dad won't notice it's gone, he hates that shit," Bobby said, pushing the bottle deep into the recesses of my backpack. I was scared to death to try it, having never taken so much as a sip in my life (my parents both grew up in alcoholic homes and were deeply set against anything that resembled recreational drinking). But a storm showed up around two that next morning, and in the flashing light outside my window I spun the cap off the rum and swallowed three mouthfuls before I could taste it. After the burning stopped, I nearly threw up but managed to keep it down long enough for a warmth to spread out from my stomach to my limbs. The thunder came down a few decibels and the lightning didn't make my breath catch like it usually did. I was in love.

The therapist had mentioned sedation only once to my parents, and they'd firmly shut him down on that front. To be perfectly honest, pills scared me too. But I was mature enough to know when I'd found a solution to my problem—if not the best one—and at the tender age of eighteen I began to self-medicate.

I was able to hide the drinking from my parents until I was a junior in college, majoring in conceptual design. They stopped by the little house I rented on the outskirts of my college town for an unannounced visit. They found me passed out beneath the dining-room table, an empty bottle of wine and two beer cans clustered around me like a miniature defensive wall.

This isn't to say I was an alcoholic at that point. I actually didn't even like the feeling of getting too drunk. For the most part I would relegate my self-medication to only when I needed it, which was sometimes three times a week and at others once a month.

Needless to say, my dad had a few choice words that day after they'd roused me from beneath the table. I understood. How could I not? And I nodded along with them once my dad stopped yelling and my mom stopped crying. We sat down on the sofa and had an honest heart-to-heart about the dangers of drinking, and I swore to them that I wouldn't touch a bottle again. I'd go back to counseling for the astraphobia, as it came to be named. It was the first lie I ever told my parents.

I realized over the years that prolonged fear does something to a person. This isn't an excuse, just a truth that I learned in time. It curls you in on yourself like paper in a fire and cuts you off from the rest of the world, which doesn't deal with the lurking terror that never truly leaves. Fear drains life of hope. It only lets you see as far as tomorrow, which might be as bad as or worse than today. It crushes you with arms that wrap you so close, you can't tell someone what normal actually feels like.

So by the time I met my wife, I'd become somewhat depressed and reserved. I'd just started at a company designing brake systems for jet aircraft, and she was a vice president's secretary. I can remember the day I first saw her. I had to go up to the executive offices to present a report for our fail analysis, something I hated to do since it involved enough questions to choke a mule. Jane was at a desk just outside the vice president's office, trying to repair a heel that had come off one of her shoes. Her legs were crossed and she was wearing a modest skirt that had ridden up her thighs as she examined the break in her shoe. I couldn't help but notice she had great legs. I told her this later when we were married, after she'd asked me what was the first thought that went through my head when I saw her. She'd slapped me hard on the shoulder and called me something equivalent to male swine, but I could always see in her eyes that she liked it. I offered to help her fix her shoe, and after some prodding, she let me take it back to the workshop downstairs, where I applied a simple bonding compound on the break. You would have thought I moved the earth an inch.

We married a year later, and nine months after that our daughter was born. We called her Sara, after Jane's grandmother, and when a baby boy followed a short time later, I got the honors and we named him Jack. I always liked the name Jack; it's a good, sturdy name, the name of a detective or a construction worker. Someone tough who wouldn't be bothered by the stresses of the world or phantom fears that came and went without boundaries or concern.

For the first few years of our marriage I tried to keep the fear and the drinking a secret from Jane. I kept a flask of vodka in the back of my sock drawer, tucked behind a divider. She knew I didn't like storms, but I usually retreated to our bedroom when one came and sipped from the flask until everything faded to an acceptable level.

One rainy Saturday afternoon she caught me slumped in the corner of our bathroom, the flask loose in my grip. There was a falling-out. A reckoning, if you will. At first she just asked questions calmly, but by the end both of our voices were raised. It wasn't until Jack knocked politely on the door to our room that we both stopped. She asked me to go to counseling and I refused on the grounds that I'd already tried that for years and it had solved nothing. I wouldn't have some quack tell me I needed a bottle of pills and to come to terms with my fears. But, in truth, I knew why I didn't want to go back. In my own way I'd found how to cope, but it was more than that—it was addiction. To put it in any other terms would be a lie. You can't drink as much as I did for twelve years and not get addicted. I knew that I was because I'd find myself having a drink even when it was sunny or when Jane and the kids were out shopping. I remember rushing to the bathroom more than once to use mouthwash so they wouldn't smell anything but pure, fresh mint on my breath. Addiction is the tiger in the grass. You don't know it's there until you feel the teeth close around your neck.

I half expected Jane to leave, to just take the kids and go, but she didn't. She stayed, and when I explained everything to her about the anxiety and fear that took over whenever there was a storm, she understood. She relented and allowed me to drink when I wanted to and, believe it or not, it angered me that she let me do it. In some insane way I always expected her to give me an ultimatum that would force me to stop, but it never came. So the tiger pounced and locked its jaws in place, and that was how we lived our lives.

I remember the last storm. I'd been tracking it on the weather radar all morning at work. My job as lead design manager dried up along with the company two years before, and we'd moved back to my hometown in the northern part of the state. At the time there was nothing resembling what I really wanted to do, what my degree said I could do, so I settled for a mechanic's position at a small shop on the edge of town. I worked with the smell of grease and oil in my nostrils every day until it felt like the only odor I'd ever known. When I clocked out that particular night, it was almost six and the evening sun was gone, lost behind pallid layers of gray clouds. The trees were beginning to tip like wavering tops in the wind. I drove as fast as I could to our small development and pulled into my spot beside Jane's minivan. A fat raindrop splattered on the windshield as I got out, and I bolted up the steps before any other cold drops could touch my skin. The wind tugged at my shirt and I shivered. It was uncommonly cool for the first week of June, even for Minnesota, where sometimes you had to wear a sweatshirt in July. Our house was a modest one-level identical to three others in our neighborhood, but Jane made it comfortable and our own in the way I think only women can.

I came inside and shut the door against the storm. The smell of cooking beef met me and I inhaled the small comfort it brought. There was the pounding of little feet and then Jack was in my arms, his six-year-old body so warm, it always felt like he had a fever.

"Dad, you're late again!"

"I know, I'm sorry, buddy."

"Are you shivering?" he asked, his little head tilted to one side.

I tried to smile. "Just chilly outside."

"Dad! It's summertime. You can't be cold."

"It's the storm," Sara said as she rounded the corner to the mudroom. Her hair was drawn back beneath a headband, exposing her mother's features. It still stunned me how much she, at only eight, resembled Jane, and I knew she would become as beautiful as her mother before she hit fifteen.

"Hi, kiddo," I said as she came to my side.

"Hi, Dad. It is the storm, right?" she asked, hugging me around the waist.

I nodded. "Yeah, just the storm. I'll feel better when I get settled." I set Jack on his feet and he rushed off to his room, no doubt remembering his Legos desperately needed to be built into something grand. Sara trailed after me into the kitchen, her eyes glancing around the room as if she would find a way to ask the question she held by searching the walls and ceilings.

"What is it, honey?" I asked as I squirted a generous amount of soap into my blackened hands. Sara hopped onto a barstool on the opposite side of the counter and smiled.

"How did you know I wanted to ask something?"

"I can read you like a book."

Again the smile. "Ashley asked me to come to a sleepover tomorrow night at her house, and I wondered if I could ride the bus there."

"Well, let me talk to Mom and we'll see. Are you okay with staying all night at her house?"

"Yeah, Ashley just got an American Girl doll for her birthday and I'm going to bring mine, and we're going to play house."

I chuckled as I attempted to scrub the grime from beneath my fingernails. No matter how many times I washed my hands the dirt never really seemed to go away. "Well, it's fine with me, but I'll check—" My voice was lost in a parade of thunder and I stopped. My heart did a funny flip, as if it were doing a trapeze act in my chest.

"Okay, Daddy?"

I swallowed as the vestiges of thunder rolled across the sky. "Yeah, just fine. Why don't you go play in your room for a few minutes?" Her eyes, the only feature she'd inherited from me, searched my face for a moment, and I wondered when she'd become so much older than her years.

"Okay," she finally said, and disappeared through the archway, into the living room.

I dried my hands and fumbled a glass tumbler from the cabinet. Without bothering for ice, I went to the pantry and pulled the dark bottle of rum from the highest shelf. I filled the glass half full and took two swallows. The burn of the liquid as it first went down was like finding the right key to a lock after searching for hours. Immediately my muscles began to unclench and my breathing deepened. I put the bottle back on the shelf and stepped out of the pantry, almost running into my wife as she rounded the corner.

"Jesus! You scared me," she said, putting a hand against the wall.

"Sorry." I leaned in and kissed her. She smacked her lips and raised her eyebrows when I pulled away.

"Wow, I think I have a buzz now."

I sighed and turned toward the fridge to pull out a bottle of iced tea. My hand shook a little when I registered a flash of lightning through the window above the sink. I topped off the glass and set the bottle of tea on the counter; I'd need it again soon enough.

"How bad is this one supposed to be?" she asked, occupying the stool Sara sat on only minutes before. Thunder grumbled nearby and my gaze shifted to the ceiling involuntarily.

"It looks pretty severe. No tornado warnings out, but I wouldn't be surprised if we got a few later." I saw a crestfallen look ripple through her features and knew what she was thinking. "I'll only have a couple," I said.

She nodded without looking at me, but managed a smile after a few seconds. "There's burgers still warm in the pan."

"Sounds great. I'm going to shower first," I said, heading for the door to our room. Before the shower got hot, my drink was gone. The storm was quieter in the bathroom and the streams of scalding water helped iron my nerves a little.

By the time I changed into a pair of sweatpants and a T-shirt, I felt almost normal. I heard my son singing a theme song to a cartoon in his room, although I couldn't place which one it was. Jane was folding laundry in the living room, and I tried to make as little noise as possible while I poured my second drink of the night.

"Sara wants to stay at Ashley's tomorrow for a sleepover," I said as I leaned against the archway.

"What did you tell her?" Jane asked.

"That I'd check with the emperor of the house before I gave her my blessing."

She shot me mocking look and stuck out her tongue. "It's okay with me."

"Good, I'll tell her." I started walking across the living room, toward Sara's door.

"Michael?" My full name stopped me in my tracks. She called me by that only when she had something important to say. "Please, just a couple tonight?" I looked down at the floor, a tumult of emotions rip-tiding through me.

"Yes, I'll try," I said. I started walking and after two steps the lights flickered. I tried to stifle the breath that my lungs attempted to heave inward in panic. The answering machine beeped to life in the kitchen, and I took a long pull from my glass, leaving only an inch of liquid at the bottom.

Sara sat on her bed combing the hair of her prize doll, Megan. She'd saved her money for nearly six months to purchase the toy, and even after several talks about the high cost, she went ahead and bought it. To her credit, it almost never left her side at home, the doll's dark hair and stylish red dress staples amongst the other stuffed animals that adorned her bed at night.

I sat down beside her on the bed, my weight pushing the mattress down so that she fell off balance and tipped into me, laughing.

"Dad, you're too heavy!"

I scrunched my face and looked at the bed. "No, this bed's just a piece of junk. We'll have to get you a stronger one."

She giggled. "I heard you guys talking."

"About what?"

"About my sleepover."

"You little eavesdropper."

She frowned. "What's an eavesdropper?"

"Someone who listens in on other people's conversations," I said.

"That doesn't make any sense. How would you hear someone if you were dropping off their eaves?"

I laughed and hugged her. "You're right as usual. And yes, you can stay at Ashley's tomorrow."

She hugged me back and leapt from the bed to her closet, her feet barely touching the carpet. "Awesome! I'm gonna pack right now! I'll have to take Megan's party dress and her brush and her shiny shoes."

"Don't forget your own clothes," I said, standing. I'm not sure if she heard me. Her head was buried beneath a pile of blankets, in search of her doll's necessary items. I smiled and left her to it.

I crossed the hall and peeked into Jack's room. He was there, in the middle of the floor, toys of all kinds spread around him as if he were at the epicenter of a G.I. Joe–Lego explosion. The wind moaned outside and nudged the house, causing loud creaks and cracks. I finished my drink and set the empty glass on the floor of the hallway. My head swam as I stood up and took a deep breath. The rum was doing its job. I pushed the door open and stood there, watching my son play for a moment. His little fingers spun a bright yellow Lego in several different directions before seating it into a makeshift wall his army men hid behind. I traced my memory back as far as I could go and tried to remember a time when I'd been as carefree as he was right then. Soft images came to me: playing cards with my father, a simple game of go fish, I think; my mother humming a soundless tune, her hands thrust in soapy dishwater while I pushed small cars around her feet. But that was all. The rest was a choppy blur of rain and low clouds that made my guts writhe. I steadied myself and stepped into his room.

"Whatcha doing, champ?"

"Playin' Joes." He didn't raise his head from the small figures on the floor. I knelt beside him, picked up a particularly frightening member of Cobra, and made the figure's knees flex wildly.

"You Joes are cowards! Hiding behind a wall!" I said in a mockingly high voice, and followed it up with a raspberry that made Jack's eyes widen and then close with belly laughs. "Laughing at me? I'll show you!" I made the figure trudge up to the wall Jack had built and aim a kick at its bottom. "Ow, oh no, I broke my foot!" I cried.

That did it. Jack fell backward in gales of laughter. I watched him, giggling a little myself, painfully aware of how brittle and fleeting this moment was. There would come a time when he wouldn't laugh so easily at his father's simple jokes. Someday the toys he loved so fervently would be packed away and forgotten. I hoped he wouldn't forget the feeling of easy laughter, or the joy he got from the make-believe worlds he created, or what it felt like to be young.

Jack opened his eyes as his laughter subsided, and sat back up. "You're so funny, Dad. You should be on TV."

"Am I better than Diego?"

He thought for a few seconds. "Yeah, I guess so."

"You guess so? Come here!" I yelled, and began tickling him. He screamed laughter again and rolled away from me. Thunder slammed overhead and echoed into the deepening night like a rockslide. I sat up, my throat tightening, threatening to strangle me right there on the floor. A small hand on my arm brought me back, and I looked down at Jack's upturned face.

"It's okay, Dad. The storm's outside and it can't get in."

Tears welled up in my eyes, and the sadness I only allowed myself in moments of complete solitude tried to rise. Sadness for feeling so paralyzed that my six-year-old had to comfort me, sadness for sitting in his room with booze on my breath, sadness for feeling like a failure.

I leaned over and kissed him on the top of his head. "I know, buddy. You're too smart, you know that?"

He just smiled and came closer. "Dad?" he asked in a whisper.

"Yeah?" I whispered back.

"Can I have a candy bar?"

I burst out laughing again. "Sure, buddy." He responded with a small whoop and raced out the door, nearly tripping on my empty glass.

Before I made it back to the living room, I heard Jack exclaim to Jane that he was having a treat at my bidding. Jane raised an eyebrow at me as I walked through, and I merely shrugged and acted as if it was the first I'd heard of it. As I came closer to her, I could smell the familiar fragrance of her shampoo mixed with her own, more subtle scent. It was the smell of her skin, organic and real and singular to her. I put my hand on the small of her back and guided her away from the laundry. Her face was close to mine and a little smile played at the corner of her mouth. I kissed her. In that moment—with my children happy, one in the kitchen, one in the bedroom, my wife pulled against me—I was content. I savored it. We finally moved apart, Jane's smile now complete.

"What was that for?"

"Because I love you," I said, simply. She hugged me close again and my eyes strayed to the window at her back. I stiffened.

Our front yard was dark. Darker than any yard should be on a June evening, a little past seven. Night had come early with the storm. Clouds thicker than I'd ever seen before coated the sky just above the tree line surrounding our home. I expected the tallest tops of the pines to actually scrape the hide of the storm at any moment. But what approached from the west cooled my blood and sent a runner of fear down my spine. A roiling whirlpool of clouds turned in a flattened spiral formation in the sky. It was enormous. Lanky tendrils of root-like thunderheads trailed up to a central black eye that rotated, swallowing the rain-laden clouds and spitting lightning every few seconds.

"Jesus" was all I managed. Jane pulled away from me and turned to the window. A hand went to her mouth.

"Is it a tornado?" she asked, transfixed by the swirling storm outside.

"I don't think so, but we can't be too sure." Thunder roared like an enraged freight train and lightning touched one of the trees across the street, creating a shower of sparks and flying wood.

I swore and pulled Jane back from the window, my hands shaking on her shoulders. "Get Sara," I said. She nodded and ran toward the opposite end of the house. I made my way to the kitchen, my knees threatening to drop me to the floor every few steps. Jack sat at the counter, contentedly chewing on a chocolate bar. "Jack, sit down in the archway, right now."

Something in my voice must have registered, because his eyes widened and he nodded. Without so much as a word, he slid from the stool and went to the main archway leading to the living room and sat at its base. I turned to the pantry, my heart leaping in alarming directions within my rib cage. The bottle of rum was in my hand before I knew it, and I put it to my lips and swallowed one, two, three gulps before I had to take a breath. I shook my head as I capped the rum and set it in its place, noting with crazed amusement that it was almost empty.

There was a loud snapping sound, like a hundred rubber bands breaking at once, and the lights went out.

"Honey?" Jane's voice was high and tight with worry. I stumbled from the pantry, amazed at how black the house was. I made out the oblong shape of the counter and the islands of stools beside it. Just a few more steps and the archway should be there. Lightning lit up my path, and in its flicker I saw my family huddled together in the archway, Jane's arms cuddling both of the kids close, their small faces white in the electric glare. They looked scared. Perhaps more frightened than me, but I doubted it.

"Flashlight," I said and turned back to the kitchen. Wind pushed at the walls and made the house moan like a ship at sea, as I finally found the drawer I was looking for. Pencils, pens, paper, coupons ... finally my fingers touched the hard barrel of the Fenix light I kept there. I clicked the bulbous switch and cool, white light flooded the ceiling. I swung the flashlight around and focused on my family again, securing them in the beam. My nerves still felt like ragged live wires, but I could breath and my heart had slowed to a normal rate. I made my way around the end of the counter as lightning strobed again, suffusing everything.

My flashlight fluttered with it.

I stopped, sure I had imagined it. The beam was steady, and I could see Jane raising a hand to block its glow. A word seemed balanced on her lips—perhaps a plea to shine it away from them? I didn't find out because lightning flashed again at that moment and my flashlight went out for good. I stood, stunned for what felt like an eternity, shock radiating through me as my mind tried to catch up with what had happened. Electromagnetic charge in the air from the storm short-circuited the minute board within the light? Batteries dead? Coincidence? I shook the light. Nothing. Flicked the switch on and off. Nothing.

A roaring began to build beyond the roof, as if a wildfire burned above us. It grew louder with every passing second, and I wondered if this was what everyone meant when describing a tornado's sound. Raising my head, I realized I was still flash blind from the combined brightness of the lightning and flashlight. There was a floating afterimage in the darkness of the living room. Three glowing, elongated shapes hung there in the black. I blinked, thinking they would be there on the inside of my eyelids too, but instead they disappeared. My stomach lurched. I opened my eyes as the golden points of light grew and sharpened in the room beyond my family. I tried to run. I tried to move to them, to pull them away from what my senses had already deemed real but my mind refused to accept.

The giant eyes and mouth hovered in the darkness. The mouth smiled.

I let out a half scream as lightning flared again, and I saw inhumanly long arms and hands scooping my wife and children into an embrace. Thunder roared and the floor shuddered beneath my feet. I lunged toward the doorway as the lights came on, in a mockery of my horror. I tripped over a stool and fell to my knees in the now-vacant archway. My family was gone.

CHAPTER TWO

AN ABSENCE AND AN OFFER

I scrambled to my feet, adrenaline speeding through my veins, everything moving slower than me. My eyes shot around the room as I spun in a circle, the booze in my system protesting at the sudden velocity of my turning.

"Jane!" I yelled. My voice was loud and strange in the house. Strange because I'm alone, I thought absently, as I scanned the living room and took a step into the space. "Sara, Jack!" I yelled, finding my legs and covering the distance to their rooms in a few strides. I burst, first, through Sara's door, and then through Jack's, the whole time willing away the tears that gathered at the bottom of my vision. I can't lose it now, I thought. Although, judging from what I'd seen in the lightning, I'd already lost it. "Jane!" I screamed, panic flooding my voice with possibilities I couldn't yet grasp, or didn't want to. I flew to our bedroom and kicked the door wide. Our bathroom was empty, devoid of life except for a solitary spider above the toilet in a gossamer web. I checked our closet, the hope that this was a prank or a joke finally dwindling down to nothing.

I retraced my steps back to the kitchen and then out to the mudroom. Their shoes were still there, all of them. Rain boots, sneakers, and sandals, all present. They couldn't have gone far. I flung the outside door open and pushed through the storm door. The deck was black with moisture and puddles jumped with splashes of rain. The wind was less than I'd expected, and my eyes shot to the sky, ready to see the vortex I'd spotted earlier through our picture window. The sky was still gray and low, but there were no twisting clouds with a black center. It was an average storm again. I ran down the steps, calling their names, despite the fear that tried to pull me back into the house. I sped past Sara's and Jack's bikes, which lay on their sides like wounded animals. Past their swing set, the chains and seats swaying and dripping water silently. Mud slid beneath my socked feet and I nearly fell rounding the next corner, which opened unto our front yard. The lush new grass of summer looked too green in the odd, failing light of the day. Glancing beneath the front porch, I saw nothing but wood chips behind lattice, and went on. The woods surrounding our house were sparse and hadn't fully greened yet, although they were well on their way. I searched the intertwining branches for movement or the shape of a person in the shadows. Nothing. A few more steps and I'd circumnavigated our property. They were gone.

My chest heaved with sobs as I pulled open the doors of Jane's minivan, knowing what I'd find but not able to help myself. Only the scent of the air freshener greeted me. Rain continued to fall as I peered in through the windows of my truck, its cold touch wetting my skin through my clothes. I spun in a small circle and then sat, not gracefully, more of a crumpling like I'd been shot. My tears began to fall, indistinguishable from the rain that soaked my clothes.

The police were no help. They showed up about twenty minutes after I called. They came in just one car, an older officer with a salt-and-pepper mustache and a protruding belly, and a younger man sporting a blond crew cut along with a sneer. They asked their questions. I answered them as best I could. Someone came into my house and took my family. Could I describe them? It was very dark but the person was tall, I said, trying to sound sure of myself, although panic tried to seep through the cracks in my voice. Both officers nodded, and the younger one eyed the mostly empty bottle of rum I'd pulled from the pantry after I called 911. They made a short sweep of the property, took our family photo from the entryway, and said they would begin a file and be in touch within twelve hours.

I watched their brake lights flare before they turned from the driveway and accelerated away. I slumped to the floor of the kitchen, the rum bottle in my hand. I drank the remainder down and tipped my head back. The image of the two arms reaching out of the darkness and grabbing my family in their too-long fingers flooded my mind. I pressed a palm to my forehead, squeezing my eyes tight against the picture. I saw the burning smile and the eyes. The eyes. They were wide and slanted, orange and black, like two holes cut in the side of a furnace.

"No!" I yelled, my voice coming back to me in a short burst from the other end of the house. My chest heaved and I felt myself on the verge of hyperventilating. I tried to stand, but my head sloshed like a jostled aquarium and I fell, banging my skull against the cupboards behind me. At least there were no handles on the drawers. Jane had taken them off when we moved in since she hated the way they looked. Why the hell had we never gotten around to putting new handles on?

I cried. Their faces floated in front of me in a maelstrom of turning shapes, terror crushing their features as I reached for them. They were in the dark and so was I, spiraling out of control. Then I could see ground rushing up to meet me, much too fast.

I awoke the next morning on the kitchen floor, drool gathered in a cold puddle against my cheek. I sat up, so disoriented that it took a few seconds to remember, and when I did, the realization pushed me back to the floor. I lay there and just stared at the ceiling, going over everything. Something had taken them from me—not someone, *something*. I tried winding my way through different explanations: I was hallucinating, I'd dreamed the whole thing, I was still drunk. But nothing added up.

I got up and ate a piece of toast, then called into the shop and told my boss I wouldn't be in. He didn't like it, but I must have sounded bad enough for him to think I was sick even though I didn't tell him I was. Looking outside, I wasn't surprised to see the neighborhood bathed in sunshine. The storm was just a memory, replaced by a cloudless cobalt sky. Puddles not yet dried up in the sun's warmth lay everywhere like mirrors strewn about.

In the bedroom I pulled down the holster from the top of the high bookshelf in the corner. The SIG Sauer was a darker shadow in the unlit room. I pulled the handgun free, unlocked the trigger guard, released the magazine to check the capacity and then slammed it home. I hadn't targeted with the pistol in over a year, but I remembered exactly how it functioned. Without bothering to lock the house, I went to my truck and climbed in, the heat of the interior a welcome feeling against the coldness that hung just beneath my skin. I sat there for a moment wondering what the hell I was doing. Where was I going? I looked down at the gun in the passenger foot space. I started the engine and backed out of the driveway.

I was going to look for my family.

I drove for five hours, stopping only to fill up on gas once. I went around our neighborhood four times, my eyes searching the yards and windows of our neighbors' houses. I stopped at each one, asking the same question—had they seen my family? The answer was always the same, no, nothing out of the ordinary, they hadn't seen them.

After our neighborhood, I expanded the search. I drove through the back streets of the town parallel to our house. I drove the main highways that intersected in the center of town. The people on the streets were the same as they always were. They went about their business between the storefronts and moved to their cars. They made deposits in the banks and walked their dogs. They talked to one another as if nothing had changed, as if my family hadn't been taken from me.

At three in the afternoon I made my final stop before going home. I got back in the truck with the bottle of whiskey and started the engine. A warming, beseeching thought came to me, and I had to restrain myself from flooring the pedal on my way out of the liquor store's parking lot. They had come home while I was away. For some reason they hadn't answered the phone the dozen times I'd called while I was out.

I drove fast to the house and slid to a stop beside the minivan. My feet barely skimmed the ground, but even before I called out for them as I pushed through the door, I knew they weren't there. A house has a certain sound to it when people are inside, especially people you love. Even silence has its own warmth, the quiet sound of breathing, of presence, of life. It's what makes a house a home. There was none of this when I stepped inside, only the hollowness of unoccupied space. I yelled their names anyway.

When I was done yelling, I went back to the truck and got the whiskey. I had three swallows gone before I came inside. The light on the answering machine in the kitchen caught my eye and my heart leapt. Stabbing the play button I listened without patience to the date and time of the call. A man's voice I didn't recognize came on a moment later.

"Mr. Brennan, this is Sergeant Davidson with the Bright Springs Police Department. I just wanted you to know that a case file has been opened and we are following each and every lead that we have. Please call us at your earliest convenience."

I responded by taking another swig from the bottle and sat on the floor. The alcohol gradually slowed my thoughts to a bearable speed. I sipped some more. The clock moved from half past three to four. I got the insane urge to call my parents and Jane's parents. Insane because what would I tell them? I lost my family during the worst storm I'd ever seen? Something was in the house with an enormous grin like the creepy fucking cat in *Alice in Wonderland*, please bring casserole and help me look for them?

A laugh slipped from my mouth that sounded so strange I stopped the rest that wanted to pour out. It was a twisted and utterly crazy noise that made me think of cliff edges and stepping into an abyss. I looked to the window and it seemed darker outside, although the sun was still overhead. Maybe another storm was on its way. I didn't care. Let it come. Maybe it would bring my family back to me. The last thing I remembered was listening for the sound of thunder in the distance.

A knocking brought me out of a mercifully dreamless sleep. For a moment I thought another storm had arrived. I sat up from the kitchen floor for the second time in less than twelve hours and squinted at the clock. It was after eight, and shadows cast by the sinking sun lengthened in the living room. The knock came again and my synapses finally fired. I jumped to my feet and nearly fell, the whiskey still with me, and it took a few seconds before I could walk again. The knocking resounded through the house, harder than before, more urgent.

"Coming!" I yelled. The mudroom was dark, and when I opened the door to the outside world, I had to squint to see who stood there.

There were two men on my porch. The one who had knocked was old, at least in his seventies if he was a day. The skin on his face was wrinkled in gentle lines that told of more smiles than frowns, and his head was bald, spotted with age, with only a few wisps of white hair that seemed to float in the evening sun. He wore a stained pair of overalls that would've looked more at home hanging on the wall at my work. The other man was slight and pale, smaller than the old man, and wore a dirty baseball hat pulled down tight over his forehead, along with a long-sleeved T-shirt and dark pants. His hands were concealed in black leather gloves and his eyes hid behind a pair of scratched sunglasses.

"Good evening, Mr. Brennan," the older man said. He was a head shorter than me, and when I looked down I saw that his eyes were brown, but a brown like I'd never seen before. They were the color of a newly fallen acorn. He held out a surprisingly large hand for me to shake, and when I did, it felt strange. My fingers registered a roughness on the back of his hand. I looked and saw what seemed to be irregular ridges on the skin there.

"You're no doubt wondering who we are and what we want," he continued, breaking me from my inspection of his hand as he let go and dropped it to his side.

"Yes," I said, trying to clear my throat of sleep and a dried coating of booze.

He nodded. "My name is Ellius, and this is Fellow." He swallowed, and I saw something in his eyes, something that bordered on regret or sympathy. "This is concerning your family."

I don't remember moving, only feeling a small twitch of my muscles. I suppose it was actually the order my brain sent down my nerves in the form of an electrical impulse. One moment I stood in my doorway, no doubt swaying from the still-formidable presence of whiskey, and the next we were on the ground, my hands around the old man's throat. His brown eyes bulged and skittered to my right, possibly asking for help from his companion, but I couldn't have cared less at that point in time. I was impervious to harm; I was steel. The smaller guy could have hit me with a chair and I wouldn't have noticed. The only thing I heard were the words inside my head: *My family.*

"What the fuck did you do with them?" I said, spittle spraying from my mouth and onto his reddening face. He gasped and scrabbled at my hands. He was strong, surprisingly so for his age, but there was no way I was letting go. I was rabid. "Tell me!" I screamed, and punctuated it by pulling him up and slamming him back down to the ground.

"Not us ... help you," he rasped. I wouldn't have been able to distinguish the words had I been farther away. I considered choking the rest of his life out right there since he might be lying—probably was lying—but I didn't know for sure. And even if he was, he was the only possible link I had at the moment.

I let go of his throat and stood up, ready to throw a fist into his tired features at the first sign of trouble. He only lay there beneath me, raggedly sucking air in through his windpipe, as if he were breathing water instead of oxygen. I glanced over my shoulder at the other guy and was surprised to see him kneeling on the porch right where he'd been standing. No, *kneeling* was too strong of a word. *Cowering* was more like it. He'd pulled himself into the smallest form he could manage and was protecting his head with his arms. A whimper floated out from his chest, and I realized he was absolutely terrified.

"I'm sorry," Ellius said as I turned my attention back to him. He worked his fingers against the bruising skin of his neck. His voice still sounded strained and rough. "I should have thought of a better way to begin all this."

"Where are they?" I asked. I still trembled with adrenaline and anger, but my mind was clearer and I no longer felt the whiskey.

He sighed and squinted up at me in the failing light, and for a split second he looked much older than seventy—much, much older. "They are far away and very close."

"What the hell does that mean?"

"I'll be happy to answer all your questions, but may I first check on Fellow?"

I stared at him for a while, indecision tipping me back and forth. Finally I nodded and gave him some space to stand. I looked to the driveway to see what kind of car they had arrived in, but there were no vehicles besides the truck and minivan in sight. When I looked back, Ellius was crouched beside the smaller man. He murmured something that sounded like reassurances to him, and I suddenly felt sorry. I wasn't a violent man, hadn't been in a fight since the fourth grade, when Sunny Goldbloom took my new hat that my parents had given me for Christmas and filled it with orange juice. Violence was not familiar and I felt strange, outside my skin.

After a few more words of encouragement, both men stood, Ellius helping Fellow up on legs that didn't look entirely sturdy. The older man looked at me and smiled for just a moment.

"What is this all about?" I heard myself say. Simultaneously I wanted another drink and didn't ever want to touch the stuff again.

"I can explain everything, but I must impress upon you that time is of the essence."

"They were kidnapped, weren't they?" I said, knowing the answer down in the pit of my stomach, where all truths reside.

Ellius pursed his lips and frowned. "Yes, they were. But it is more complex than that, I assure you. I now must ask for something from you, Mr. Brennan. I must ask for your trust if you are to ever see your children and wife again. Can you give me that?"

I felt as if I'd been slugged in the guts, hit with a bat and left to marinate in my own misery. "How do I know you didn't take them?" I asked, my voice wavering just a little.

"You don't, but I can assure you we didn't. We would not be here if it was not of the utmost importance." He watched me from the top of my porch, gauging my reaction. Perhaps he knew what my answer would be even before I did. Looking back after everything that happened, I wouldn't be surprised.

"Okay, I've got nothing else. I'll listen to you," I said.

"Good," he said, stepping down the stairs. "Come, Fellow, there's no time to spare." The smaller man followed in his footsteps, not looking at me or Ellius, watching only where his feet landed, as if he were afraid the ground would fall away before him.

"Where are you going?" I asked as they walked past me, toward my truck.

"You must drive us. I'll direct you," Ellius said, examining the passenger door of my Dodge. Gingerly he reached out and pulled on the handle. The dome light came on and Fellow backed up a step from the vehicle. Ellius glanced at him with something like annoyance.

"Just a light, Fellow. Electricity and all."

The statement was so strange I didn't even try to compute it at the time, and merely walked toward the truck. After climbing inside I started the engine, which elicited another cringe from Fellow, who sat pressed against the passenger window. I gazed at him and determined it wasn't an act; the man was truly petrified.

"Is he okay?" I asked Ellius.

"Yes, yes, he'll be just fine. He's not used to many things."

Again the oddness of the old man's words. I shook my head and reversed out of our driveway.

My eyes traced our yard, recalling chasing the kids beneath the maple tree in the front yard, Jane and I reading together on the deck in the sunshine, the laughter echoing in rooms that were now empty.

We backed onto the road, and I put the truck in drive, but held my foot on the brake. "Where are we going?" I asked.

"Not far and very far," Ellius said. When I didn't drive, he looked over at me, the wrinkles on his face feathered with shadow in the last light of the day. "I'll direct you, just please hurry, your family needs you."

I drove.

We passed through the heart of Bright Springs and continued on, the middle of town controlled by the giant retailers promising big savings and lower prices in poly-acrylic letters lighting up against the darkening sky. Grocery stores were mixed in here and there, their entryways glowing, inviting and welcoming. Gradually the north side of the city became older, buildings devolving from cinderblock to brick, composite siding to mortar and brownstone. Ellius said very little, merely pointing in one direction or another when we came to an intersection. When he motioned straight ahead after the last stoplight on the north end of town, I glanced over at him. He wasn't just giving directions at random. There was a destination in mind; I could see it in the way his eyes searched each street, each sidewalk, each tree. Yet not once did I see him read a street sign.

"Are you taking me to them?" I asked as we sped past a housing block and a multitude of parked cars in front of what must have been a raging party.

"Yes, in a sense," Ellius said, his eyes never leaving the road.

"Enough with the Zen shit!" I said more loudly than I meant to. Fellow cowered against the far window and turned his head away. The dark glasses still obscured his eyes, but if I were a betting man, I would put my money on them being squeezed shut. "I've done what you asked when I really should've called the police. Now tell me where we're going!"

To the old man's credit, he didn't flinch, not once. He didn't even look at me. "It's just up there," he said in a quiet voice.

I looked at the street we were on. A hundred yards ahead another road intersected our path, a sweeping curve that went on for nearly half a mile around the edge of a small lake. Barren Lake it was called, if I remember correctly. Its name was in honor of never, in the history of Bright Springs, producing a fish. Its flat surface now stared back at me from across the road as I pulled to a stop, the last rays of the sun catching on its skin in flashing shimmers.

To our left the road continued into the final neighborhood on the north end of town. Lights illuminated windows, the families therein settling down to a quiet evening of relaxation and peace. I swallowed and looked right. The road before us curved away and disappeared behind a stand of trees that lined the far edge of the lake. On the opposite side the county fairgrounds sat empty, eerily somber, the simple white structures boarded up against the weather until the last weekend in August, when the fair would visit and the entire place would come alive with smells of caramel and cotton candy.

I panned the scene again, checking the rearview to make sure we weren't blocking anyone, and then turned to my passengers. "Where now?"

Ellius pointed to the right. "There," he said.

I followed the path of his finger and realized it pointed at the empty fairgrounds. I scanned the parking lot one more time to see if I'd missed any cars parked along its edges in the lengthening shadows, but saw nothing.

"The fairgrounds? That's where they are?"

"No, but that's where we're going," Ellius said.

"But there's nothing there."

"Look again."

I did ... and froze. There was something there.

CHAPTER THREE

THE RIDE

At first I didn't know what I was looking at, and then the object began to materialize. It was like peering through a thick fog and finally seeing what you were searching for take shape in a cloud of moisture. Lines sharpened and rose high into the night air. Smoky walls hardened. Material flapped in the gentle breeze coming off the lake. I held my breath. It was a fair, but not *our* fair. The rides that sat behind the low fences lining the property were desolate and dark. I could see, even from a distance, that the carnival wasn't active and looked like it hadn't been for years. No—not just years but decades. A cloud blocked the last rays of sun and details in the fairgrounds deepened, forcing away the thoughts of denial that flooded my mind.

"How?" was all I managed.

"You see it?" a soft voice said from near the passenger door. I turned my head, almost more surprised by Fellow actually speaking than by seeing a carnival emerge into reality where there hadn't been one before. His face was turned toward me, the scant eyebrows above his glasses raised.

"Yes," I said. "Yes, I see it." Fellow nodded and I saw a slight grin tug at his mouth. When I looked back the cloud covering the sun fled, leaving the fairgrounds in better light. The rides and tents dimmed a little and took on the look of a mirage floating just above the ground, there but not there.

"Please," Ellius said and put a weathered hand on my arm.

I glanced at him and saw the same look he wore on my doorstep: pity barely concealed. I nodded and turned right, parking in the far right corner of the lot. Dust billowed from around my wheels as I shut the engine off and opened my door. I heard Fellow and Ellius exit on the far side, but by then the rest of the world had faded. I took one step, two, and then stopped just inside the fence.

The midway was set up almost exactly like the fair that visited our town every August. A main alley wound through a maze of booths and tents, their openings bare and unmanned. Ropes and black scraps of cloth dangled from posts and poles, swaying like beckoning fingers. An empty ticket booth sat a few yards away, its interior lined with stained pennants and flags. Steel girders grew from the ground and twisted upward into strange rides that, at first, I'd thought were familiar. Now I could see they were dark doppelgangers of the carnival I knew. Their frames were bent and broken in places. There was a tilt-a-whirl, slanted and pitted with rust so deep it was the color of ancient blood. A merry-go-round with a solitary headless horse rotated so slowly I thought it would stop at any moment, but it continued emitting a tinny shriek every quarter turn. The black mouth of a funhouse yawned in our direction, a tongue of rotted and falling stairs leading into a pool of shadows that seemed to dance and move. And beyond it all, a roller coaster nearly three stories high stabbed at the evening sky with black rails and a row of three oversized light bulbs perched over its entrance. All were lit, in stark contrast to everything else on the grounds.

I tore my attention away from the carnival and looked at Ellius. The old man's face was set in a near grimace as he gazed at the midway. "What is this place?" I asked, my voice barely above a whisper.

Ellius stared for a few more seconds and then turned his eyes my way. "A dark place of traverse. Somewhere no soul should tread." I saw movement just behind him and realized Fellow huddled a few inches from the old man's spine. A tremor ran through his small form and his hands clenched and opened inside the gloves he wore. "Follow me closely and do not stop, no matter what you see or hear. Do not speak to anything, do you understand?" Ellius said.

The sun finally slipped below the tree line in the west and evening stepped closer to night. The details of the carnival sharpened before us and I blinked, opened my mouth to say something, then shut it again. Ellius took it as a sign of agreement and began to walk. Fellow went next, his steps falling in Ellius's footprints exactly, like a child walking behind a parent in deep snow. I trailed after, throwing a glance over my shoulder at my truck, alone and abandoned in the empty parking lot. The sight of it saddened me to no end and I turned away, not being able to put a finger on why I would feel morose at leaving my pickup. We entered the midway, the rides towering over us on the left and the open fronts of the carny games on our right.

"Tickets?" a voice hissed.

Looking toward the origin of the voice I saw that we'd drawn even with the ticket booth. It was still dark inside, but now there was a silhouette seated on some sort of stool behind the cracked glass. A gray hand emerged through the ticket slot, pressing a thick sheaf of dripping papers across the counter. The nails on the hand were black and very long. There was an intricate design on the soggy paper beneath the hand, and I wanted to see it. It was strange but familiar, and in the dying light it was hard to make out. I began to step closer when Ellius's voice made me freeze.

"Michael! Do not stop."

I started to tell him I hadn't when I saw that he and Fellow were several paces ahead of me. I turned away from the booth, but not before I saw a multitude of tiny hairs glistening on the papers beneath the hand. When I was within a few feet of Ellius, he leaned forward and grasped my wrist.

"Do not stop again, or I won't be able to call you back." He let go and began walking once more in a straight line.

I felt cold all over, as if I'd just stepped into a meat locker. A gust of wind came across the lake and pushed its way through the rides, its hollow voice talking amongst the flaking bars and beams. Several plastic bags skittered past us, as if fleeing from something. A tinkling sound like falling icicles drew my attention, and I saw that a game booth to my right was full of hanging knives suspended from the ceiling by twine. Their blades flashed as they spun in the breeze, and when I looked down at the sash of the booth, I saw row after row of teeth jutting from the rotting wood.

I snapped my eyes back to the grass beneath my feet and walked in time with Fellow's shorter steps. Just breathe, I told myself. Don't look up again.

"Dad?"

I stopped, transfixed by the sound of my son's voice.

Beside me a pointed tent with pinned flaps that opened unto darkness smiled. Without thinking about it, I stepped up to the counter and peered inside. "Jack? Is that you?" I called. Something tugged at my sleeve, trying to pull me back, but I yanked my arm away. "Jack?"

"Dad?" It was Jack, but something was wrong. His voice was different, lower, with guttural tones just beneath the boyish curl of his words.

"Michael!" I didn't want to look away from the tent because something was moving in there, something short, about Jack's height. It was coming closer, and I was afraid if I looked away, he'd disappear. "Michael!" I risked a glance over my shoulder and saw that Ellius and Fellow were right behind me on the path. "Come here now!" Ellius yelled. I looked back into the tent and saw the shape again, but now it was too wide, with short, piggish arms at its sides.

"Dad," it called again, but now it was laughing and didn't sound like Jack anymore. Its voice bubbled, as if it were talking through a layer of mud. I sprang backward just as a single claw sank into the counter where my hand had been. I felt Ellius grab me by my shirt and haul me onward. Watery laughter trailed after us through the tent flaps.

"What was that thing?" I asked, fear hacking my words off unnaturally.

"Not your son, that's all you need to know," Ellius said over his shoulder as he led me on. We neared the entrance to the roller coaster, and Ellius passed through the gates without pause.

"Get in," he said, pointing to one of the canted cars on the track a few yards away. Fellow surprised me by reaching out and taking one of my hands in his own. The flesh beneath the glove felt odd, as if it were made of ropes and hard segments instead of skin and bone. I followed him across the grass and stepped into the car, the smell of mildew and decay wafting up to me as I sat on a cracked seat. Fellow reached forward and pulled a heavy bar toward us, which snapped down painfully across the front of my hips. I looked at the uneven tracks ahead of us. Some of the bolts and rivets were missing, and the rails ran askew of each other at multiple places before vanishing over a steep crest in the distance.

A jolt of movement from the cars snapped us back in the seat, and the coaster rolled forward. "No way," I said, trying to push the locked bar away from my lap. "This thing's gonna come off the rails." Hearing a snapping sound behind us, I turned in my seat and saw Ellius in the car to our rear. "Are you crazy? You're going to kill us!" I yelled at him, my stomach dropping as the train of cars began to climb the rise.

"We will be fine," he said. "Now hold on tight."

I faced forward just in time to see the first car fade from view, into the drop on the other side. My hands gripped the ragged steel bar as my teeth ground together. I hated roller coasters.

For a moment we hung high above the ground, and then descended in a drop that lifted my lungs and shoved the air from them. I couldn't have screamed if I'd wanted to—and I wanted to. The rattling of the cars on the rails was unholy and I felt my eardrums waver with the noise. We hit the bottom of the hill and swooped up and to the right. The force of the turn slid me sideways into Fellow, who whimpered as I tried to move back to my space. Then we dropped again, into a left turn that dug the edge of the car into my ribs. I moaned with fear, even as deep inside me I felt of rush of something, the speed and the turns igniting my blood with exhilaration. We corkscrewed straight up, and that's when I began to think that maybe we wouldn't die. A tunnel approached after two more sickening drops that pushed a maniacal laugh from me, and then we were inside.

The light didn't just dim, but vanished entirely. I felt light, as weightless as fog. We had crashed and I was dead, I realized. There could be no other explanation. I tried to touch my face but found that I couldn't feel my hands. I wiggled my toes but couldn't feel them either. I consciously tried to breathe in, but there was no air.

An unyielding force pressed upon me, gentle at first and then harder, until I could feel pins and needles pricking every inch of my body. Heat bloomed around me like a warming oven, and then a point of light appeared in the distance. It was only then that I realized how fast we were traveling. The light grew exponentially and my head snapped back with an even higher burst of speed. I thought my skin would be flayed from my bones with the passage of air around us.

There was a vacuum of sound, and I drifted away into an ether devoid of sensation. Then everything rushed back in, slamming me into my body from somewhere far away. I sucked in air through my teeth, which felt like they'd recently been taken out and replaced, and blinked. My vision swam in layered pools of light and shadow, but I could tell the coaster was still. I rubbed my eyes and felt Fellow touch my arm, his hand barely there.

"Are you okay?" he asked.

"Yeah, I think so. I feel like I was taken apart," I said.

"That's because you were," Ellius murmured. I turned toward him. He was a dark smudge emerging from the car behind us. I focused on him and slowly my vision cleared. I felt an overwhelming sense of vertigo and swallowed down the urge to vomit.

"Feeling sick?" Ellius asked.

I nodded, squeezing my eyes shut again. "Yeah, I hate amusement-park rides."

"It will pass soon enough. Do you think you can walk?"

I blinked, looking around for the first time. We were in some sort of hollow. A steep, tall hill rose beside the coaster and ended with a line of trees at its peak some forty feet above us. The ground was grassy, but there was something wrong. All the grass was brown and dead. Not a single green blade could be seen. A layer of fallen leaves littered the tangled ground and shifted in a wind that curled into the hollow and pushed at my back. I felt cold. Colder than it should have been in June, much colder. The air bit with a sting that spoke of fall, and when I looked to the sky it was a gun-metal gray, an October sky if there ever was one. From what I could tell it was nearing dark, and after turning in my seat a little more I spotted the sun. It was almost in the same place as when we'd left, just behind a stand of trees, with only a few spokes of light poking through. Something began to dawn on me then, a feeling of unease that spread outward from my center, as if my stomach knew a secret my mind didn't.

I shifted in my seat, facing the rear cars, knowing what I'd see because I had seen it once already while looking at the surrounding area. My eyes traced the two lines of the tracks we sat on. They were in even worse disrepair here, rust so thick in some places I was surprised it didn't derail us. The tracks curved away for a hundred yards and then disappeared beneath a portion of the hill behind us. My mind tried to grab hold of the information, but it wouldn't fit. Each time I blinked I thought I saw a tunnel where we'd exited, but the side of the hill remained solid and whole. Dead grass lay on the tracks as well as a few broken branches and brambles. There was no sign that a ten-car roller-coaster train had just driven over them.

I turned my head and threw up.

I felt Fellow's hand lightly on my back, patting just between the shoulder blades like a mother comforting a sick child. My stomach heaved again, revolted at the impossibility of everything. I could see the short, squatty thing in the tent, could hear it speaking to me in my son's voice. I saw the knives hanging by strings, smiling their steel grins. Oh God, I missed my family, my home.

I wiped my mouth, weak from expelling whiskey onto the dead leaves beside the car. "Where are we?" I asked without looking at Ellius.

I saw him shift from one foot to the other, debating something. "Let's get a fire going and we'll talk. I'm sure you're cold."

"We're not on Earth, are we?" I asked, the words trying to stick in my throat amongst the phlegm and bile.

Ellius paused, his head turned so that I could see one deep brown eye studying me. "No, not anymore."

CHAPTER FOUR

EVERFALL

The fire snapped and bit at the wood inside the small ring of stones. I held my hands out, letting the heat seep into my fingers and touch the bones therein, hoping warmth would soothe the cold that continued to creep beneath my skin. Ellius mixed something together in a wooden bowl with a peeled twig where he sat across the fire, pausing every few minutes to peer into its depths before stirring some more. Fellow rested a few feet away from me, the flames dancing in the twin mirrors of his sunglasses.

Nothing was said after I climbed from the coaster save Ellius's warning not to stray too far. He'd disappeared immediately into a nearby copse of trees in search of firewood. Fellow had busied himself with building a ring out of a group of thick, gray stones he found beneath a pile of black leaves. I'd walked out of the hollow and onto a flat plain that extended out in every direction. To me it looked like a freshly cut straw field with chaff sticking up almost uniformly as far as I could see. The woods we had arrived in looked to be a half-moon shape, following the depression and then the rise of the hill where the tracks sat. All of the trees were bare, their branches twisting in strange patterns toward the low sky. To me it looked like they'd never had leaves on them at all; they looked dead. The air was full of the withering scents of fall—dry leaves, cold soil, and a promise of winter.

Ellius returned a half-hour later wearing a brown smock similar to something a monk might wear. A black belt stretched around his middle furthered the similarity. I said nothing at seeing his change of clothes. I suppose I was in mild shock, but I didn't mind. It was almost comforting not to be alarmed anymore, to feel a bit of numbness surrounding me like a bubble.

The fire found a knot and sprung it free with a crack. Ellius stopped his stirring, satisfied with the mixture. He stood and walked around the fire to my side, and held the bowl out to me.

"Drink this, it will help with the sickness and shock you must be feeling."

I leaned toward the bowl and looked at the cloudy substance inside before sitting back. "No thanks, I'm fine," I said.

"Please, Michael, it will help you focus on what I have to tell you." The old man's eyes beseeched me in the firelight.

I almost slapped the bowl out of his hand, but instead relented and took it from him. The odor wafting off the liquid inside wasn't as unpleasant as I'd imagined. It held a soft sweetness and a tang of earthy undertones. It smelled a little like Guinness. I put the bowl to my lips and took an experimental sip. It was so cold I thought I'd swallowed liquid nitrogen. It raced down my throat, sucking the heat from inside me. I coughed and sputtered. Fellow had a small smile on his face, the first I'd seen, and anger immediately flooded my system.

"You poisoned me," I said, still coughing.

Now it was Ellius's turn to smile. "No, it's not poison, but the first sip is always a different experience. Try it again, I think you'll like it."

If it was poison, I'd already swallowed it, so there was no harm in having more. Perhaps I'd wake up realizing this was all a nightmare. Perhaps I wouldn't wake up at all. The lack of fear at the latter thought scared me. I needed to stay alive to find Jane and the kids, I couldn't be careless anymore. Or maybe the absence of fear was a premonition, a message from the inner eye telling me that they were already gone and the only way I'd ever see them again would be to follow them.

I put a hand to my eyes, casting the thoughts away, and poured more of the liquid into my mouth. It wasn't cold anymore, just cool, and this time it tasted like iced tea with a hint of coffee, but sweet. I drank more. The more I swallowed, the more I wanted, until the bowl was straight up and the last of it dripped onto my tongue. I set the bowl down on the log I rested on and stared at Ellius.

"That was the best thing I've ever tasted."

The smile again, but less this time. "I'm glad I haven't lost my touch."

"What is it?"

"A blend of tree roots, water, an assortment of other odds and ends. Do you feel okay?"

I took inventory of myself. The first thing I noticed was the cold was gone; it had vanished the moment I downed the last swallow. Heat flowed through me now, not uncomfortable, just warmth from within. The unease was also less, not gone entirely, but faded to a manageable level.

"I feel pretty good," I said at last.

"Good."

I waited a beat and then leaned forward. "Ellius, I need you to tell me where we are and what this has to do with me and my family, and I need you to tell me right now."

The old man's head bowed and his naked scalp shone in the firelight. I was just about to say something again when he spoke. "A question of where may be the wrong thing to ask. Inside, outside, around, these are all irrelevant. We are not on Earth anymore, as you have already guessed for yourself, but we are not far. The best way I can explain it is we are on the border of Earth, within it and beside at the same time."

I studied him to see if he was lying but saw no sign. "You're not making any sense. What do you mean, in it and beside it?"

He sighed and pursed his lips. "Imagine that the Earth is a house, an enormous moving and ever-changing house with the surrounding universe as its walls, roof, and basement. If you can imagine this in your mind, then the place we are now would be the house's ventilation."

"Ventilation?" I asked.

"Yes. Every house needs airflow—heat in the winter to warm it, windows in the summer to cool. This place provides the Earth with ventilation for balance."

"I'm still not following you," I said. My mind felt clear, but Ellius's words glanced off it like stones skipped on a pond.

"Everything must have balance," he began again, holding his hands out, palms toward the sky. "Without balance a tipping would occur that would destroy the world you know. This place gives balance by leaking through the vents of the world, creating a type of harmony."

I rubbed the side of my face and glanced at Fellow, who merely stared into the fire, absorbed by its dancing flames. "So what does this place give off that balances the Earth?" I asked, feeling absurd by even contemplating what the old man said.

"Evil."

I froze and looked at him across the fire. "Evil?"

He nodded. "There is good and evil in your world, in many forms. There is devastation and rebirth, darkness and light, cruelty and kindness. Good and evil are counterparts on a scale greater than even I understand. They are cogs in a machine so vast it defies the imagination of any mortal being. I don't pretend to know all the answers or how everything works, but I can tell you this: your world would topple without this place." Ellius raised his hands with the last words and gestured to the surrounding forest.

"Where did it come from?" I heard myself ask. I was beginning to feel strangely sleepy, as if I would tip forward at any minute, my head weighted down by the thoughts that spun through it.

"It has always been here, as long as the Earth existed."

"You say it provides evil ... how?"

Ellius swallowed, and stirred the fire with a nearby stick. Plumes of smoke and dancing sparks twirled away above our heads. "This place is a realm of forgotten nightmares, of lost things and malignant thoughts. It has changed over time, evolved along with the Earth and its inhabitants." His eyes flashed up to mine and held them. "This place mirrors your world in some respects, and is utterly alien in others. Nothing grows here, nothing can. Everything that would normally live on Earth perishes here. There are things here born of the churning void that I will not speak of, and darker forces without will or mind that swallow light only because they exist."

I felt my hands tremble and pressed them together. The heat of the drink still sat inside of me like a softly burning ember, but it did nothing to quell the shiver that ran from the bottom of my spine to my shoulders. "So this is hell," I said.

"No, it is not a place of sinners, if that's what you mean. People are not supposed to come here, but some do." He paused, a strange look just behind his eyes. "In a basic sense this place is energy, black, cancerous energy, but energy nonetheless. Without it there would be no mass murders or tornadoes. There would be no plagues or disease or famine."

"So this place exists to cause pain and suffering?" I asked.

"Suffering is a by-product of the venting. The Earth must be balanced by good and evil or it will fall, simple as that."

"What do you mean, 'fall'?"

"It would cease to be, along with this place and the other that provides anything good."

I rubbed a hand across my eyebrows and wondered if I'd made a mistake by coming here. Maybe I was still asleep on the kitchen floor. I pinched the back of my hand until a blood blister formed there. I looked down at it, waiting for the pull of consciousness to drag me from my dream. It didn't come.

"Why do you do that?" Fellow asked, his shaded eyes looking at the spot I'd pinched.

"I was hoping this was all a dream." He looked up at me and I saw his eyebrows draw together. Perhaps he didn't dream, but I didn't care enough to ask.

"I'm sorry, Michael, but this isn't a dream," Ellius said.

"Then what does this have to do with my family? What does it have to do with me?" I asked loudly. My voice rebounded off the forest walls and a flock of black-winged birds exploded from the treetops. Ellius's face was a rock, immovable and without expression.

"I said that this place is the ventilation for your world. The energy that resides here has to transfer somehow. It needs vents to do so."

"Vents," I repeated. "Like doorways? Like that roller coaster back there that looks like it hasn't moved in fifty years?"

"Something like that, yes. But *doorway* is a terrible word for the vents. Doorways imply that they should be traveled through," Ellius said. His eyes looked black. "Sometimes people can become vents. There are various people that have become famous, and infamous, in your world because they are a host to this world or its counterpart. You would know them as mass murderers and saints."

I shook my head. "So you're saying the people who do wrong or right on Earth are only conduits for another dimension?"

"No, there are many people who are inherently good, just as there are some who are evil, but there are a select few who become something more. Sometimes an act so vile occurs in your world that a semblance of it is born here—not the same, mind you, but something like it. Do not be surprised if you see something familiar here.

"But most of the time the vents are not people but obscure places that move constantly so people and animals will not stumble into this realm. The storm above your house was a vent of sorts, but in this case ..." Ellius paused, and for the first time since I met him he looked unnerved. "It became a doorway."

My throat felt constricted. "A doorway for what?"

Ellius leaned forward, his voice nearly a whisper. "It has no name because it needs no name, and to name it would be blasphemy. It has been here since the creation of the world, growing, adapting, and changing with time. It is the utmost evil that calls this place home, and even the vilest creatures that live here fear it and pay it homage. It thrives on suffering and pain, and it knows no mercy." Ellius spit into the fire, and I saw Fellow draw in on himself, shrinking into nearly half his normal size.

"It's what took them, isn't it?" I asked. Ellius gazed through the flames and nodded. "I saw it that night, I saw its face." I felt tears brimming on the edges of my eyes. The horror set before me was mind numbing in its disconnect with the reality I knew. Something from another world had taken my family. Its alien fingers found them in the darkness and pulled them here, screaming and terrified and wondering why I hadn't saved them.

A sob escaped me. I pressed a palm to my forehead and shuddered with the hopelessness that rolled through me. I felt close to death, almost at one with it. A breath could've pushed me into its embrace, and I would've gladly gone at that moment. I felt Fellow's hand on my shoulder again, a dragonfly's alighting touch, reassuring somehow.

I raised my face, felt the fire warm the tears on my cheeks. "Are they all right?"

"I'm not sure," Ellius said. "We believe they are still alive."

"How can you know?" I asked.

"Because everything is still here," he said.

I sniffed and pushed the tears away with the heel of my hand. "What do you mean?"

"It is one thing if a person wanders into this place. Have you heard of the Lost Colony of Roanoke?"

I frowned. "The colony that disappeared in North Carolina?"

Ellius nodded and pointed to his right, over a stand of trees. "Their bones lay in a field a mile from here."

"Jesus," I said. "What happened to them?"

"They were driven here through a vent by an attack of some sort in your world. They ended up being devoured by something far worse." I swallowed, my gorge rising once again. "To take a person or animal from Earth by force is forbidden, and until this point I thought it to be impossible, but somehow it has found a way," Ellius continued. "I gathered the identities of your family from several sources that are loyal to me who saw them here. When I realized what had happened, I took Fellow with me to find you. The lasting power of the vent led us right to you, and your name was on my lips as soon as we came through. No doubt your family being here will upset the balance, and I think that is exactly what it wants. Chaos and destruction of everything, not just this world but every world, including Earth."

I blinked, my mind finally working again. "But if it's forbidden to take someone from Earth, how did you both bring me here?"

Ellius offered the smallest of smiles. "You came here of your own free will, Michael. We only had to show you the way. Besides, you are the only one that can bring your family home. A person either has to wander back out of a vent or must be led out by blood."

I sighed. "This is a lot to absorb." I stopped mid-sentence and looked at Fellow beside me, and then across at Ellius, a strange feeling drawing over me like a cold sheet. "How is it that you both are human and have survived here?" I asked. Ellius grimaced and Fellow shrank away.

"I hoped you wouldn't ask that question until later, but there's no choice now," Ellius said. He stood and moved forward until he almost touched the licking tongues of flame. He looked like a man lit from within. His eyes held mine for a few seconds, and then he looked away to the gray sky above us—and changed.

His skin roughened and became darker. The white hair clinging to his scalp fell away and points began to rise beneath the age spots like fingers trying to escape. His eyes deepened in color, from light brown to deep chestnut. The ridges I'd felt on his hand earlier became exactly what my mind had suggested—bark. Tips of branches broke through his scalp and grew several inches before stopping. The rough texture, similar to an oak's skin, flowed over him until he was completely covered. Pieces of moss grew on the fringes of his skull and draped down his back.

"My God," I said, not sure if I should be terrified or in awe. I felt a little bit of both tugging at me.

Ellius looked at me, judging my reaction. When he seemed sure I wouldn't run screaming into the nearby woods, he sat. "As you can see, I am of the forest. It is my family, and I know every tree that has ever stood. I am bound to the woods." He shifted his eyes to my right and nodded at Fellow.

I rotated on the log and watched as the quiet man stood and pulled off the hat and sunglasses he wore. Beneath them I saw that Fellow's skin was not only pale but deformed. His skull was knobby and encrusted with scabrous lesions. His eyes were light orange, and either reflected the fire perfectly or glowed of their own accord. He pulled off his gloves and I saw why his touch had felt strange through the leather. His fingers and hands were composed of ropy vines and intertwining gray stalks. He flexed their knotted joints and turned them this way and that for me to see. When I looked down I noticed he'd also removed his shoes, exposing two knurled hunks of wood with articulating claws on all sides.

"I am Fellow, born of the speaking trees and soil. I am glad to reveal my true self to you. In disguise I felt like a lie." With a small bow he sat back beside me, his posture more relaxed than I'd seen it.

"You understand that we had to disguise our natures prior to this?

We couldn't risk frightening you," Ellius said.

I laughed as my eyes shifted between them. "So what now? You guys call something out of the woods and let it eat me? Is that it? You said yourself that this place is evil and you're both from here." I could feel hysteria growing in my chest, the kind of panic that won't allow steadiness or reason.

"There is balance everywhere, Michael, and this place is no exception. Yes, there is mostly evil here, I won't deny that, but there is also good. There are some here who will help you because they have chosen to be kind and peaceful, and they have been hunted because of it," Ellius said.

"You just need me to get my family out since you can't do it yourself, to save your precious world, is that right?" The panic I felt shifted to anger. Anger at the two beings before me, anger at what had taken my family, anger at myself for being weak and unable to help them.

"Yes, I would be lying if I said I didn't want to save my world, but you would be saving your own also," Ellius said.

Fellow touched my shoulder again, a few burs and thorns poking through the cotton of my shirt. "I want you to find them," he said, the sincerity in his voice speaking more than the words.

I nodded finally, dropping my chin to my chest, and I felt like crying again. "I'm sorry, I'm just lost without them," I whispered. They said nothing, and only the fire replied while it forced its way deeper into a log. "Where are they?" I asked after a while.

Ellius looked into the sky, the top of his head reminding me of our maple tree back at home in the winter. "It lives a long distance away, in a place it's made inhospitable to most things native to this land. You must journey there and bring them back if you can. If you can't ..." He let the sentence trail off into the breeze.

"Which direction?" I said, standing from the log.

"You can't go now, you're exhausted and you need rest. We will sleep and begin later."

"Bullshit, my family's out there and I need to find them, now!" I said, stepping around the fire.

"You'd die before you crossed that field," Ellius said, gesturing to the open plain I observed earlier.

"He's right, Michael," Fellow said. His timid eyes still glowed, but implored me to sit.

I trembled like a plucked guitar string. I needed to move, to run, to hurt something. I wanted to tear a hole in the earth, in the universe. I let out a short yell and kicked a rotted stump, sending pieces of peth flying in all directions. My chest heaved and I stared into the twilight, looking for something to guide me, but to where I didn't know. I turned and looked back at the fire. Neither Ellius nor Fellow had moved. I walked back and sat down beside the fire once again.

"When can we leave?" I asked.

"Very soon, very soon," Ellius said. "We're actually waiting on one more. He's—"

The words were cut off by a resounding belch that echoed back and forth in the hollow behind us. There was the snapping of branches and a few curses in a gravelly voice from the edge of the trees, and then a wide figure emerged.

"God-awful fuckery in there," it said in a baritone voice that strangely held the drawling tones of an Australian accent.

"And here he is now," Ellius said, closing his eyes as the figure approached behind him.

It stepped into the light of the fire, and I could see that the newcomer was manlike, a flat slab of a head sitting atop two hulking shoulders any NFL lineman would have been jealous of. He wore a tattered cloth vest and a threadbare pair of canvas pants. Both might have been black once, but were now a muddy brown. A thick chest bulged beneath the vest and two legs the width of the log I sat on supported his massive frame. I studied his face in the dancing light and saw that his skin was a dark gray, like that of the stones around the fire. His lower jaw jutted forward, and I was immediately reminded of the cartoon *The Iron Giant*. I'm pretty sure my son would've made the same comparison.

"The fuck are you lookin' at?" he said when he noticed my eyes upon his face.

"Nothing," I said, glancing at Ellius.

"Michael, may I introduce you to Kotis, he'll be accompanying you on the journey."

"Hello," I said. Kotis just stared at me with glinting onyx eyes.

A form swooped out of the forest and flapped an enormous set of wings before landing lightly on Kotis's shoulder. It was an owl, but an owl like I'd never seen before. Its shape and feathers were familiar, but its eyes were wide set and narrowed as though it was squinting. Its beak, instead of a short hook, was long and curved like a scimitar.

"Fellow, didn't see you there, thought you was part of the log," Kotis said, a crooked grin tilting his heavy jaw to one side. Fellow blinked and then smiled. Kotis turned his head and whispered something to the bird, which tucked its beak beneath a wing and seemed to go to sleep.

"Well, now that we're properly met, let's retire for the night and get an early start," Ellius said.

"That's something else I wanted to ask you," I said as everyone stood. "I've been here for over three hours and the sun hasn't set." I motioned to the orb that still hung just behind the tree line, its feeble light never letting the day turn to complete dusk. "How long are the days here?"

"The sun never sets here," Ellius said. "It rotates on the horizon around us. Time passes differently in our world. Here, it is always evening and never night."

I shook my head, glancing at our surroundings. "So it's forever fall."

Ellius nodded and turned away.

The thought of the sun never setting and seasons never changing was a bit too much for my mind to absorb, and as soon as I lay on the ground beside the fire, my arm tucked beneath my head, I was asleep.

CHAPTER FIVE

THE FIELD OF LIES

I awoke to the same gray of an October afternoon. The fire was still going, or rekindled since I couldn't see any of the others around me. I rolled onto my back and studied the churning clouds overhead. It was like looking at the muddy bottom of a river, constantly moving and swirling, making near recognizable shapes before absorbing them again into the gray mass.

I'd dreamed something in the night, or what passed for a dream. I had been young, playing with my childhood dog, a bruising German shepherd named Gunner. We were roaming my parents' property near a small river that dried up each fall and flooded each spring. In the dream the river had been a curving bone of mud and cracked earth. Darkness was falling, just on the edge of becoming black, and I felt the pull of the house beckoning me to come inside, into the light and warmth that waited for me. But Gunner and I were exploring, and there was just one more bend that I wanted to see that night. We rounded it and I felt a cold breeze spring up where there had been none before. Gunner began to growl, his hackles rising, making his considerable size look even bigger. There was something at the border of the streambed, something shimmery like heat rising off a highway in the summer, and I felt my stomach tighten. I took a step toward it and stopped, thinking I saw something move. I heard Gunner's growls increase, and there was another sound beneath it. Someone was calling for help, a child's voice, Jack's voice. I turned to tell Gunner to be quiet, but he wasn't there anymore. I realized the growling was coming from the space in front of me and there were eyes there in the darkness, long and slanted and full of burning hatred.

That's when I awoke, and for a few seconds I thought I was still there, on the bank of the stream, and I'd somehow fallen onto my back. I closed my eyes, letting the weight of my family's absence settle into me. The air squeezed out of my lungs with the pressure, and I thought it might crush me into dust.

"Michael," Ellius said. I looked up at the grainy, bark-laden features of his face. "It's time to go."

I stood and dusted my clothes off, shivered. Ellius stepped closer, holding out the same bowl I'd drank from the night before. "Drink this, it will help keep you warm since I have no clothes to offer you here."

I drank the contents, immediately feeling the effects of the mixture. Heat spread from my center to the ends of my limbs, making me feel like I was wearing fleece on every inch of my body.

"For hell's sake, is he up yet? We need to move," Kotis said as he walked into the clearing.

"I'm up," I replied.

"It's about fucking time, it's near midmorning and they'll be out soon enough," Kotis said. He stepped over a log and put a giant, bare foot directly in the licking flames of the fire. Hissing erupted from beneath his sole, and he stared at me without moving, the beginning of a challenging smile on his blocky face.

"Who'll be out soon enough?" I asked, trying not to show my discomfort at the method he used to extinguish fires.

He stared at me for a moment, lips pulled back from a set of very straight, gray teeth. "You'll see soon enough," he said, and stomped away.

I turned to Ellius, who shook his head and shrugged. "I make no apologies for him, he is the way he is and nothing will change him. Give him time, he's merely angered at the fact that I've asked him to go with you."

"Why did you ask him?"

"Because you need protection that I cannot provide and he is one of the few in this world that I trust."

Fellow stepped from the bank of trees to my right, and I greeted him with a tip of my head. He walked toward us and stopped a short distance away, wringing his ropy hands.

"As far as I can see, the way is clear ahead," Fellow said.

"Good, we'll leave immediately," Ellius replied. Fellow struck out in the direction of the field, his misshapen head turning in every direction, as if expecting an attack. "Fellow will be your guide. His timidity is outweighed by his sense of direction and compassion." I nodded and breathed deeply. "Can you carry on, Michael?"

"There's nothing in this place that could stop me," I said, and headed toward the clearing where Kotis and Fellow waited.

We walked into the dusky light of the morning, which was the same as the night before except now the ever-present clouds covered the sun, masking it with their gray bodies. The field we walked in was large, larger than I'd first thought. It stretched away to the left, and for all I could tell, it might have gone on forever. To our right the line of trees continued, and I studied them as we walked. Shadows grew only a few feet inside the forest and nestled themselves in every available space. Dead reeds slouched forward at the edge of the woods, and a brown bramble covered with thorns completed what looked to be an impenetrable mass. The air was crisp, but the mixture Ellius gave me did its work and I was comfortable in just my T-shirt and jeans.

Fellow led the group, his thin, gangling legs pulling him forward in a strange gait. His head still swiveled on his neck, but his direction was clear and he did not deviate from it. Kotis was next, his hunched shoulders and massive back swaying to and fro as he walked, the owl-like creature on his shoulder continuing to sleep despite the movement. Ellius was behind me and followed at an easy pace, glancing every so often to the forest, as if he were listening to a conversation only he could hear.

After a few miles I began to notice a change in the landscape ahead. The forest became composed of smaller trees, then brush, and then ended completely. At its border the field opened up, but a white wall of fog concealed what lay ahead. I'd never seen fog so thick. The old comparison to pea soup came to mind, and for the first time it seemed applicable, though the whiteness of the fog deserved a more appropriate description. It was more like clam chowder, blank and so thick I imagined I could scoop some away and hold it in my hand. Fellow stopped a few feet from the haze and waited for us to catch up. I gazed around at the group, measuring their reactions to this new development. Kotis remained stoic, while Fellow began to rock on his wooden feet. When Ellius spoke, the muffled sound of his voice startled me.

"I'm afraid this is where I must leave you."

I turned to him, incredulous. "What? You're leaving, now?"

"I cannot stray beyond the boundaries of the forest, but I will meet you again soon. Wherever there are trees I may travel." His brown eyes held mine and told me that there would be no negotiation, that this was the way it must be. I nodded, not knowing what other choice I had. I faced Kotis and Fellow.

Kotis turned his head to the bird on his shoulder. "Right, shit-feathers. Get airborne and earn your keep." At his words the owl raised its head, blinked its round eyes several times, and leapt clear of its perch. Its long wings caught air, and in two flaps it vanished into the white murk. I looked after it for some time, trying to see if I could spot its shape in the fog, but I saw nothing. I glanced at Ellius to ask what was happening and found only empty air. He had gone.

"He will join us soon," Fellow said. "He has not forsaken you."

"Oh, just like the old tree lover, get gone when things get shaky," Kotis said, lowering himself to the ground.

Fellow frowned. "Kotis, you shouldn't speak of him like that."

"Ah, complete fuckery this is my little friend. A wasted cause trampling into who knows where for some trespassers," Kotis said, jerking thumb in my direction.

Anger boiled in me, and even Kotis's intimidating, muscled frame couldn't cool it. "Listen, my family was taken by something from your world. I didn't ask to come here and my family didn't either, so don't put this shit on me," I said, taking a step forward.

Kotis turned his flattened head in my direction, studying me with the glinting points that were his eyes. "You wanna be careful, mate, who you talk to like that. Might just end up in a bad spot."

I was about to fire something back when a form materialized out of the fog and landed on Kotis's shoulder. The bird ruffled its wings and pulled them tight to its body. Its beak opened and a soft clicking punctuated with a few high squeaks issued from its bobbing throat. It sounded like a telegraph in fast forward. Kotis nodded and brought something out of the pocket of his vest and fed it to the bird. Its long beak scissored a few times and then it was still.

"He says it's clear ahead for almost a mile, ground and sky," Kotis said.

"Clear of what?" I asked, fury still heavy in my voice.

Kotis rose from the ground and dusted the seat of his pants off. "It's clear of the nasties we don't want to meet in there, that's what," he said.

I was about to ask exactly what he meant when Fellow approached and drew close to me. "Michael, stay within a few feet of us. Do not speak, and tread softly. Do not stray like you did in the carnival on the border of your world, we won't be able to protect you, and you won't survive."

"Fellow, what's in there?" I asked, staring into his orange eyes.

"Do not stray," he said, and without hesitation stepped into the folds of the fog. The area where he vanished swirled and spun. Kotis raised his dark eyebrows and followed Fellow.

For a heartbeat I was alone, standing in the silent field. I looked over my shoulder once, hoping I would see Ellius striding from the trees to join us after all, but instead I saw only the shadowed forest and the dead plains we'd crossed. Taking a deep breath, I took two strides and stepped into the clinging mist.

It was like being thrust into a padded room. All sound became null as the fog closed around me—even my footfalls were distant and muffled. I could just barely make out Kotis and Fellow ahead waiting for me. When they saw me following, they turned and moved away, their departure so quiet and featureless it was unnerving. I turned my head from side to side, trying to distinguish something, anything that would ease my sensory discomfort. I looked for a rock and listened for the wind; I breathed deeply, trying to pick out an odor of some sort. There was nothing except our footfalls on the dead stalks as we moved.

We might have walked for hours, or days, or minutes. The passage of time was inscrutable and lost all meaning. I recited my children's names along with Jane's and their birth dates over and over in my head. I pictured their faces smiling, laughing, sleeping, all the expressions that made them who they were.

I wanted a drink. Oh, how I wanted a drink. A Jack and Coke? No, too plain. A vodka cranberry? No, too bitter. Beer? A cold glass of beer, I would've killed for one right then. To feel it sliding down my throat and warming me. It would have been beyond grand. I could taste it and was about to begin contemplating my favorite brand when I saw something out of the corner of my eye.

It was a quick movement, and when I snapped my eyes to where I thought it was, it was gone. I paused mid-step and turned in a full circle, looking for what I'd seen. It was a small shadow, not much more than three feet off the ground. Nothing moved around me except the forms of Kotis and Fellow, which became increasingly hard to see as they walked away. I hurried to catch up, remembering Fellow's warning.

"Michael."

I stopped and spun around, looking for the voice that had spoken my name, had whispered it no more than a few inches behind my back. The fog was unyielding and thick. I felt my heart pump harder as adrenaline flooded my system. I hadn't imagined it, the voice had been real, as tangible as a touch in the dense mist.

"They're dead, Michael."

I jerked around, my eyes bulging and my fists clenched. My fingernails dug into the palms of my hands, but the pain did nothing to loosen them. This time the voice had been beside me, right in my ear, the passage of breath on my skin like a lover's caress. Goose bumps spread over my body in a rolling wave. I backed up and, stumbling, turned and fled, my feet much too heavy and my legs weak, as if I'd been doing squats for an hour. After only a few steps I realized that I could no longer see Kotis and Fellow. Was this the way we'd been going? I couldn't remember and there were no landmarks to go by. I slowed some but kept a brisk pace, glancing over my shoulder every few seconds. A shape emerged from the gloom, and I nearly sobbed with relief as Kotis's silhouette appeared.

"Kotis, Fellow!" I called, my voice dying in the fog after traveling only a few feet. I remembered Fellow saying not to speak, but I needed to tell them what I'd heard and seen. I took two more steps and then stopped, my stomach shriveling in on itself like a balloon losing air.

The thing I'd thought was Kotis rippled in the dim light of the mist. It looked like a black sheet tacked over a doorway in the middle of the field, with a breeze blowing through it. The form undulated and bulged as though something desperately wanted to escape from beneath it. I began to back away, slowly at first and then with more haste. I was about to turn and run when the form exploded into dozens of small, fleeting shapes that ran, laughing, into the coiling fog. My bowels threatened to release and my eyes bulged at the spot, where there was only blank mist.

A hand grasped my shoulder.

I tried to scream but another hand clamped down over my mouth, stifling my yell. Kotis pulled me close to him and brought his face within inches of mine.

"What in the blue shits do you think you're doing?" he said. His black eyes spoke of murder and I thought he might kill me on the spot, when Fellow appeared at his side and pulled his giant hand from my mouth.

"Michael, what is it? Did you see anything?" Fellow asked, his eyes wide.

I nodded dumbly. "Over there, something big. It broke apart and the pieces ran away."

Kotis glanced at Fellow before hauling me closer to him again. I could smell his breath and it was fairly rank. "You move right behind Fellow, don't stop and don't look around." He squeezed my shoulder to emphasize his point and I winced in pain. With a murmured word to the owl on his shoulder, the bird took flight and was gone into the fog. "Let's go," he said and began to run.

Fellow sprinted ahead of us, and I followed with Kotis at my heels. The air whistled around my ears and my breathing became ragged as I tried to keep pace with Fellow. He ran with fluid ease, his ropy legs pumping and his oblong head pushed forward. More than once I felt Kotis jab me in the back with a finger, urging me faster.

After a few minutes of running, I became aware of a rushing sound all around us. It was like a breeze growing before a storm. Just as I began to look over my shoulder I was flung to the ground, the air knocked loose of my lungs as I landed on my chest. When I managed to raise my head, I saw that Fellow was also prone. A shadow passed over us and I blinked, trying to follow it. It was massive and triangle shaped, but that was all I could gather because in another second it was gone.

"Up," Kotis whispered and hauled me to my feet. We ran. I felt hunted. I knew then what the first mammal must have felt like hurrying across a primordial plain with something monstrous only a few steps behind.

"They're dead, Michael. Just lie down." The voice echoed now, and I nearly stopped to figure out where it had come from, but Kotis pushed me onward.

"I hear it too, just keep moving and we'll be out soon," Kotis breathed through clenched teeth.

"Can't you feel that they're gone? Lie down to sleep and we'll show you."

I'd been wrong. There wasn't an echo; it was a chorus. The voices spoke almost in unison, but several were delayed, causing an eerie reverberation. Jesus, how many were there? I glanced to my left and saw a shape zip away into the fog and nearly screamed. I only caught a momentary impression, but it looked like the shape was serpentine with a distinctly human-like head.

I forced myself to look forward and focus on keeping pace with Fellow. He never wavered in direction, and we seemed to be traveling in a straight line. I prayed that he knew where he was going.

"Daddy?"

My daughter's voice stopped me. Kotis grabbed for my neck, but I shrugged his hand off like it was a gnat. In the fog I saw a small outline I would have known anywhere. Sara was there in the mist. She was only steps away, her arms hanging limply at her sides, her face turned toward me.

"Sara!" I called, and felt Kotis's hand encircle my arm just below the shoulder. I swung a left hook as I turned and must have caught him off-guard, because it connected and his hand loosened just enough for me to pull away. I ran to Sara, but when I looked again she was farther away, but still there.

My little girl. As I ran I remembered the time she'd ridden on her bike out to the road by our house without me knowing it. I recalled stepping onto the deck and seeing her hair flying out from beneath her helmet as she pedaled into the street, right in front of a car rounding a nearby corner. The next instant I was bleeding from both knees, having dived into the road and tackled her off her bike before it was mowed beneath the front of the speeding Ford Taurus. But in that interim of lost time I felt fear unlike anything else I'd experienced before, an emotion so pure and powerful it drowned out all else except the need for it to go away.

I felt that same fear now as I ran toward her small shape. The ground pounded beneath my feet and I leaned forward. I'd gather her up in my arms just like before and tell her it was okay, that Daddy was there, that everything would be all right.

The laughter was what stopped me, because it was not hers. My daughter's outline came closer, became clearer, and dread filtered down through my stomach.

Her face was gone.

Only flat, leathery skin coated the area where a nose and mouth should be, and the hair that should have been smooth and honey blond was tangled and black. An amorphous face shifted on either side of the head, a nose pressing out and then receding, eyes surfacing and then descending again. A slit opened on both cheeks and an obscenely long tongue lolled out, licking the air as the thing spoke.

"I'm dead, Daddy. You should die too."

I backpedaled too late, and the thing that was not my daughter lunged forward with a swiftness of a striking snake. I smelled rot and burning hair before two wings beat past me and landed with clawed feet on the shifting, faceless creature. Shrieking filled the air, making my hands shoot up to cover my ears. The owl hovered over the thing from the fog, its long beak darting forward to strike at where eyes should have been in the creature's face.

A hand grabbed my arm and pulled me away. I was thrown forward and somehow kept my feet underneath me as I began to run. Kotis ran at my side while Fellow sprinted ahead, the sounds of the fight fading in the mist as we left it behind. Two hissing shadows appeared to our left, and Kotis cursed as I saw him reach into the pouch he'd fed the owl from earlier. He drew out the same substance and tossed it at the approaching forms with a bellow and hurried on, his large hand shoving me faster.

"The bridge!" Fellow called over his shoulder, and for a few seconds I didn't know what he meant. Then a structure took form ahead. I could see a flattened area on the ground and newel posts growing up like leaning headstones, with drooping rope hanging between the supports. As we fled onto the wooden planks, I spotted the river. It wasn't wide, but I had never seen anything like it before. The water was as black as tar in the deep ravine below us. Every so often a gout of flame would erupt and light the earthen walls with swimming shadows. But the strangest and most disorienting trait the river held wasn't its color or flammability, but its speed. I gaped at it as I ran, trying to judge how fast the black liquid flowed. But each time I found something to focus on, it washed away out of sight. However, I knew the river could outrun any express train I'd seen on Earth.

The fog at the far end of the bridge thickened, and I resisted the urge to hold my breath as we plunged into it. There was a disorienting moment when everything vanished into the dull gray and sound ceased completely, then we were out of it. The mist fell away, and we were in a field identical to the one we'd left on the other side of the fog. The horizon was unchanged except the sun's half-lidded eye sat farther to the right than it had that morning.

Fellow slowed his pace, and then stopped and turned to face me. Despite the weakness in my legs, they wanted to continue on, driven by the terror that still vibrated in the back of my skull. Fellow put out a hand and braced me before I could tip forward to the ground. I swallowed a rush of bile that flooded my mouth, and coughed. Flitting black snowflakes danced at the corners of my vision, and I wobbled but remained standing with Fellow's help. The air tasted almost sweet, and I sucked it in greedily as I turned and gazed back at the bridge.

The fog ended at the first board and shot straight up until it became one with the clouds. Kotis stood only a few feet from the wall of fog, his dark eyes searching the folds of mist. Without warning the owl exploded into view and landed awkwardly on the giant's shoulder. Its feathers were ruffled, and when I looked closer I saw that many were missing from its wide wings. Kotis murmured to it, and the bird clicked a few times and seemed to shudder.

I turned to Fellow, who still stared at the fog, his eyes watching the curtain intently. "Fellow, what were those things?"

"Lies embodied. The field we crossed is called the Field of Lies. It exists only to destroy those who try to travel through it."

I heard Kotis's heavy footfalls approaching and turned to say a word of thanks to his bird, but all that greeted me was a close-up view of four immense knuckles, followed by darkness.

I wasn't surprised to find myself facing the sky when I opened my eyes. I'd dreamed of being hit by a truck, and as my memories came flowing back to me, I realized I wasn't too far off. I sat up and rubbed my jaw, which felt like a rusted hinge. I worked it up and down a few times to make sure it still functioned and my teeth matched up.

"Are you okay, Michael?" Fellow asked. I turned my head and found that he sat only a few feet to my right. His vine-like arms rested on his knees and his fingers held two stalks of chaff.

"Yeah," I managed, blinking back a bout of double vision that made my stomach flop with nausea. "I think my jaw might be broken."

"Oh, fuckin' nonsense! I hit ya half speed, if that, you little bastard," Kotis called from my left. I looked to where he sat and studied his face, which was drawn down in disgust. The owl sat on his shoulder, its head tucked beneath a tattered wing.

"I'm sorry," I said. "I shouldn't have run off, but I heard my daughter in there—Christ, I saw her! I couldn't help myself."

"Yeah, well, you almost got us all killed!" Kotis yelled. "Fellow tells you to stay close, you run away! Maybe next time we say get gone and you'll stick around!"

"Look, I said I'm sorry. If you both knew what was in there, why didn't you warn me?" I asked. I tried to keep the anger out of my voice, but only partially succeeded.

Kotis stood up and took a few steps forward, pointing at me. "We didn't have any forsaken clue as to what we'd find in there. Shit, I've never stepped foot in that blasted place before today."

"He's right, Michael," Fellow said, kneeling beside me. "The Field of Lies is a cancerous spot even in this world, and it's destroyed many who've tried to traverse it. The creatures that live there are unique to each life that passes through the fog. I could have guessed at what you'd see or hear, but there was no way of telling for sure."

I mulled this over. Fellow was right, and I begrudgingly admitted to myself that Kotis was too. I'd endangered everyone, including my family. The words that the shadows spoke in the fog floated back to me, and I stood without thinking.

"Does that mean that Sara's ... that she's—" I couldn't bring myself to say it, and looked from Kotis to Fellow, my eyes asking, pleading.

"If something is said or seen in the Field of Lies, it is untrue. Your daughter is surely alive," Fellow said as he stood and placed a gentle hand on my shoulder.

Relief swam through me and I nearly staggered. Sara was alive. And if she was alive, then I could hope that Jack and Jane were too.

I walked in an unsteady line to where Kotis stood. He studied me with open contempt, and I braced myself for another blow, but none came. "I'm truly sorry," I said after a moment of meeting his gaze. "I would like to apologize to your owl and thank him for saving me."

"He ain't an owl, whatever that is," Kotis said, but I saw his brow soften. "He's a reacher, one of the last of his kind. And he's missin' feathers now because of you, and they won't ever grow back."

I studied the empty spots on the bird's wings where the monster in the fog had broken or pulled the feathers out during their battle. The brown and black tones of the feathers that seemed familiar before now looked strange up close, and I saw that they were all bordered with a metallic silver. In fact, the edges looked sharp, as if they could slice not only air but flesh and bone. "I'm sorry," I said. "Could I please say thank you?"

Kotis remained stoic for almost a minute, and just when I thought he wasn't going to answer, he tilted his head to the side and whispered something to the mass of feathers on his shoulder. A few seconds later, the bird unfurled its wing and its head appeared. I saw that its eyes were black and ringed with gold, the color of the last escaping rays of a sunset. Its beak opened and an impatient click issued from within.

I looked the animal in the eyes and spoke as though I were apologizing to a person. "I'm truly thankful for your help earlier, and I'm very sorry you were injured." Any absurdity I felt at speaking to a bird was dispelled when its eyes blinked and the rounded crown of its head titled forward in a small bow. Without meeting my gaze again, it promptly re-covered its head with a wing and was still.

"He's more forgivin' than I am," Kotis said as he ran a hand in a gentle stroke over the bird's frame.

"What's his name?" I asked.

Indecision battled on the giant's wide face, as if telling me would concede something he didn't want to let go of. "Scrim," he said at last.

"Scrim," I repeated. "What's it mean?"

"It means, it's his bloody name, that's what it means," Kotis said, shaking his head as he turned away. I glanced at Fellow, who hid a small grin beneath his hand.

We rested for a while at the edge of the fog, although we moved a little farther away despite Fellow's assurances that nothing could cross the bridge from the field. We could make no fire since there was nothing really to burn except the dead stalks covering the ground like spiny whiskers. Instead, we sat in a semicircle, speaking little as the rotating sun moved clockwise around us.

"What did you throw out of your pouch at the shadows before we crossed the bridge?" I asked Kotis after an extended bout of silence. He merely looked at me for a time before digging into the little bag at his side. He drew out a handful of dark chunks and tossed them to me. A few landed on the ground, but I caught the majority of the round lumps. They were fibrous and black, about the size of quarters. When I brought them closer to my face, I smelled strong spices and smoke.

"Dried cobble," Kotis said. "Cured meat," he offered after I tipped my head to one side.

"Do the things in the fog eat this stuff?" I asked, picking up the jerky that lay on the ground.

"I've no clue, but it was all I had to throw at the demons," Kotis said.

I glanced at him, waiting for an insult to fly from his lips, but to my amazement a wry smile bloomed there. I looked at Fellow, who grinned, and then back at Kotis, who chuckled deep in his chest. I laughed then, realizing that Kotis had been as terrified as the rest of us. Soon we were all laughing together, the tension of the day easing out naturally through a conduit that seemed to transcend not only races but worlds as well.

I lay back on the ground, flattening a spot large enough to encompass my body, and let the mirth fade away. Sleep pulled at me, and within minutes my eyes fluttered closed and I was gone.

Fellow nudged me awake sometime later. Time seemed inconsequential, yet was also the most precious thing in the world to me. It was fluid and slipped away with only the variance of the sun passing around us, rubbing me raw with thoughts of how long my family had been gone. As I rose from the ground I tried to envision where they were, in what hell they subsisted, and what horrors they endured. The enormity of the sorrow that pushed down on me was almost too much, and I shoved it away to the wings of my thoughts, where it waited to smother me again with its wet blanket darkness.

"Which way next?" I asked, brushing myself off.

"Not that way, that's for sure," Kotis said, jerking a thumb in the direction of the fog. "If I never go through that place again, it'll be too soon."

"This way," Fellow said and pointed at an angle just to the right of the line we'd been traveling.

"How can you be sure?" I asked as we began to walk.

"Because that's the direction we'll find the next forest," he responded.

I frowned. "How can you know? Have you been through here before?"

He shook his head and turned his orange eyes my way. "I've never set foot past the edge of the bridge before today. The trees call to me."

Kotis drew even with me, his long stride equaling two of mine. "Little ropy bastard can find a tree in a thousand-mile desert, he can," the giant said.

"But is that where my family is, near the next forest?"

Kotis shrugged. "It's the best we've got to go on."

Scrim's head appeared from beneath his wing and he eyed me with his brilliant gaze. I marveled at the intensity of the look, the intelligence that shone out like two beams of light.

"He really understands what we say, doesn't he?" I asked, motioning to the bird.

"Oh, he understands more than you know there, wanker," Kotis said, giving me a glance. Four hours before I would have bristled at the insult, but something had given a little after sharing the laughter in the field. Though my jaw still hurt where he'd punched me, I knew that there was no venom in his words now. "He's the only thing in this land that can touch those demons in the mist."

"Please quit calling them that," Fellow said quietly ahead of us.

Kotis opened his mouth and then shut it. I looked at him questioningly, and he merely shook his head and stroked Scrim's head before clearing his throat.

"I raised Scrim here from an egg. He was a gift from my father when I became old enough to hunt and defend our home. We been side by side ever since."

"But he's not really a pet, is what you're saying," I said.

"No, he's not even really bound to me at all. He could fly off at the first whim he had and never return, but he always comes back, don't you, you flying shitbag!" Kotis poked Scrim in the ribs, who responded by clicking his long beak with a sound like a pair of scissors closing. Kotis leaned closer to me and cupped a hand conspiratorially around the side of his mouth. "I think he comes back because of my shinin' personality."

I laughed and Kotis looked ahead, his black eyes gleaming. I thought I caught a shake of Scrim's head before he leapt from his perch into the air and soared away.

We walked in silence for miles after that. The ground rolled in familiar-feeling plains that I knew from growing up in the Midwest. I could imagine the unending fields studded with rows of corn or barley. Other than the slight rises and falls of the ground, the fields we trekked across were unremarkable. I strained my eyes and turned several times, trying to spot something, a bird, a rock, a tree, anything, but there was nothing, just an ocean of brown stubble that may have existed at the same height for a millennia.

My thoughts returned to Jane and the kids as we walked, the chorus of our feet a drumbeat to the soundtrack of a life that seemed impossibly far away. For some reason I kept thinking of the last time Jane and I had fought. I'd been drunk, and it hadn't rained for weeks. I remembered how she'd looked at me, pinned me to the wall with a gaze that every person in a relationship comes to hate: the look of true hurt. Her eyes now floated before me and blotted out the dismal landscape that surrounded us. They'd shone with barely restrained tears, tears that begged to fall but couldn't, somehow held by the curvature of her eyes or by sheer will, I wasn't sure which. The words she said lingered in my ears and drowned out the light breeze that ruffled my shirt. *It just hurts, Michael, that's all. I won't leave you, but you've got to do something for me. Find a way to fight it that won't destroy you, or us. Please.*

I swallowed and wiped away a tear, hating myself for wanting a drink at that moment. I saw Kotis glance at me, and I turned away to look back the way we'd come so I didn't have to meet his gaze.

A shadow stood on the last rise behind us.

I sucked in a breath and felt my muscles flinch. The figure wavered like a mirage and then folded in half, then in half again, until it was gone from sight. I heard Kotis stop, noticing I'd quit walking.

"What is it?" he rumbled as he stepped beside me.

I pointed to the last hill we had come over. "There was something there. It was there and then gone."

Fellow moved to my other side and gazed at where I pointed. "Are you sure, Michael?"

"Yes, I'm sure, it was standing there watching us, it almost looked like—" I stopped, fear closing in on me like a tide. "Are you sure they can't come out of the fog?" I asked hoarsely.

"Their kind cannot cross the river," Fellow said. His voice was low and reassuring, but I felt a chill run through me as I remembered how the black thing in the fog had broken apart and capered away.

"Let's keep an eye on our tails, eh?" Kotis said. Scrim flew from the sky, and Kotis put out a thick forearm for him to perch on. Several long clicks and a short screech stuttered from the bird's open beak, and Kotis squinted, listening.

"He says there's something ahead, less than a mile over the next hill."

"What is it?" Fellow asked.

"I'm not sure, he keeps saying." Kotis paused, looking at Fellow and then me. "He keeps saying 'death, death.'"

CHAPTER SIX

THE HOUSE OF BONE

It took us ten minutes until we crested the last hill and saw it. At first, we thought it was a massive forest growing in serrated angles that prodded the twilight sky and that Fellow's sense of direction was dead-on. But as we drew closer it became apparent that it wasn't a forest at all. The first thing I noticed was the smell. I'd gotten used to the autumnal air—the smells of cold earth, fallen leaves, and organic decay. The new smell on the wind was one of death, the potent stink of spoiled flesh, and it brought the sound of flies buzzing, even though there were none in sight. The color was the next thing that struck me. The shapes ahead were white. There were no soft browns or blacks to indicate trunks or bark. There was only a monochrome, devoid of color.

We walked several more steps before Fellow froze and spoke without looking at either of us. "Kotis, is this what I think it is?"

Kotis looked at Fellow for some time before realization dawned on his face and his eyes widened. "You got to be shittin' me," he said.

"What?" I asked, glancing between the two of them.

Fellow finally turned and looked at me, his face holding an undeniable amount of fear. "This is the place of death in our world. It is where all things come to die, and those that don't come are brought."

"Brought? Brought by what?" I asked. Fellow pulled his gaze from mine and looked fleetingly at Kotis before walking away. Kotis followed, and I had no choice but to do the same.

The closer we got the more detail began to take shape. What looked like trees before now became sharper, more curved. I noticed a few gray tinges here and there within the white. The mass before us stretched away in either direction until I lost sight of it, and I was reminded of the fog. I wondered if the world I stood in now had no solid dimensions, the vision of those seeing it being its only real limitations.

I was again about to ask what it was we were approaching when I saw something that I recognized, and stopped. What I thought was some sort of structure or abstract architecture became identifiable, and I felt my mouth open as my aching jaw slackened.

Bones.

Millions or trillions, perhaps more. They were stacked with wild abandon in crisscrossing patterns, interlocked in a macabre jigsaw puzzle. They were polar white, with patches of gray age setting in on some. Some were broken and twisted, leaving jagged edges to catch the low light and spray their uneven shadows onto their brethren. The pile was at least fifty feet high and relatively uniform except for a few places where several rib cages towered over everything, unfathomable in their height because I knew no animals that possessed bones of that size.

"Oh my God," I said. Fellow and Kotis stood staring at the spectacle for some time before turning to me, their faces holding no reassurances. "What is this?" I asked.

"Like I said before, this is death's gathering. Everything that lives here comes to die in this place," Fellow said in a low voice. He spoke as though he was afraid something might hear him.

"I almost didn't believe it existed," Kotis said with a small amount of awe. "I mean, I knew, but seeing it is something different."

The number of bones was so staggering my mind faltered trying to comprehend it. I looked at the skeletal wreckage and tried to pick out something familiar, but saw nothing that resembled anything on Earth. Many of the bones were so massive they defied logic to a mind that considered dinosaurs and blue whales large. I spotted a bleached skull with two spiny horns sprouting from each side that was the size of a compact car. Its forehead was riddled with what I thought was decaying holes at first, but then saw that they were eye sockets, all twenty of them.

"We have to find a way through," Fellow said.

"Scrim, find us a passage, eh?" Kotis said to the bird, which flapped away down the face of the twisted mass. We began to walk in the direction Scrim flew, our heads turning constantly to gaze at the pile beside us. It was only a few minutes later when Scrim returned, speaking to Kotis of a break in the wall, but by then we could already see it.

There was a wide swath through the bones, forming a V channel that shot up on either side like an enormous hall. The ground was packed solid as though many feet had trodden there, pressing the dirt into a highway between death's walls. The passage twisted away out of sight a hundred yards in, and a quiet hush fell over us as we gazed inside.

"There's no other choice," Fellow said, seemingly reading my mind. "We have to go through."

Kotis grunted and I licked my lips. Even the fog hadn't instilled a sense of dread like the one that coiled within my stomach as I looked at the path. But Fellow was right, there was no other way through. The words of a song came to me then. Something about walking through hell on feet made of glass.

We stepped into the canyon, our footsteps echoing off the walls around us. I had the feeling of walking into a cave, even though the sky above us was open. The smell I noticed earlier only increased with each step, and soon I was resisting the urge to pull my T-shirt over my mouth and nose to block it.

There was something else too, and at first I couldn't put my finger on it. But then I noticed Kotis turning his head back and forth, examining the gaps in the bones around us. The feeling was of being watched. I was about to say something when a clatter and movement drew my eyes past Fellow, who stopped and braced his feet on the hard ground.

A few bones fell end over end down the edge of the passage and came to rest on the path. I scanned the wall where they'd fallen from and saw nothing in the stacks. Scrim let out a small cry and then hissed as he ruffled his wings. All of us watched for something more, but after several minutes of silence we moved on. The trail twisted like a snake, first right, then left, then back again, almost in a full circle before straightening out. The entire time I felt eyes on my skin, pushing against it and raising goose bumps more than once as I glanced over my shoulder expecting something to be there, inches behind me.

After nearly an hour of walking, a clearing appeared ahead, with a dark spot at its center. The dark area gradually took form, and I saw that it was a house, of sorts. Its walls were made of the largest bones I'd seen yet, their ends disappearing into the ground like tent stakes. Here and there windows were cut out, opening unto perfect squares of darkness. A spire shot from the top of the structure and looked like an auger shell my uncle gave me when I was nine. He'd picked it up on a beach in Vietnam during his tour there, and placed it in my hand, telling me it was from a country where monsters lived. My father had reprimanded him, saying not to fill my head with nonsense and things I didn't understand. His words chilled me as I gazed at the bone house. *There are places where monsters live, Michael. Don't ever go where your heart tells you not to.* Everything in my being told me not to walk into the clearing, but Fellow and Kotis continued on, and I followed.

The clearing was circular, like a meteor had plummeted and burned a hole in the bone field, and pools of dark water sat in depressions. We avoided these without words, an unspoken agreement that only heightened my fear when I looked down into one and saw no bottom. The bone house was also circular, and for a moment I was reminded of Stonehenge. This place was desolate and alien, and I wanted nothing more than to circumvent the house and continue past it, to run from there with all the strength I had left; but we walked on, each of us controlling our fear in our own way.

We stopped at the building's wall and looked up. The nearest window was cut through the center of a femur twice the size of a redwood. An idea struck me then, and I put a hand on Fellow's shoulder to pull him close.

"Could this be the place my family is being held at?" I asked. My hope withered as Fellow shook his head.

"This is a place of legend that only the dead know. The one we seek is beyond here."

"Think someone's home?" Kotis asked in a whisper. I shrugged and was about to suggest we not investigate when we heard footsteps from behind.

We spun as one and watched the cowled figure that emerged from the path. It was short and humped and wore a frayed brown cowl draped over its head, obscuring any features in the dim light. It walked with a sure steadiness that spoke of many trips in and out of the yard we stood in. The most unnerving thing about the figure, which pushed me back until my shoulders met the solidity of the house, was the bone it carried over one slumped shoulder. It was long and arced like a sickle, and a polished edge that looked sharp enough to cut flesh with ease shone.

The hood shifted and the open darkness beneath the hanging fabric took us in, perhaps seeing us for the first time. It stopped and regarded us for a few long seconds, and then reached up to its cowl. Before the withered hand grasped the hood and drew it back, I saw something move in the darkness where the face hung. There was a shifting, a *rearranging* of shadows, and then it stilled as the hand pulled the coarse cowl away.

An old man stood before us, his head smoother than an eight ball, with sallow cheeks that hung down like a hound's. His lips were dark red and dipped in middle of a smile that appeared warm but made my stomach drop.

The man looked at each of our faces and held steady when he came to mine. Our eyes met, and I realized his were the color of newly formed ice. "Good evening," he said in a singsong voice that dipped with each syllable. "I didn't expect guests tonight, but it is a delightful surprise."

"Hello, we are just traveling through and will not burden you with our presence. We're sorry to have intruded—" Fellow said, but the old man cut him off in mid-sentence with a wave of his hand.

"It's no burden at all. I was just out for a walk and in the mood for supper. Will you take part in a dinner?"

"We must be going, we're expected by friends at the other side shortly," Fellow said in a steady voice. Inside my head, I sang his praises because of the calm front he portrayed and prayed he could keep it up to get us out of here. Something was wrong, and deep inside me an instinct reserved for survival shouted warnings that kicked my heartbeat into high gear.

"Nonsense," the old man said, coming closer. "Supper won't take but a breath, and I can see you're hungry. Especially this one," he said, pointing at my chest.

"We'd be very much obliged," Kotis broke in. The giant stepped in front of me, partially blocking my view of the old man. I saw a flicker of annoyance cross the cowled man's face, and then he broke into a smile.

"Come inside, friends. You'll be on the path again in no time." Instead of leading the way, he motioned to the opposite side of the house, herding us ahead of him. I hoped I wasn't the only one that noticed how he gripped the sharpened bone over his shoulder tighter as we began to walk.

We made our way around the side of the house, and I studied the walls as we went. The bone was black, and only when I looked closer did I see that it had been burned. The charring was only on the outside of the house, and I could see the whiteness resume where the heat hadn't reached. A door appeared after a few more steps, and we moved aside to let the old man enter first. His eyes moved over us as he walked past and threw the door wide without pausing. I felt Fellow grip my arm and tip his head toward the far side of the clearing. Another path led away, through the field, and looked almost identical to the one we had just left.

I understood what he wanted and prepared myself to run, when Kotis's hand gripped my shoulder. "No, there are things in the bones, I saw them moving behind him when he came near us," Kotis whispered. My eyes shot to the surrounding walls and searched for movement but saw none. "We have to go in," he said, and glanced at Fellow to make sure he understood.

"Come in, friends, come in. No need to stand outside," the old man said from deeper in the house. Fellow hesitated and then nodded his assent. Kotis entered the house, and I followed, with Fellow a few steps behind.

The inside of the house was spacious, the air above us open where a second story might've been. Looking up I noticed that the spire on the roof was partially hollow. The walls were bare and white, in stark contrast to their reverse sides. There were no adornments anywhere, and the only furniture was a small table and two chairs in the center of the room. I took one more step and stopped, my bowels squeezing painfully inside me as I saw what sat in the chairs.

Two human skeletons.

They were bleached whiter than any of the other bones I'd seen, and sat stock-straight, as if they were held to the chairs by invisible strings. Their sightless eyes stared at the opposite wall, and their jaws hung open almost to their breastbones.

My stupor broke with a slamming sound behind us, and I spun to see that the door was shut and the lock turned closed, twisted by an unseen hand.

"Alchemy, magic, whatever you'd like to call it, that's the center of all things. It's where it all originated. Flung from the center of the void it came, and I caught the strings of it, pulled it down, and kept it here, inside my head." The old man stood at a narrow shelf beneath a window, his hands working on something I couldn't see.

"I guess we don't rightly follow, sir," Kotis said as politely as he could. I saw him stretch his shoulders. Scrim's eyes were trained on the old man's back.

"No, I wouldn't think you would. Feeble minds think alike, they say. Addled by weakness, pah! So fitting you should wander here, but delightful for me and my children."

I took a step back and tried to calm my breathing, which had begun to pick up speed. The old man's voice changed as he said the last words, gathering depth. *My children.* I noticed Fellow and Kotis glancing around the room. I searched for something I hadn't seen when we entered, some kind of weapon or a window low enough for us to climb out of. But there was nothing; not even the sharpened bone was anywhere in sight.

The man turned, and I saw that his eyes were larger and the pupils had disappeared. They were solid gray-blue and filmed with a milky substance. "This, my friends, is what life is about," he said, holding a glass vial half full with a black fluid. "This is life, but it's lacking one thing." The huge eyes found me, and I felt a pull, like something snagging my clothing on a hook. "Enough blood to sustain, not just imitate."

He tipped his hand and poured a few drops of the liquid onto the skull of the nearest skeleton. The bones on the chair thrashed into life, and a bloodcurdling scream ripped from the tongueless mouth.

All three of us backed away, and I felt the door latch dig into my back. I reached back without turning around, unwilling to look away from the old man, who was not a man at all, and tried to open the door. It was stuck tight, and when I struggled to yank it open, the thing in the cowl laughed in a deep voice. The skeleton he'd poured the mixture on moved with an eerie similarity to real life. It whipped its head from side to side, as if searching for something, and when it opened its mouth again, a panicked voice issued forth.

"Where am I? Oh God, what happened? Alice? Can you hear me? Please, answer me! I can't see anything!"

The thing in the cowl wasn't even remotely human anymore, and I saw that only the two bulging eyes and wide mouth remained on its face. Dagger-like teeth flashed in blackened gums as it walked around the table and grew taller by the second. "I need all the blood in your body," it said, pointing a ragged fingernail at my chest. "To make my children whole."

Kotis launched into motion, and threw a kick at the thing's chest so fast it wasn't able to react in time. The giant's foot sank into the brown fabric and met something hard. With a howl, the creature flew backward and nearly fell when its back connected with the table. The skeleton that hadn't reanimated fell limply to the floor and scattered in several pieces, while the other continued to scream for Alice.

"Window!" Kotis yelled, and shoved Fellow and me toward the far wall, where an open square hung in the bone almost ten feet above the floor.

I ran and stopped below it, looking up at the dim outline that was our only way out. Kotis grabbed me roughly and hoisted me up. I felt like a toddler being tossed into the air by the strong arms of a father. I reached as high as I could and grasped the sill with the tips of my fingers. I strained against the weight of my body, and finally found enough purchase on the smooth wall with my feet to push me higher.

There was a grunt of pain from below, and I looked over my shoulder to see the creature brandishing the sharpened bone in its hands. There was a slick of blood, intensely red on the white of the bone, and I saw Kotis holding his chest. Scrim flapped wildly around the room, and then dove and zoomed straight at the creature's head. The thing swung its weapon, but it was too slow for the bird. As Scrim passed by its shoulder, I heard the tearing of cloth. A gout of blood spewed from the wide gash near the creature's throat, and it staggered, holding a palm to the wound, a look of disbelief shining in its enlarged eyes.

"Up!" Fellow cried.

I turned back to the wall. With a yell, I heaved myself up and into the large window. The outside air washed over my face and it had never felt so good. I crouched and turned back, reaching for Fellow, who stood below the window. Our eyes met and he jumped, extending his knurled fingers toward me. Our hands locked and I pulled, surprised by how light he was. I stood and yanked him into the broad window, almost losing my balance as I did. We both looked down at the scene below us.

Kotis circled the border of the round room, while the creature stood at its center swaying the bone sickle in the air. Scrim flapped about and seemed to bide his time for an opening in the thing's defenses. The wound on the creature's neck was gone, leaving only a gaping hole in its cowl and unblemished white flesh beneath.

Kotis paused, his eyes shooting up to where we stood. "Go! Leave me!" he yelled, thrusting his arm out in a shooing gesture.

I searched the area around us and saw nothing of use. My eyes traveled up to the ceiling high above, and I saw a few slivers of light around the base of the spire. Something clicked in my mind, and I scrambled out to the edge of the window.

"What are you doing?" Fellow asked, his orange eyes wide with fear.

"Just give me a boost," I said, reaching out and grasping the overhang of the roof above us. There was just enough of a lip to grab on to, and my fingers found purchase in a cracked bone. I raised one leg and felt Fellow's hands interlace beneath my foot. At the same time, I pulled and he flung my foot up and away.

I swung out and onto the roof, my upper body landing heavily on the steep incline. The rough contours of bone dug into my ribs and I gasped. I felt gravity begin to do its work, and lunged higher in one last effort before I fell. My hand scrabbled against smoothness, and then clenched on a narrow opening in the roof. I strained as hard as I could, my muscles screaming in protest. My legs slid up and gained footing on the overhang.

A bellow of pain came from below, and I knew Kotis had sustained another injury. I hoped he could hold on a few more seconds. I awkwardly climbed up the roof until I was eye-to-eye with the base of the spire. My assumption had been right. The massive bone was barely fastened in the chimney-like opening of the roof. A few bone wedges jammed into the gap prevented the spire from falling inside.

I worked my fingers into a small space and pulled a wedge free. I felt a vibration and saw the spire list to one side several inches. Encouraged, I grabbed another bone and yanked it back and forth until it popped loose with a dry crack. The entire spire slid almost a foot before jamming tight with a short squeal, a long, broken bone stopping its progress. My heart punched the inside of my chest, and I blinked the moisture from my eyes to clear my vision before putting my face down to a crack in the roof.

Kotis shifted slowly from one foot to the other at the far side of the room. A rivulet of blood ran down the inside of his bicep and dripped from the tips of his clenched knuckles. Scrim flitted into and out of my limited field of vision. I strained to see where the creature stood. A flash of bone whipped through the air just below me as the thing slashed wildly at Scrim, who continued to fly in circles. It took another step, and I saw the bald gleam of its skull below.

I snapped the wedged bone sideways, and watched the spire plummet past me.

There was an inhuman screech and then a wet thump, the house vibrating beneath me. The spire's tip jounced and rattled in the hole left by its base, then broke off and disappeared inside with another dry crash. Dust flew up through the hole, and I coughed, tasting the osseous particles. After a moment I leaned over and peered inside, terrified that I'd missed.

The spire was in two pieces on the floor, as was the creature. The huge bone had caught the thing in the mid-back and punched it to the floor, severing its body in half. Blood washed the dirt with a black fan, and one of the creature's arms twitched, as if reaching for something.

"Fuck me runnin'," Kotis said, leaning against the wall, his big hands splayed on the bone behind him. When his eyes looked up and found my face poking through the hole in the ceiling, he smiled. "Nice shot, mate!"

"Thanks," I said, the shock of the last few minutes grinding into me. I steadied myself and swallowed down the taste of bile in the back of my mouth. Shuddering, I sat on the roof and tried to calm my breathing. I felt sick and triumphant all at once.

I heard Fellow speaking to Kotis below, telling him to drag a chair closer to the window so he could climb out. Another sound invaded my ears, and I looked around the house for its source. It was a hissing whisper punctuated with short tinkling like a wind chime makes in a soft breeze. I stood and surveyed the path we'd entered from, and saw nothing in the shadow thrown by the high wall of bone. I turned again and looked down the avenue leading out of the yard. Nothing moved there either. The sound continued, and I noticed it came from all sides, the hissing thump and violin scratch getting louder and louder. Then I saw it.

The piles of bones all around the clearing were shifting.

Something moved beneath them, *burrowed* through them. I saw bones being forced apart and then falling back together with the passage of whatever moved our way.

I found my voice after a second. "Guys! Get the fuck out of the house! Now!" There a pause, and then I heard hurried movement below me. I half walked, half slid down the roof until I sat perched on the overhang. I scanned the surrounding walls, but I wasn't high enough to see the progress of whatever drew nearer. I could only hear the rattle and clack of bones from every direction.

Kotis appeared in the window, pulling himself up next to Fellow, and glanced at me. "Swing down, I'll catch you," he said, extending his tree-trunk arms.

Without thinking too much about trajectory or speed, I lay down, scooted to the edge of the roof, shimmied my legs over, and swung toward the window. My hands lost their grip, and I let out a terrified squawk reserved for the unique sensation of falling. Kotis snatched me from the air as I passed by the window and pulled me in with ease, setting my feet on the window opening.

"What is it?" Fellow asked, grasping me by the shoulder.

"There are things coming toward us through the bones, they're everywhere," I managed.

Fellow looked at Kotis and then at the ground. "We'll have to jump," he said.

I glanced down and saw we were still more than fifteen feet up. With a quick breath, I stepped into the air and fell. The ground flew up and smashed into my feet, sending rivers of pain from my heels to my hair. My legs collapsed and I rolled, remembering to tuck into a ball. The dirt bit into my spine, and then I was back on my feet, trying to catch the breath that had been yanked from my lungs. Fellow and Kotis leapt from the window at the same time, both landing with much more grace than I'd managed.

"Go!" Fellow yelled, and we ran toward the opening on the far side of the clearing. Our feet hammered the ground and blood flew from Kotis's arm as he pumped it at his side. Scrim zipped past us, flying low without a flap of his wings.

We passed out of the yard and were enveloped by the high walls of the path. I heard a wall of bone behind us clatter to the ground and knew whatever chased us was in the clearing. I didn't dare look back for fear of tripping.

The trail veered left and then right. The wind whipped into my mouth and tore down my throat. Bones shivered and fell away along the incline on our right side, and something wiggled loose. I glanced in its direction and received an impression of a bulky skull working itself free of the bone field. A few streaks of black, shiny musculature extended from the rear of the skull and stretched to a long spinal cord that slipped free, letting its bulk fall to the path. The thing immediately began to slither in our direction at an alarming speed.

I tore my gaze away from the abomination and increased my pace. Fellow and Kotis raced along beside me, none of us looking back as more bones broke loose of the slopes. My fractured thoughts flew back to the creature's words in the bone house: *my children*. Perhaps they knew that their father was dead, killed by the four that fled from them.

All of my thoughts abruptly ended as the wall to our left bulged a few yards ahead of us. A tooth-encrusted snout nosed its way out of the bones, shoving femurs, rib cages, and pelvises aside. It was huge and horse-like, easily twenty feet across at its forehead, and its sabre teeth gnashed at the air as we ran by. The black holes of its eye sockets followed us with paralyzing accuracy, and I had no doubts that it somehow saw us. With a roar that made my eardrums reverberate, it flung itself free of the wall and landed on two long front legs that pulled it forward while its curving spine slid like a giant tail along the ground. The same tendinous striations stretched back and wrapped around its snake-like body.

We rounded another curve, and I nearly collapsed with relief. There was an opening ahead, and I could see a swath of trees growing beyond. But what made me rejoice inside was the sight of Ellius standing at the mouth of the passage, his shoulders thrown back in a posture of courage and his eyes smoldering as he looked past us.

We ran, the ground trembling beneath our feet. A stitch in my side threatened to double me over, but I kept going, each leg speaking of denial and collapse with every step.

We broke free of the pathway and rushed toward Ellius, who stretched out his arms and lowered his head. His eyes were closed, and his lips moved with soundless words as we neared. I risked a look back, continuing to jog sideways, unwilling to stop completely.

There were hundreds of the beasts behind us, slithering and scampering. Some were small and some towered over the rest. All were composed of bone and were missing vital pieces, like eyes, lungs, and brains, yet they continued on. I saw one creature composed of nothing but two rear legs, a spine, and a rib cage. It ran almost upright and reminded me of a Jesus lizard sprinting across a watery surface.

The creatures moved in a wave toward the path's opening, and at that moment I prepared myself to die. I couldn't run much farther, and the things that emerged from the bone field seemed to be tireless. They would eventually catch up to me and snatch me from my feet, to crush me inside their bleached jaws. I'd pictured death before, but not like this. I'd watched *The Notebook* with my wife, and that's how we'd agreed to go: together after we'd spent a lifetime with our children, who were happy and healthy with children of their own. We wanted to slip away simultaneously, two lovers escaping to a new dawn that we hoped would bring eternal happiness.

Now I imagined my family dying here, it this nightmare world of monsters and evil, without hope, without even my comfort. I closed my eyes, praying that everything was a dream. A rushing sound filled my ears, and I looked back again and came to a stop, as my legs refused to take another step.

Two gigantic tree roots pushed their way through the bone pile at the mouth of the passage, their brown trunks twisting and turning as they grew like the fabled beanstalk in the stories of my youth. They shot up from the ground and created an avalanche, as thousands of bones rolled downward, covering the entrance to the field. The monolithic horse creature in the lead turned its long head just as it was swallowed by the wave, and fell beneath the bones with a severed roar.

The roots continued up toward the sky, and just when I thought they would extend forever and pierce the hovering clouds above, they hooked down and flew toward the ground. Their tips dug into the earth and drove through it like two trains passing into a tunnel. The pile of bones continued to cascade into the passage, filling it until the roots fell still after creating a double archway that crossed near the center.

Ellius dropped his hands to his side and raised his head, looking in my direction. The smallest of smiles played across his lips. "Michael, so good to see you again."

"Woo! That's the stuff right there!" Kotis called, throwing a bloody fist high in the air. "Clunking wankers got their rights! Woo!"

Scrim swooped down and landed on Kotis's forearm, careful to avoid the nasty gash on his shoulder. He raised his head and let out a triumphant cry from his long beak.

Fellow smiled and walked to Ellius. The two stared at each other, and then clasped in a tight embrace. After a moment Fellow stepped back, looking Ellius in the face. "You had no trouble traveling here?"

Ellius threw back the branches on his head and laughed. "I'm sure my trip was unremarkable compared to yours, and we were only apart a day and a half! Come, let's sit near the trees and we'll talk over a fire." He turned, regarding me for a moment. "Michael, I'm sure you're hungry."

I was about to say no, that I'd been nauseated only minutes ago, but then I noticed the ravenous gnawing at the base of my stomach and realized I was starving. Weakness overcame me and fatigue settled on my back. I nodded. "That would be great."

Ellius smiled again. "Come then, we'll rest and recuperate for a bit." He spun on his heel and headed for the tree line a short distance away. Without another word, we followed him up the hill, in the shade of the everlasting evening.

CHAPTER SEVEN

THE VALLEY OF SOULS

The fire crackled and leapt into the air, attempting to take flight into the twilight above us. We sat in a circle around it, each chewing a piece of sinewy meat from skewers Ellius produced from inside his shawl. I didn't know where he'd gotten the meat, and I didn't care. The hunger I'd repressed until that point was painful, a burning ball at my core, and I wolfed the greasy food down as though it were lobster. In all actuality, it tasted a little like venison, and being from Minnesota, I was used to the flavor.

Ellius set down his clean skewer and sighed. "Nothing like a bit of feltson to tide you over, is there?"

"What is feltson?" I asked, popping the last of the meat onto the back of my tongue.

"Up until an hour ago he lived in a little hut just over the hill," Ellius said, jerking a thumb toward the trees behind him.

I froze mid-chew and felt the insides of my cheeks almost blister with revulsion. The warmth in my stomach that had been so satisfying a few minutes ago was now a lead brick, yearning to get out. Vomiting wasn't a conscious thought, but I must have turned white, because at that moment Kotis broke into deep, rumbling laughter that shook his mammoth frame. I swallowed and looked at Ellius, whose eyes twinkled with wicked mirth.

Fellow smiled and patted me on the back. "He's just having fun. Feltson is a type of animal here, soulless and heavily muscled. One animal provides food for a man for a month."

I nodded, willing my galloping heart to slow down, and reassured myself that I wasn't a cannibal.

"I'm sorry, Michael, couldn't resist," Ellius said, his eyes still glinting.

"It's okay," I said. I massaged my stomach and spit off to one side. My mouth was full of saliva after the receding threat of being sick.

Ellius reached forward, prodding the fire with a stick before tossing his skewer into the flames. "Tell me what transpired on your journey here," he said at last.

I breathed out and glanced at Kotis and Fellow. Fellow nodded and began to speak. He related our passage through the fog where we initially parted ways, telling of the lying shadows that we encountered. His description of me straying was mercifully brief, and Ellius's eyes flitted to mine and then away. Fellow continued, finishing up with our flight from the bone field. Silence fell over the group, except for the snapping of the wood in the fire. Ellius pursed his lips and rubbed the side of his face. A few particles of bark flew free of his rough skin and floated on the heat above the flames, until they drifted away out of sight.

"You were very lucky, Michael," Ellius said at last. "You must take care not to endanger yourself again, your family's lives depend on you reaching them in time—not to mention the fate of the worlds. Remember, if you perish, no one else can bring your family home. Only blood can bring blood out."

I nodded. "I'm sorry, I let my emotions get the best of me in the fog. It won't happen again." I turned to Kotis and Fellow. "I'm sorry." Fellow smiled and patted my shoulder before turning back to the flames. Kotis dipped his head, his eyes more soft than I'd seen them. I looked back at Ellius, who gave a small smile of approval. "What was that thing in the bone house back there?" I asked after a few seconds of quiet.

Ellius sighed. "It is the death collector. It carries the bones of the fallen to the field, adding to its piles, always adding."

"Where did it come from?"

"The fog you traveled through, it once was the King of Shadows there, the chief liar, so to speak. But it had more ambitious ideals than merely presiding over untruths and feeding upon the odd traveler who stumbled into the fog or tried to cross its land. It wanted power, power to govern over another domain. It wanted to be death incarnate. It devised a way to cross the Damning River by persuading another soul to take its place as the King of Shadows. But when it left the fog it realized that it had lost its power to bleed life from living things by just lying to them. So it began to collect the bones of the dead, amassing what you saw earlier."

"So it's something like the Grim Reaper?" I asked. Ellius tilted his head to the side. "Like death itself? On Earth death is sometimes represented by a hooded figure carrying a scythe."

"It may be a mirroring of your world, yes," Ellius said after a time.

"Those things that chased us, those were its children, weren't they?" I asked.

"Yes. Irony, it seems, is fluid and defies boundaries. The death collector was alone when it left the mist in search of more power, and soon it was driven mad, if it wasn't before. Its only solace was creating life from death, a strange circle that power has a habit of constructing. The semblance of life you saw today was its attempt at creation."

I felt sick again as I recalled the shambling bones, animated by a power I didn't understand. "It wanted my blood," I said, gazing across the fire. "It said my blood would bring its children life."

Ellius shifted his eyes to Kotis and Fellow before looking at me. "Human blood is a precious commodity here for those who know how to use it. It was unfortunate to run across such a creature, but I doubt it will forget the impression you left on it—literally."

I frowned. "You talk like it's not dead."

Ellius's face became grave. "That is because it isn't. You merely disabled it by crushing it beneath the spire. It cannot die. Like all things here, the collector has its function and place. To kill it would be the same as attempting to kill death in your world."

I blinked. The idea of the thing alive in the field that I could still see was unnerving. I imagined the mouth of the path erupting in a hailstorm of bones as the thing rushed out to claim me and drag my lifeless body back to its children, to make them whole. I shuddered.

"Best not to think on it too long," Kotis said, leaning forward. Scrim let out a short screech, seeming to agree. "You can get lost in your own head easier than in the wild, that's for sure," he continued, rubbing the wound on his shoulder with his opposite hand. Ellius had cleaned the gash before supper and announced that the behemoth would survive.

"'The wild,'" I repeated, glancing at Ellius. "Is that where you traveled to meet us here?"

He laughed and shook his head. "No, Michael. I move amongst the trees as their brother, but I am confined to only where they grow. As you noticed, there were no forests anywhere that you traveled, thus I cannot exist there either."

He stood and stretched his arms out, the bark beneath his shawl rustling with the movement. A gust of wind blew and threw a flurry of leaves into the air around us. I shivered and scooted closer to the fire.

Ellius clapped his hands together with a dry crack and then pointed at me. "I bet you're cold, Michael. I found something for you." He spun and hurried away from the fire's light, and returned a few minutes later carrying something.

"I found it at the base of a tree while traveling here. It blended in fairly well, so it was only happenstance that I spotted it. Hopefully it fits." He handed me what was in his hands, and I unfolded it.

It was an olive-drab wool jacket with two large breast pockets. Stains covered nearly every inch of it, but it wasn't torn anywhere I could see. Something brass on one collar caught the light of the fire, and I looked closer, rubbing my thumb across the textured surface.

"Fifth Division, Victory," I read, staring at the symbol engraved in the pin. I could make out the design of a tank's track emblazoned with a lightning bolt. I shook my head.

"What's it mean?" Fellow asked quietly.

I shrugged, rubbing the pin, cleaning it of dirt and grime. "It's from a war of my world, the last of two."

"See if it fits," Kotis said, gesturing toward the jacket.

I swung it over my shoulders and slipped my arms inside. The wool whispered against my skin, and I smelled a hint of mildew. But the material instantly warmed me and felt wonderful against the cool air. I felt a bulge in one of the chest pockets and reached inside. After some digging, I pulled two objects out and studied them in the firelight. One was a small package about the size of a deck of cards. I could barely make out the faded letters with a little crown above them.

"Chesterfields," I said, opening the pack of cigarettes. The tobacco within smelled almost fresh, as if the soldier whose coat I wore had only stepped away briefly.

The other item was heavier and reflected some of the wavering flames. I flicked it open and closed with a loud click.

"What's that?" Kotis asked.

"Zippo lighter," I said. "Portable fire."

Kotis looked offended. "We can make fire wherever we go. All we need is the right rocks and kindling."

I smiled. "Call it a little magic of my own, then." My thumb hovered over the small wheel, the urge to rotate it almost irresistible. But I hesitated. If the flame somehow didn't erupt from the wick, I knew I would feel sad. Perhaps more sad than I'd felt so far. I flicked the cover closed and returned the two items to the same pocket.

I buttoned up the front of the jacket and shifted in my seat. "How's it look?" I asked.

"Fits you nicely," Fellow said.

"You look like a prick," Kotis said and grinned.

I laughed and turned back to Ellius. "Thank you."

Ellius smiled, his brown cheeks crinkling. "No problem, Michael." He looked up and then turned in a short circle until he spied the sun. "Well, we should get some sleep before we continue on."

We all agreed, and I watched Ellius move away to bed down on the ground a few yards outside of the firelight. For some reason I wasn't particularly tired, so I remained sitting. After a moment I noticed that neither Kotis nor Fellow had moved. I glanced at them, the shadows dancing with the light on their strange faces, and felt a sense of wonder at where I was. The ache of my family's absence still throbbed in my chest, but I was awestruck that I sat within a few feet of beings that were not human, in a world founded on evil and misfortune. I shook my head, gazing up at the ever-present clouds. Fellow's soft voice pulled me from my reverie.

"What do you think is above them?" he asked, pointing at the swirling grays overhead.

I stared upward for a while, remembering all the nights that Jane and I had sat on our deck staring up at the clear summer sky, crickets and frogs singing their harmony in the grass, just out of sight. The memory was so poignant I had to blink away a layer of tears before answering.

"Stars," I said.

Both Fellow and Kotis looked at me. "What are stars?" Fellow asked after a beat.

How could I explain something so elemental and beautiful to someone who didn't, perhaps couldn't, understand? "They're ..." I faltered, but then I felt Jane's hand in mine, and I swallowed. "They're points of light in the sky, things so far away you'd never reach them, but you can still see them." I breathed in the fall air, tasting leaves and dead grass. "They're beautiful."

"Maybe it's different here," Kotis said in a quiet voice. "Maybe they're not there at all." His words were indifferent, but his tone said anything but.

I continued to gaze at the gray sky, searching for a break in the desolation, even though I knew better. "They're there," I said finally. "They're always there, even if you can't see them."

We sat in the quiet evening light with our own thoughts, the shadows of the nearby trees falling on us like dark blankets. After a while, Fellow stirred and rose from the log he rested on.

"I'm turning in," he murmured after offering a sad smile in my direction. His lanky form receded and disappeared as he lay down in the brown grass that coated the field.

"He's a gentle soul," Kotis said, as he stood and moved to the log closer to me. With a grunt he sat down again, and shrugged his shoulders, causing Scrim to readjust his hooked feet. "Gets emotional fairly easy," the giant said, lowering his rumbling voice.

I looked in Fellow's direction and nodded. "He's very kind," I offered.

Kotis blew a breath between his heavy lips. "Oh, never find another that would help you more. We've been friends since we were knee-high."

I nodded, then laughed. Kotis turned toward me, his eyes narrowed. I noticed his expression and shook my head. "I'm not laughing at you.

It's just … it's so strange listening to you speak about your childhood friend. It's very much like where I came from."

Kotis rubbed his wide jaw. "What Ellius said about mirroring? It's like that a lot here. Our world, your world, they reflect each other a bit, you know. It only makes sense since they're connected. Not a day goes by that something from here doesn't affect something there, and vice versa. Things appear here that weren't before, like that coat," he said, pointing to my chest. "That's been sittin' in the forest for who knows how long before Ellius picked it up."

"At least sixty-five years," I said.

"Yeah, that's it exactly. How'd it get here? What's the story with it? Who wore it before?"

"A soldier," I said. "Someone who drove a tank."

"What in the bleedin' hell is a tank?" Kotis asked.

"It's like an armored …" I searched for a way to convey how a tank looked. "It's like a big, rolling beast that breathes fire."

Kotis's eyes widened and his eyebrows shot up. "That sounds like it belongs here, not in your world."

I huffed laughter. "Yeah, you're probably right." I let my thoughts ruminate for a while before turning, something nagging me in the back of my mind.

"Why did Fellow ask you not to call the things in the mist demons?" I asked. Kotis stiffened, his back straightening as he looked off into the darkness. I waited, thinking I'd offended him somehow, and was about to apologize when he spoke.

"He believes there's only one demon." He paused. "The one that took your family."

"Like, he thinks it's actually from Hell?"

"Yes and no. It's kind of a … religion, I guess you'd call it. You see, it's just like Ellius probably told you—there's good in every place, just like there's a bit of evil everywhere. You think that beautiful place he spoke of that's all good and light, that vents into the Earth opposite us, doesn't have its share of evil? You can bet it does."

"Just like you three are the spots of good here," I said.

Kotis chuckled. "You talk like you know us."

"Just what I've seen so far, you three seem better than a lot of people I know back home."

"Can you say you're completely good?" he asked, his dark eyes shifting toward me.

"Well, no, I have my flaws, just like anyone."

He nodded. "Me too. I ain't perfect, neither is Ellius or ... well, Fellow just might be, but you get the idea. There's some of us here who try to live peacefully in the midst of all the evil. We're few and far between, but we're still here. Now the one that took your family, that's a different story. The ones like us fear and loathe it, but you could guess there's a right many others that worship it like a god."

"And Fellow just doesn't want things that aren't as malevolent lumped in with something he thinks—"

"Is pure evil," Kotis finished. "He hates the evil one with as much malice as his little body can produce, and right now he doesn't look it, but he's scared down to his soul of this journey we're on. But he's going anyway because he believes it's the right thing to do."

"And what do you think?" I asked.

"I think I try to do what I believe is right, as much of the time as I can."

I closed my eyes and soaked in the information Kotis had provided, as fear came over me. It was a creeping sensation of distant doom, of a failing yet to come. How would I fight something that was pure evil? How could I win against something that was as old as the Earth? My family's faces swam through my mind, each smiling or framed in a memory of everyday life, which was now precious. Jane doing dishes, her hair falling over her forehead; Jack bounding across the living room to jump into my lap; Sara gently combing the hair of her doll, no doubt imagining the wonderful mother she would grow up to be.

I opened my eyes to the fire, which burned low. I made a silent promise: I would save them, or I would die trying.

Kotis slapped my back with a meaty hand and sent the air in my chest flying from my mouth. "Better get some shut eye, mate. Dawn'll come early, no doubt." He pointed at the sun that never dropped below the horizon and laughed before standing and moving away from the light.

I sat for a while longer, listening to the breeze in the forest before throwing another chunk of wood on the fire. I lay down and drew the coat of a soldier long departed close around me, and when I closed my eyes to sleep, I pretended that the air speaking in the branches nearby was the familiar wind of home.

A gentle hand shook me awake, and I opened my eyes to see Fellow stooped over me. "It's time to get up, Michael."

I nodded and stretched, feeling the soreness of muscles overworked by adrenaline the day before. I sat up and accepted a cold piece of feltson meat from Ellius and chewed on it, letting the salty striations dissolve on my tongue.

"You could actually probably sell this in my home state," I said between bites. "Tell people it's venison, they wouldn't know the difference."

"If a person ate it in your world, they would die almost immediately," Ellius said, looking over his shoulder.

I paused, another bite almost to my lips. "But I can eat it," I said.

"Yes, here it is fine. On Earth it becomes poisonous, like most other things brought from here," Ellius said. A strange look danced across his features, and he turned away. I wanted to ask him more, but he moved away toward the belt of trees that lined the middle of the field.

As Kotis passed by me, he jabbed a light elbow to my ribs. "It'll just give ya rotten gas here." His laughter rang out against the trees, startling a few birds from the lower branches.

We followed the tree line all morning. The ridge that it rode upon maintained a steady incline that wasn't noticeable but for the ache that began to bloom in my calves just before we stopped for lunch. The clouds looked higher and the sky seemed brighter. Maybe I was imagining things, or maybe I was actually getting used to how time passed here. As we set out again, our footsteps the only sounds save for the rustling of some small, unseen animals in the underbrush, I looked at Kotis, Ellius, and Fellow in turn.

"None of you have weapons," I said.

Ellius glanced back at me before replying. "No, typically there's no need for them. Especially since we live mostly on the other side of the fog. It's a place of relative peace, except for the occasional traveler from this area."

"I don't ever carry a weapon," Kotis said, stroking Scrim's feathers. "Got all I need right here, don't I, piss beak?" Scrim squawked and nipped at Kotis's ear, eliciting a chuckle from the giant.

"You don't need any weapons, you're as big as an ox," I said.

Kotis eyed me before turning his gaze forward again. "How big's an ox?"

I grinned. "They're big," I said. Kotis nodded, a pleased expression on his slab-like features.

I looked ahead and saw that the ground rose abruptly before falling away into a panoramic view. The trees became more sporadic as we neared the drop, and when we crested the rise, I stopped, my legs locked tight by the sight below.

The ground ended in a sharp cliff of tan rock. A valley stretched out a thousand feet below us, and the sheer size of it addled my mind. To the right I saw a forest of dead trees on the valley floor, which must have covered hundreds of thousands of acres, their spiny branches like a nest of sea urchins. A dark river flowed from the center of the forest and wound its way through the valley, sometimes disappearing for what must have been miles, only to reappear again and then fade out of sight. To the left was a field of stone, with towering buttes and boulders that were almost level with our height. Much of the valley lay in shadow created by the low sun at our backs.

"My God," I said.

"Yes, it's a sight," Ellius murmured at my side.

I tore my gaze away from the immense basin to look at him. "You've been here before?" I asked.

He nodded imperceptibly. "Once, a long time ago."

Fellow approached the edge of the cliff and looked down, then turned back to us. "There's a trail that heads down, looks safe enough."

"Well, lead on, you viny bastard," Kotis grumbled, nearing the edge.

The path was narrow and pocked with holes that opened into gaping depths I tried not to look into. Every hundred yards it switchbacked, leading in the opposite direction. The air cooled as we dropped out of the sun's light, and I fastened the topmost button of my coat and rubbed my hands together to dispel the chill. Several times we stopped to climb over various rock piles and parts of the wall that had collapsed, and, once, we were forced to sit down as the rock beneath out feet rumbled with a ferocity I was sure would throw us off the face of the gorge. After several minutes, it quieted and we resumed our descent.

When at last the path switched one last time and we could see where it merged with the valley floor, I breathed a sigh of relief. My legs ached from climbing, and my eyes were sore from the stinging wind that constantly pelted the side of the valley. We stepped onto a rough landscape of parched rock and cracked soil. The ground looked like it had never seen a drop of rain. For all I knew, maybe it hadn't. The thought of a storm made my insides cringe.

"Does it storm here?" I asked.

"Storm?" Ellius repeated.

"Yeah, does it rain and thunder, lightning, that sort of thing?"

"Well, yes, we do get a storm from time to time. Nothing much, a little moisture and noise, but that's all." Ellius regarded me for a second, his eyes questioning, but then Fellow spoke and we all turned our attention to him.

"Stop," he hissed, tilting his head to one side.

We halted. The shadows on the valley floor seemed to move on their own accord, and I waited for something to spring at us, claws and teeth open and waiting. A noise caught my attention as I surveyed our surroundings to see what had Fellow spooked. It was a high whining that came from our left. The rocky wall extended in a hip that branched several hundred yards out, obscuring our view of the sound's origin. It rose in pitch and then dropped, and I felt my heart beat faster. Something in the noise was familiar, and I strained my ears to discern it.

Screaming.

The deep guttural sounds of people dying echoed to us from around the corner. The high shriek of a woman and the baritone yells of men intermingled in a cacophony of suffering that made the skin on the back of my neck bristle. It sounded as though they were being eaten alive.

Fellow spun, his orange eyes wild. "Hide!" he yelled, pointing to a break in the valley wall behind us. I turned and ran as the volume of the screams became louder, until the whole basin rang with them. There were a few garbled words amongst the cries, emphatic pleas for relief that surpassed the eardrum and knifed directly through the heart. Part of me wanted to turn back, to run to the aid of people obviously in desperate need of help, but something else pushed me on. Fear throbbed through my veins, a steady pulse that told me to run and hide.

The crevasse in the wall was wide enough to house all of us, but it was not much over five feet high, and Kotis nearly had to crawl on hands and knees to fit. We scrambled into the darkness, our breathing rebounding off the walls, each of us trying to control it. Fellow crouched at the mouth of the cave, with Ellius at his side. I shuffled forward, flanking both of them. We watched for movement as the screams became louder and more hysterical.

A mass of swirling air filled with dust and debris emerged around the rocky hip to our left. It looked like a whirling tornado, but smaller and more concentrated. Strands of twirling air stretched out and touched the ground, making the dust storm resemble a shifting spider. Screaming emanated from it, and as it drew nearer I squinted, seeing forms within its clouded exterior.

Faces leered at us through the haze.

Elongated and amorphous, they were like blotches of oil on water. I could see men's, women's, and even a few children's features pressing against the skin of the funnel, as if they were trying to escape. As soon as one face came into focus it would release a scream of torment. I assumed the same things was happening on the storm's opposite side, since I could still hear many other voices. Then the face would recede, letting another take its place.

The cloud tipped and spun closer to where we hid, and I had a vision of it beelining toward us, smothering our hiding spot with its spitting dirt and choking wind. The screaming rose to a climax in a symphony of pain and despair. I clapped my hands to my ears to block it out, but merely muffled the sounds of agony. I watched as the stirring storm swung away from our hiding spot and continued toward the distant edge of forest that was barely visible, the arms that extended from it seeming to pull it along.

I slumped to the cave wall and felt my stomach slosh sickeningly. I'd heard of alarm systems for homes emitting a high-frequency sound that, if listened to for any longer than a few seconds, would make a person nauseated. After hearing the screams for less than a minute, I could relate. The unbearable urge to have a drink hit me again, and my throat constricted. For a sip of wine or whiskey I would've traded the same amount in blood.

I pushed myself off the wall and put a hand on Ellius's shoulder. "What in the hell was that?"

"A soul storm," he said. "There are several of them here in this valley. They're a product of the one who took your family." Ellius's face sobered to the point I thought it might crack. "The people who accidentally come here never leave. They eventually die one way or another, killed by something native or by their own hand when they can't find a way back. But the worst is, their souls cannot escape. They are bound to this world in death. When the one that took your family finds them, alive or dead, it weaves them into a storm of anguish like the one you just saw. It feeds on their suffering and they are bound to it, to forever wander this place in unbearable pain."

My hand fell to my side. I glanced at Fellow and Kotis. Both of them looked like I felt inside, sick and unsteady. The ground shifted beneath my feet. "Do any of you have anything to drink?" I asked.

Fellow pulled a small water skin from his belt and offered it to me.

"Something stronger?" I asked. He tilted his head and looked to Ellius.

"He means alcohol," Ellius said, waving Fellow's water skin away. "We have nothing like it here, Michael, I'm sorry."

"Not as sorry as I am," I said with a quaver in my voice. "What happens if you touch one of the storms?" I asked.

"You join their ranks of torment," Ellius said.

"Right, so don't touch the bleedin' things," Kotis said gruffly.

"Exactly. Avoid them at all costs. You cannot fight them. If you see one, just run," Ellius admonished.

"Is it gone now?" I asked.

Fellow stepped out of the cave and swiveled his head back and forth. He waited nearly a minute before turning back to us. "I can't see or hear it anymore," he said.

"Good," Kotis said, crawling forward. "This abode leaves a lot to be desired. Let's get the hell out of here."

We exited the cave one by one, and stood abreast of each other. Without another word, we moved forward into the valley. After only a few steps, I heard the clack of rocks falling behind us and turned.

A figure stood framed in the sunlight at the edge of the canyon.

"Guys!" I yelled, and stared at the outline above us. It wavered and then folded, just as before, into half, and then again.

Kotis stopped at my side, staring up to where I looked. "What is it, mate?"

I scanned the rim, looking for anything that would betray the figure's location. Nothing moved; it was gone.

"The shadow I saw before, it was right there above us, watching us," I said, pointing to the spot where it had been. I could feel Fellow and Ellius behind me looking for the outline I'd seen.

"You sure it was there?" Kotis finally asked.

"I'm not seeing things," I said, looking at his wide face. "It was there, I heard a rock fall behind us, that's why I turned. There's someone following us."

"We believe you, Michael," Fellow said. "Let's all keep a lookout from now on, we don't know if it might be an agent of the one we seek."

"Come on, mate, let's move," Kotis said, placing a giant hand on my shoulder.

Psalm 23 came to me as we turned and made our way across the burned ground, around slanted piles of rock. Yea, though I walk through the valley of the shadow of death, I will fear no evil: for thou art with me. The words were shallow and didn't hold the power I hoped they would. No matter, I sent up my own prayer: Be with my family instead of me if you have to choose, amen.

We walked for several hours through a winding maze of rock outcrops, which opened into a wide field of the familiar cut straw. The forest we'd seen earlier ran close to the field, and after another mile we stepped into the weak rays of the sun, leaving the shadow of the gorge behind. The sun crept clockwise to a seven o'clock position, and I mused on the idea that it actually was seven on Earth. The idea seemed right somehow, and I was going to voice my opinion about the time when we crested a small hill that dropped away into a gorge with a flat bottom.

An enormous ship lay in the center of the depression.

I stopped, my breath catching in my throat as I took in the ship's shape. It lay sideways to us, its broad hull partially buried in the dirt. Its bow tilted down, as did its stern, giving it the look of a dying beached whale. Its upper decks heaved toward the sky, and a massive crack ran down the side of the hull. The ship was a dull brown where it met the ground, faded to a poisonous green at its top. I could see the leprous etchings that aquatic sea life leaves on a ship that has been underwater for some time. A bit of seaweed hung from the foremost railing and waved in the slight breeze. I looked for the four steam stacks, but realized they would have toppled off as the ship sank. Even without them I recognized the ocean steamer in an instant.

It was the RMS *Titanic*.

"Oh my God," I managed, staring at the impossible sight. "What the fuck is that doing here?" I felt my mind tremble with the ramifications of what lay before me. This was a ship that had sunk in the Atlantic Ocean a century ago. I'd seen the movie, I'd watched the documentaries. It was at the bottom of the ocean. How could it be there, lodged in the ground just the way it was in all the photos of where it came to rest on the ocean's floor?

I fell onto my ass. I'd always thought someone's legs giving out was melodramatic and didn't actually happen, but I couldn't help it. I'd tipped over from drinking too much, but never when I was stone sober. I didn't even feel the sting in my tailbone as I touched down, only noticed the change in the view of the ship. Fellow knelt at my side, and then Ellius was there too.

"How?" I asked finally, tearing my gaze away from the ship.

"It appeared here some time ago, Michael," Ellius said. "Sometimes when something terrible or evil happens on Earth it materializes here, like an afterimage from looking at a bright light. I assume you recognize it?"

I nodded, feeling like I'd consumed a bottle of cheap vodka much too fast. My head swam and my hands shook. After all I'd seen and experienced, the vision of the *Titanic* sitting in the depression was the most shocking.

"It was an accident, a terrible accident a hundred years ago," I said. "Lots of people died. This is ... unreal ..."

Ellius nodded, a concerned look on his face. "Can you stand?"

I grabbed his offered hand. Even with shock still buffeting my senses, I marveled at the wood-like hardness of his palm as he pulled me to my feet.

"All right?" Kotis asked.

I nodded, and felt Scrim's wing fan my shoulder. The bird flew out ahead of us as we walked down the sweeping drop of the valley. The wreck grew in stature with every step, and the vertigo from seeing it tried to pull me to the ground again. *How?* kept echoing in my mind, but soon I gave up trying to understand the principles of a world that defied logic.

We were passing through the ship's shadow when we heard the voice.

"Hello, lovelies." The words drawled with an English accent.

My head snapped to where the voice came from, and I saw a figure leaning nonchalantly on the closest railing near the top deck. It was wreathed in shadow, but I could make out a long, tattered overcoat with pearl buttons adorning the front. Black gloves covered the fingers wrapped around the railing the figure leaned upon, and dark hair hung to its shoulders, obscuring its features.

"What the flamin' shit?" Kotis said.

"Come to look at my beauty?" the figure asked, bending perilously over the railing. Some of its hair shifted, and I saw talcum-white skin stretched across angular bones. Too-red lips were pulled into a rictus grin.

"Don't speak to it," Ellius said, trying to guide me away from the wreck. "It's just a wraith tied to the ship in some way. It can't hurt you."

"Oh, I'm much more than that, old soul," the figure said. Suddenly it was gone from the upper deck. Movement near the yawning break in the hull drew my attention, and I took a step back when I saw the man dangling, monkey-like, from a shattered floor. "I created this, wonderful—" He vanished and reappeared on the ground at the edge of the ship's shadow. "—sight," he finished with a small bow.

I took another step back, shocked at the flickering movement. Up close I could see more of his features. Sunken eyes peered between the bars of stringy hair. The skin of his face was even whiter than I'd thought, and when he smiled I saw that his teeth were square and even. The smell of a waterlogged carcass floated to me, and I nearly gagged.

The man put out a hand and extended a gloved finger at Ellius. "You look familiar."

"Do not speak to it," Ellius repeated, and began to walk away with me in tow.

"Oh, but I want to tell you how I crashed this ship," the man said in a cold voice.

I stopped and turned, halting Ellius's progress. "What?" I asked.

The man smiled, his teeth now yellow and uneven. "I did this, my good friend. I turned that ship into the iceberg on purpose."

Kotis had a hold on my other arm and dragged me backward.

"Killed the crew, I did. Nasty shades of red the walls became that night. It was meant to be, that berg floatin' so pretty in the fog. What a sound it was, the rending of steel and the screams. I can still hear them." The man cocked his head to one side, as if listening to something we couldn't hear.

I found my feet and began to walk backward on my own, the horrible implications of the man's words wreaking havoc with my thoughts. "Who are you?" I heard myself say, my voice coming from somewhere far away.

The man grinned, and now his teeth were split, some missing, their color mimicking the sulfurous green of the ship behind him. "Oh, I've had many names. My father called me John, and to some I was known as Pint. But I earned my favorite name in Whitechapel some years before taking this voyage." The man's smile stretched much too wide for any human. "You can call me Jack ... the Ripper."

With a laugh that bubbled up from deep within his chest, the man flickered and was gone.

My stomach rolled and churned as I swallowed and turned away from the *Titanic*. I put my head down and stared at my feet, one step after another, until we rose up the far side of the depression and were out and away from the terrible spectacle. We walked in silence, and I tried not to let my thoughts roam back to the ship and the thing that inhabited it.

The land soon became rocky and wild, with several large trees dotting the hills around us. My feet ached from walking, and the shoes I'd deemed comfortable back home felt like they were full of tacks. Scrim returned to Kotis a short while later and told him that the way was clear to the river.

"We'll be able to rest there and fill up on water," Ellius said, urging us on. After another half-hour of walking, we saw it.

The river ran between two sweeping banks of gray stone. Pictures of Alaskan beaches immediately came to my mind as we started toward it. The river was dark and flowed at a quick pace, but didn't even come close to matching the speed of the one we'd crossed at the border of the mist. But what it lacked in speed it made up for in size. It spanned at least a quarter mile, the opposite bank climbing up and ending in a short cliff. A few trees lined the other shore, and I felt relief at knowing Ellius could continue with us.

We stopped at the river's edge and waited while Fellow filled three water skins. When he handed me one, I drained it almost immediately, feeling the icy water chill the skin of my parched throat. Fellow grinned at me, and returned a minute later with more. I drank half of another skin before dropping it to chest level. Water dripped from my chin and soaked my T-shirt.

"This water's safe, isn't it?" I asked.

Ellius smiled. "Yes, it's safe to drink."

"Why is this water okay and other water isn't?"

"It's just like anything here, Michael. There is always some good within evil," Ellius said. He turned his head and gazed downstream. "We'll be able to see the bridge soon, it's not far."

The river ran fairly straight, with only a few jags to the left and right. At first I thought the relatively level beach would be easy walking, but soon found that the smaller rocks twisted beneath my shoes. Kotis and Fellow didn't seem to have a problem since their feet were bare and oversized, while Ellius moved with the grace he always possessed, never faltering or running short of breath.

I gazed past Kotis's lumbering form and strained my eyes for something that would tell me that we were close to the bridge. I was rewarded with what I first thought was a large boulder but soon saw was a rounded pillar mortared together with many smaller stones like the ones that littered the banks of the river. There were two of them standing like sentries, and when I looked across the river's expanse, I noted two more adorning the opposite shore. The space in between them troubled me.

"Where's the bridge?" I asked as we stopped a few yards away from the pillars.

Ellius walked forward and laid a hand on the stone structure. With a tip of his head, he motioned me closer. I stepped beside him and looked through the gateway formed by the two pillars.

"It's there, Michael. Can you see it?" he asked.

I looked at the flowing water, and was about to shake my head when something caught my eye. Beneath the surface I saw a line, and only after following it did I realize what it was. The bridge's walkway was about three feet below the water. It was composed of large cobblestones, and the reason I hadn't seen it before was because there were no rails on either side. It was merely a walkway a few feet wide that a man would be swept from if he tried to wade in.

I faced Ellius. "This is the bridge? How do we get across?"

"The river ebbs and flows, much like your oceans but at a much greater depth. In a few hours the water will recede and drop until it reaches its lowest point, several miles below the bridge."

I started. "Several miles?" I asked, sure that I'd heard him wrong.

He nodded. "This river sits in a chasm that drops straight down. In some places the bottom cannot be seen when the river is at its lowest."

The thought of a river miles deep was staggering, but the impatience that had been building during the last two days was about to spill over. "How much farther to where my family's being held?" I asked.

"It is not too far," Ellius said.

"Can't we cross now?"

"We'd be thrown downstream by the current, Michael, it's not safe."

"I need to get to my family!" I shouted, and was surprised by the vehemence in my voice.

Ellius grimaced and looked at the ground. His expression made the striations of bark stand out on his face, and for the first time I wondered how old he really was.

"I understand, Michael but we must be cautious."

I thrummed with anger at the feeling of utter helplessness that coursed through me. Never in my life had I been filled with so much angst, not even when I thought my fear of storms would drive me insane. The worries that I tried to hold in check broke through a dam inside me, and I felt tears flood my eyes.

"You don't understand, they're mine. I was supposed to protect them. Jack's only six and Sara's eight. They're terrified right now, and I need—" My breath hitched in my chest. "I need to find them," I said, choking. Fellow approached and stood a few paces off to my side.

"We will find them, Michael, I promise," Ellius said. I wiped my eyes with the heel of my hand, feeling weak and ashamed.

Fellow's rough hand rested on my shoulder. "Sometimes all you can do is wait," he said. I sighed and nodded.

"Let's get a fire going, but a small one. We don't want to attract anything," Ellius said.

The sun ran its clockwork path around the horizon. The steady wind abated somewhat, and the constant chill that came with the fall air dispersed a little with the heat of the fire that Kotis made. We sat around the flames and ate a mush that Ellius concocted from a few berries, some dried leaves, and river water. It tasted like bitter oatmeal, but my stomach welcomed it even if my tongue recoiled. When we finished, I watched Kotis shift on the ground. For the first time since I'd met them Scrim dismounted from his perch on Kotis's shoulder and didn't fly away. Instead he settled onto a stone warmed by the fire.

"Fellow, give us a story, you were always good at that," Kotis said as he tried to get comfortable.

If Fellow could blush, I think he would have at that moment. "I'm not a storyteller by any means," he said.

"Oh, bollocks on your forehead!" Kotis chided. "You're the best I've ever heard."

"Then you haven't heard many," Fellow said with a smile.

Kotis leaned toward me. "He used to entertain us for hours at night when we were just little shits. He's just shy, that's all."

Fellow's smile widened a bit. "What would you like to hear?"

Satisfied, Kotis lay on his back, his huge hands interlaced behind his head. "Oh, just go with it. You always do quite well."

Fellow looked at the fire and his orange eyes reflected the dancing flames. "A very long time ago, in the forest where we come from"—he motioned to Kotis—"there was a sentinel of the trees. He was the largest tree of the forest, and if truth be known, he originally spawned the entire woods that surrounded him with his massive roots that grew off in every direction. He stood a thousand feet tall and spanned an entire field with his branches outstretched.

"One day a woodcutter came to the forest. It was a massive beast that ate nothing but trees, tore the bark from their trunks and gnashed their knots into paste. Although woodcutters were rare, if one came to a forest, no tree would be left standing. The sentinel watched the cutter approach, and when it was close enough, he spoke to the beast. He said, 'Stop, woodcutter, for I know your only purpose here. These trees are of my flesh and they are not to be harmed. Go away in peace and leave this forest be.'

"Well, the cutter looked up and sneered at the sentinel, since it too was old and powerful, with long jaws that could clip a full-grown tree off in one bite. 'I'll tell you what, wooden heart, you let me pass and I let you stand, since you and I are kings of our kind. Let me eat my fill, and you can spawn another forest here someday.'

"The sentinel was appalled. The forest was his children, his friends, his family. They were part of him, and he wanted no harm to come to them. But he saw that the cutter was powerful and terrible, so he said, 'Come back tomorrow and I will give you my answer.' The woodcutter wasn't pleased about waiting for his meal, but he agreed, knowing deep down that the old tree had no choice.

"For hours and hours the sentinel thought deeply on how to save the forest. They could not pull up their roots and move. They could not rightly defend themselves against such a threat, and had no other mighty allies to call upon. The sentinel was about to give in to despair when an idea struck. He pondered on it for a long time, and realized that it was the only way. He then spoke to the animals in the forest, the small creatures in the ground and even the wind. He held council with them because he was ancient and wise.

"They then left him and went to work, though none could see them. Time passed, and soon the ground shook with the woodcutter's approach. It stopped in the sentinel's shadow, just like the day before, and looked up with hateful eyes. It said, 'What have you decided, tree of the forest?'

"The sentinel looked down upon his foe, and said, 'I choose for you to take my life and to leave my children be, for their time has only begun and mine has long since passed.'

"The woodcutter laughed at this, rolling on its bladed back until deep furrows were cut into the ground. When it finally regained its feet, it said, 'You do not get to choose whether I eat you or all of your family, for you are a tree and I am a hunter. It seems you've made your decision, and I will feast upon you and then the rest of your woods.'

"The cutter stepped forward and prepared to bite the sentinel with its powerful jaws, but then the old tree spoke to the wind, and the wind answered. It came across the fields and hummed in the branches of the forest, and when it touched the sentinel with its strong embrace, the old tree toppled and crashed down upon the cutter, killing it beneath its weight. For, you see, the sentinel knew there was no way to save his family, so he asked the creatures of the forest to dig in the ground and weaken the hold his massive roots had in the soil. He asked the wind to help push him to the ground when called, so that he would die and his forest would live."

Fellow paused and gazed at me across the fire. "It is said that the sentinel's trunk and branches became the mountain beside the forest that we're from and that its soul still watches over the family it perished for."

Silence draped over us, except for the popping of the fire, and I looked down at my feet, absorbing a story that no other human being had heard before. I was about to speak when Kotis beat me to it.

"Well, aren't you a cheerful fucker?" Kotis propped himself up on a thick forearm and looked across the fire.

I glanced at Fellow, who scowled at the giant for a few seconds, and then watched as his lower lip began to quiver. A few seconds later the smile he held back burst onto his face, and he leaned forward as honking laughter poured from his mouth. The strange sound elicited a giggle from me, and when I looked at Ellius, he was also laughing.

It felt good to laugh after so many hours of solemn contemplation. In fact, it felt good to laugh without the aid of liquor. I couldn't remember the last time that I'd laughed because I was truly happy; my anxiety and fear were constant companions even when the skies were clear. I sat for a few moments, in awe of the fact that I felt freer than I had for many years. The craving for a drink was still there, prodding at my mind intermittently, but otherwise I felt better somehow.

"You live close to each other?" I asked as Kotis and Fellow quieted.

Kotis nodded as he sat up. "Grew up together, me on the side of the mountain he spoke of, and Fellow down in its shadow."

Fellow's eyes became distant as he looked into the shade of the evening light. "The forest is wider and longer than any we've seen so far. It's beautiful in its own way, as everything is."

"Fellow there's got a nice little meadow all to himself, with a brand-new bride. I think he built his home there just so he can have extra time alone with her, if you know what I mean," Kotis said, raising his eyebrows.

I smiled, then faltered as I turned to look at Fellow. "You're married?" I asked.

Fellow smiled shyly and nodded. "Over a year now, I suppose it is."

I was appalled. I swung my gaze back to Kotis. "But you aren't, are you?"

Kotis looked at the fire and smiled in a way I hadn't seen before. "Oh, yes I am. Got a little son too, he's seven now and cranky as his mother."

I dropped my chin to my chest and shook my head. I heard Ellius shift in his seat, and felt their eyes on me. "I didn't want this," I said.

"What, Michael?" Ellius asked softly.

I raised my head to look at them in turn, their faces framed in the light of the fire, each watching me without anger or resentment, which actually made me feel worse. "I didn't want you to leave your families for me. You're risking your lives to come with me, and it's not your battle."

"But don't you see, it *is* our responsibility, for our family, for everything," Fellow said, gesturing to the surroundings. "Ellius says if your family is harmed, our world will fall as well as your own. I owe it to my wife and myself to do what I can."

"As do I," Kotis said.

"And I as well, even though I have no other kin," Ellius said. "Michael, we want to help you, not only because of the gravity of what may happen if we don't but because it's the right thing to do."

I felt tears spring to my eyes again. The sheer selflessness of their words and the good they embodied, cast against the backdrop of such evil, left me speechless. I could only smile at them, imparting gratitude through my eyes.

I looked to where the pillars sat, two monolithic molded casts, and watched the water level. It looked lower, and I willed it with all my being to move down faster.

Not long after that, both Kotis and Fellow bade goodnight and walked a short distance away to make their beds in the softer soil higher up the bank. I heard Scrim issue a short cry and Kotis grumble a colorful insult beneath his breath. I felt fortunate to have them near in a place so hostile. I shot another glance at the river, hoping to see a drastic change.

"It will drop, Michael. It only takes time. When it does, it will drop fast," Ellius said, noticing where my gaze kept straying to.

"I know, I just want to keep moving. Stopping seems like a betrayal."

"I understand. And do not fret about Kotis's and Fellow's families. They are well aware of where their loved ones are and why they had to leave. They are both very good, the only two that I would trust to travel with us."

"They obviously trust you," I said. "How long have you known one another?"

Ellius smiled again, the bark of his cheeks crinkling. "A long time. Since they were very young. I travel to the forest Fellow spoke of regularly, and befriended Kotis's father many years ago. When he passed, I agreed to watch over Kotis. Surprising as it is, Kotis needed very little guidance. As harsh as his words are, his morality is only challenged by Fellow's."

I smiled. "I guessed that a little while after he knocked me out."

Ellis looked horrified, but I assured him I deserved it. After a bout of silence punctuated only with the gurgle of the river and the intermittent breeze, I was about to rise when Ellius spoke again.

"I know what follows us, Michael."

I stopped, hovering above my seat. "What?"

"The shadowed figure you've seen trailing behind us. I know what it is."

I sat back down, my attention riveted to him. "What is it?"

"How long have you been addicted to alcohol, Michael?"

The question caught me off-guard. The only people that knew I had a problem were Jane and my parents, although I think both my mother and father tried to believe that I changed after the day they found me drunk beneath my table.

I sighed and realized there was no point in lying. "Probably five years, maybe more."

Ellius nodded, his face growing grave. "I assumed so."

"What does that have to do with what's following us?"

"Michael, your addiction *is* what's following us."

I stared numbly at him. "What?" was all I managed after a few seconds.

"You said you saw it the first time shortly after emerging from the field of lies, correct?"

"Yeah, it was behind us before we went through the bone field."

"I'm afraid when you crossed the river that guards the field, the worst aspect of your personality emerged from the black water. There is a reason it is called the Damning River."

I furrowed my brow. "So you're saying that my alcohol addiction is, what? In physical form now?"

"Yes, that's exactly what I'm saying. The Damning River sees the worst in those who pass above it and creates a likeness composed entirely of their failings. That is why none of the creatures that live in the fog can cross it, they would be consumed instantly by their lies."

I shook my head as doubt pleaded to have its voice heard, but after all I'd witnessed I knew there was no room for disbelief in this world. You either believed or you died. "What does it want?" I asked.

"The same thing it wants in your world, Michael—to destroy you."

"Listen, you don't really know me. I have reasons why I drink, and if I want to drink, it's my business. I can control it." I hated the words for the lies they truly were, and I saw Ellius's lined face fold a little beneath my harsh tone. I was going to apologize, knowing exactly where the defensiveness came from, where it lived and what controlled it, but Ellius cut me off.

"I can't change you, Michael, all I can do is warn you of the dangers this world holds. Your addiction will follow us until the time is right for it to strike, and it has only one target," he said, holding up a wooden finger. "And that is you. It will not tire or cease to give chase. It eventually will catch up, and when it does, neither my guidance nor Fellow's kindness, or even Kotis's strength, will save you. And if you fall, all is lost."

I opened my mouth to respond but closed it again. I knew what I would say, and it would be nothing but fallacies, false bravado to condone the prodding I felt even then to have a drink.

Ellius gave me a long but not unkind look, then left the warmth of the fire's light. I sat by myself pondering what he'd said. Jane's voice spoke in my mind after what seemed like hours of mulling over endless thoughts. *Michael? Please just a couple tonight.*

I looked at the river and thought I could see the bridge's shape beneath the current. A deep fatigue settled over me, the entire day's exercise compounding within my muscles at once. I lay down on the

poking stones near the fire, not willing to abandon its light, and closed
my eyes.

I awoke to screaming.

I'd been dreaming about the shadowed figure that followed us. It had
appeared out of nowhere, grown from the very ground, and stood
beside Kotis. It bit the giant in the back, pulling out a huge chunk of
dripping flesh. Blood spurted from the wound, and Kotis fell to his
knees, screaming a death cry. Fellow leapt to his aid and tried to pull him
away from the figure, but it was too fast. With a swipe of a black arm, it
sliced through the ropy cords of Fellow's neck. He fell beside Kotis,
trying to stave off the running fluid that flowed from the gaping hole in
his throat. The figure roared in triumph and turned in my direction, and
I felt fear unlike anything I ever had before, because when it rushed
toward me, intent on tearing me limb from limb, it was my own face
that I looked into.

As I drifted up from sleep, I thought it was the screams created by
my own mind that I heard. But then I realized there were too many
voices yelling, too many overlapping sounds of misery to come from just
our group.

I sat up just as the soul storm crested the nearby hill. It still swirled
and leaned with its tendrils of wind, but this time the faces that cried out
as they surfaced looked directly at us.

Kotis and Fellow sprinted toward the fire ring, the last dying flames
just beneath burned cinders.

"Up, Michael! The bridge!" Fellow yelled, angling past me.

My body ached from the few hours spent on a bed of stones. I
looked to my right and saw that not only had the river receded below
the bridge's walkway, it was completely out of sight.

I ran away from the howling storm of faces, feeling a few specks of
sand and dirt patter against the back of my jacket. Ellius waved Kotis
and Fellow past him where he stood at the pillars.

"Hurry, Michael!" Ellius cried, urging me onward.

I ran for all I was worth, dreading the touch of the thing behind me.
I wondered what it would feel like, to be enveloped by the spinning
debris. Would it be instant darkness without suffering, or would the
transition be strobed with pain until my face fell in alongside the
undulating others that took turns gracing the storm's surface? The
thought of being trapped in eternal agony spurred me onward, and when
I was near enough, Ellius ran ahead of me onto the bridge.

The cobblestones of the bridge's surface were wide and flat, smoothed over time by the passage of feet and flowing water. Bits of green algae hung off the side that faced the water's flow, while the rest of it was clean and clear. The bridge itself was built in a great arc that swept up beneath the walkway to support it and feathered out in its middle, where it became almost too thin for comfort, before widening toward the opposite shore.

I raced onto the bridge just as the storm hit the pillars behind me. Comforted by the sound of gravel clacking off the gateway, I risked a glance over one shoulder, thinking the bridge's boundary would stop the ravenous souls from moving onto the narrow surface.

The pillars were gone, and the storm was right behind me.

A mouth like a car's open hood appeared within the roiling storm and reached for me. Teeth composed of rock, leaves, and sand emerged from beneath a curling lip and slammed shut. I turned back and leaned forward, gaining on Ellius, who ran with surprising speed ahead of me. For the first time I looked down to my left side, over the edge of the bridge, and the sight made me flinch with vertigo.

The river was at least fifty feet beneath the bridge's walkway and receding fast. I saw a large boulder exposed on the far bank, and within seconds it hung in the open, free from the touch of water. I heard a snapping sound, and a rush of air pushed against my hair, as if a door had closed directly behind me. I looked ahead, praying that the far bank was close, and saw with some relief that Fellow and Kotis were almost there. I could make out a thick stand of trees at the top of the bank, and knew that Ellius could hide us there if we reached it in time.

The splash that shot up from beneath my left foot told me, even before my mind registered I'd slipped, that I was going to fall. A depression in one of the wide cobblestones held less than a half inch of river water, but it was enough to make my shoe slide to the edge. My arms pinwheeled and my stomach lurched. I felt the bottom of my shoe fly sideways into open air and the scrape of the bridge as it slid up the inside of my leg. My weight tipped, and I made a grab at the side of the walkway as it flew by, my hands catching but instantly snapping free.

I fell.

CHAPTER EIGHT

CAPTURED

People say the instant before death your life flashes before your eyes, or what passes for your life. Bits and pieces of experiences, happy or sad, snippets of words, all coalesced into a barrage that makes up your existence.

They're wrong.

The few seconds it took for me to drop from the bridge to the river below were nothing but a terrible, whirling free fall. My mind conjured no comforting pictures of my family or images of God, only stomach-tearing suspense as I waited to smash into something hard. I saw the river's walls rip by and the bridge above me turn crazily as I flipped over backward, and I had the impression of a dark wall coming up to meet me.

The river water bit into my skin like a thousand needles, and I suddenly felt as though my entire body burned in a cold fire. I tried to suck in air, and realized that I'd done half a belly flop from higher than any Olympian dared to dive. For my efforts I received a lungful of water so cold it made me convulse before the lack of oxygen did. I coughed, trying not to inhale again as I strained for the surface, my coat and pants no longer shielding me against the cool air but pulling me down as they soaked up water. I kicked again, and the roaring silence of being underwater broke.

Screams met me as soon as the water drained from my ears. They echoed down to me from above in a cascade of sound. Some were my name, but most were just cries of the damned. Water rushed over me, and I stroked toward where I thought the bank should be. The current rushed around me, a physical thing that pushed and pulled, sweeping me along at an alarming rate. My shoes felt like anchors, and my fingers burned with cold. The screams grew distant, like the screech of hawks far overhead. When I managed to look back where the bridge should have been, it was gone, replaced by a turn in the chasm.

Terror tapped the back of my brain with a sharpened fingernail. I was being carried farther and farther from my group, and if I didn't stop myself soon, I would be hard-pressed to find them. The walls to either side of me were at least a hundred feet tall, and getting higher by the minute. I managed to maneuver myself so that I pointed downstream, and saw that in the distance the river made another turn. Maybe I could use its curve to my advantage and get a hold on the wall when I got close enough.

I swam as hard as I could toward the rocky wall. Weakness sapped the energy from my limbs with each stroke. The water wasn't as cold as before; it was warmer, more welcoming. I shook my head until my neck hurt, clearing the thoughts that whispered of resting just for a moment. My foot struck something solid beneath the water, and I spun, facing the way I'd come. A rock, I told myself. That made the most sense. But then Ellius's words came to me, making my scalp prickle. He'd said the river was miles deep. There wouldn't be a stone that tall in the middle of the river.

I swam harder downstream, beating the water with all I had, my muscles flaring with pain. I tried to breathe as my swimming instructor had taught me in high school. Stroke, breathe, stroke, breathe. Don't break the rhythm.

Glancing forward, I brought my head up. The bend was approaching, and the wall was only a few yards away. With all my power, I put my head down and kicked, pulled, fought the clutches of the current, which threatened to yank me back to the center of the river. My hand brushed rock.

I rubbed my eyes free of water. The wall was there in front of me, sliding by. The river's speed was faster on the inside of the curve, and I reached to grab a protruding stone as it moved by. My fingers caught and held. With the last of my strength, I pulled myself up and grasped a fissure in another boulder. I cried out and heaved my sopping body free of the water, and found a narrow ledge to stand on, hugging the wall like an old friend. My breath puffed out before me, something I hadn't noticed on the journey before. I rested, relishing the feeling of being free of the river. With trepidation, I looked up.

The edge of the bank was out of sight.

"Fuck!" It felt good to speak, although it came out as a croak; it meant that I was alive.

I sorted my options. I could climb and risk falling, or I could stay where I was and wait for my friends to find me. I blinked. When had I started to think of them as my friends? I didn't know, but they were and there was no time to contemplate it. Looking up again, I scanned the wall above and around me. It was made up of jagged rocks like the one I clung to, interlaced with muddy soil that dripped and ran. I felt a tremor run through my right arm, and imagined dropping back into the water. Looking down I nearly did fall.

The water was at least two stories away.

I shut my eyes, leaning as close as I could to the rock. I wanted to become part of it, to seep into the wall and rest. Without debating anymore, I reached up and found another handhold. I couldn't wait for the group to find me, and since it looked as though the rocks above jutted from the wall, they might not spot me even if they walked directly over my position. I had no choice. I climbed.

Hand over hand, with disciplined effort, I found handholds and shelves to brace my feet against. The ever-present cold hanging from me in the folds of my clothing was no longer staved off by adrenaline. Shaking with every movement, I couldn't feel my hands, and had to check each hold they grasped to make sure I was secure. I was without a body, merely a freezing piece of meat hanging from the side of a bank. Every few minutes I checked my progress. The first few times I made the mistake of looking down instead of up; the river's steady descent gave me false hope that I'd made great progress. From then on I kept my gaze up, always looking for the next point to grab while making sure my hands did what they were told.

Eventually I reached a shelf that stuck out like an underbite. It was wide enough for me to turn and sit down. The relief of my body was unlike anything I ever had experienced, and I sighed with pleasure. The thought of the shelf giving way beneath me crossed my mind, but for a few seconds all I could do was relish the feeling in my muscles. As I prepared to maneuver back toward the wall to continue, something touched my foot. It was such an odd sensation that I froze at first, wondering if a rock had fallen from beneath the shelf and brushed my shoe. Then I felt a tapping against my shin, and I recoiled, feeling skin tear free as I dragged my calf over the ledge. Pressing my back against the stone, I tilted my head forward to look over the shelf.

A tentacle the width of a flagpole shot from beneath the rock and jabbed at my head. I saw a flash of opaque green and felt something wet flick my face before it slammed into the wall over my shoulder, tearing out a piece of stone the size of a television. I yelled, my center of gravity tipping out toward the river before I pulled myself back. The tentacle lashed away, yanking the chunk of rock with it. Spinning around, I scrabbled my shaking hands along the wall until I felt a small crevice. I did a fast pull-up, my muscles fueled with fear-induced energy once again, and found a brace for my feet. I climbed faster, knowing how far down the water must be, and in turn, guessing at the immensity of the thing attached to the tentacle.

With a hurried glance upward, I saw the edge of the bank was only fifteen feet away. I doubled my pace but tried to maintain a careful hold with my raw hands, in case the stones I grasped were loose. A gulping sound rose from below, reminding me of water draining from a sink plugged with pieces of wet food.

The chasm's edge was only five feet away. I could see the tops of tall trees lining the bank, and the sight of them spurred me onward. Two more lunges and I climbed free, pulling myself onto the sloping bank.

I crawled across the rough stones as fast as I could, away from the edge, away from whatever chased me. I fell onto my side just as the bank began to rise higher, the slim forest of dead trees greeting me. My breath came out in shuddering bursts; I couldn't get enough oxygen. My hands and forearms were useless as bowling pins below my elbows, and my feet were no longer there. I stood, half delirious with cold and exhaustion, and felt something wrap around my leg.

I fell to the ground with a scream, as the green tentacle slithered back over the edge of the bank. It was wound twice around my knee, and dug painfully into my thigh just below my groin. As I slid I noticed a distinct pattern within its flesh, something akin to the design on the back of certain playing cards, circles and ellipses intertwined. In other circumstances it might have been beautiful, paired with the dark green of its skin. My useless hands flung out to either side of me, raking the ground for something as the canyon drew nearer and nearer.

I didn't notice the rock clutched in my fist until I slammed it down onto the tentacle. The rock was the size of a softball, with a broken edge revealing a quartz shine. The serrated teeth of the stone bit into and through the hide of the thing gripping my leg with amazing ease. The flesh parted and spread, white syrup erupting from within, bringing with it a carrion stink. My stomach clenched from the smell, and I struck again, and again. With a sound like wet fabric ripping, the ropy arm snapped in half and raced backward out of sight, over the bank. The portion on my thigh uncoiled. It flopped to the ground, but not before I saw an unlidded eye on the end shift in my direction.

I ran with all the grace of a wounded animal, until I was at the boundary of the trees. I turned and sat, ready to scramble up if anything moved below. The amputated piece of tentacle wriggled a few times, and even turned in the direction of the river, before falling still. I could still smell the foul odor of its blood, and when I looked down, I saw a few white globs stuck to my pants. Disgusted, I wiped them away before rising to my feet.

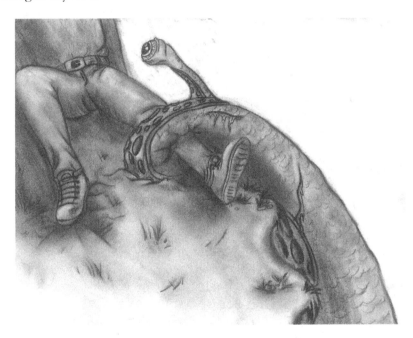

Studying the woods I almost expected something to rush out from the darkness to devour me. But the only sound was the wind shifting branches against one another, clacking wind chimes without tune. I moved closer to the trees, shivering with each step, my legs threatening collapse. I looked down the bank to my right, hoping I would see the familiar outlines of Fellow, Ellius, and Kotis. Only the gray knobs of stone and emptiness of the beach met my eyes.

My feet crunched across dead leaves and sticks. Finally, my legs gave out. I fell to my knees and then sat on my ass, bracing with my hands to keep me from falling straight to my back. It felt very good to sit, to rest. My mind drifted in a haze of nothing. There was only flaming cold that felt like heat. I tried to wiggle my toes, but couldn't tell if they moved within my shoes. Stories of hypothermia replayed through my mind, how survivors described the urge to lie down and fall asleep, how the concern of death became dull and lost its menace. I contemplated it—death. My wife and children were probably dead; I didn't know how long they'd been gone. Without the rest of my group, I wouldn't find them anyway. I would wander the wasteland at the heart of evil forever, until I succumbed to death anyway, by force or by their crippling absence, which would eventually crush me into madness.

I didn't feel my left arm give away, and only realized that I'd fallen onto my side when something poked into my chest and ribs. I grunted, no longer wanting to stay awake. I wanted to float away, unbridled and unchained by the life that pulled me down. I shifted, and the object prodded me again. Something in my pocket, something hard and unyielding.

My eyes shot open.

Managing to get an elbow beneath me, I shoved myself into a half-sitting position, enough to balance, to reach around and fumble with the pocket on my jacket. I looked down and guided my hand by sight, rather than touch, until I was sure I must be holding something. I drew my clenched fist out and opened it, looking at what lay in my palm.

The Zippo was covered in white goo, and for a moment I thought some of the tentacle blood had gotten into the pocket. Then I saw the faded letters on a few pieces of the paste, and knew the Chesterfields were no more. I brushed away some of the cigarette wrapper and managed to flip open the lighter. Several drops of moisture flew out from inside the cap. I turned it upside down and waited for water to dribble out and extinguish my hope. None did.

With more energy than I thought I possessed, I rose to my knees and piled the nearby dead leaves. Each stick or twig I found I added, and soon I had a mound of dry fuel that was knee-high. I stared at the lighter in my hand. It wavered, or maybe I did as I placed my thumb against the little wheel. I prayed against the voice in my head that said the flame wouldn't appear, and flicked my thumb.

The Zippo lit instantly.

A flame nearly two inches high bloomed from the wick. I laughed and held the flame under the edge of a leaf at the bottom of my pile. It smoked for a few seconds and then caught, the fire smiling beneath the leaves and sticks with a widening grin.

I shut the lighter and leaned over the heat. It felt blessed. Careful to not put my hands too close to the flames, I rubbed them over the growing fire. The leaves wrinkled and curled almost as soon as the fire touched them, and soon the sticks on top were burning. Shuddering, I gathered more and more twigs until the blaze talked and snapped. Soon the ground was clear of any leaves and sticks around the fire, and I stumbled to the edge of the forest, where I found larger pieces of wood. I carefully fed them to the flames. A humming vibrated within the centers of my hands, not true feeling but close. I imagined my fingers smoking and curling like the leaves, and at that moment it would have been okay.

After one more trip to the trees, I sat down and placed a large, gnarled chunk of hardwood on top of the pyre before pulling off my shoes. They still dripped water as I set them aside, and peeled off my socks to dry. Next I unbuttoned the coat, and although I dreaded taking off its protection, I pulled the heavy garment away and draped it over me as I lay down only a few feet from the edge of the fire.

Exhaustion sank its roots deep into my bones and tugged my eyelids down. Still shaking, I curled an arm beneath my head and closed my eyes to the ache in the tips of my fingers.

I awoke to a fluttering sound and something hitting the ground nearby. I sat up, choking on dread with thoughts of a slithering tentacle meandering its way toward me. I blinked and stared at Scrim, who sat a few feet away, his head cocked to one side.

"Scrim!" I yelled and jumped to my feet. My legs wobbled and my head felt two sizes too large. The bird squawked once and leapt from the ground, only to hover before me, his long wings beating the air. It was a few seconds before I figured out what he wanted, then I extended my forearm. With surprising grace he landed on the perch I provided, with a gentleness I didn't expect. His long beak clicked several times, and a whirring sound came from the back of his skull.

"Where are they?" I asked, feeling better by the second. I turned and strode to the top of the bank. There was no one on the strewn rocks in either direction. I listened, waiting for a branch to break in the woods or the sound of stones shifting. I heard nothing.

I lifted Scrim to eye level. "Where are they?" I asked again. The bird clicked a few more times and blinked. I thought I saw a hint of something in the golden rings of his eyes—a warning? Then he jumped from my arm and soared up the shore before coasting back.

"You want me to follow?" I asked. He replied with a long tittering that sounded like a red squirrel ferreting an acorn. "Let me get my shoes," I said, and headed back to the fire.

The flames were low but not entirely out. My socks were fairly dry, but I realized they wouldn't stay that way as I placed my shoes over them. The inserts inside the sneakers were two sponges filled with cold moisture, and I tore them out. When I wiggled my toes they were chilled, but the feeling was back in the form of nettling pain whenever I put weight on them. The wool jacket was almost completely dry, and it felt reassuring as I pulled over my shoulders. My fingers were the most concerning. They were mostly thawed, but the tips remained white, with only slight sensation as I buttoned the coat. Scrim swooped low, past the trees, and called out again. With nothing else to carry, I set off after him, in the direction of the bridge.

A light mist hung a few feet off the ground, as if suspended from the bridge pillars, when I approached the structure. I assumed that the others searched for me and went back to the bridge to regroup when they didn't find me, so the elation I felt when I crested the hill soured at their absence. Scrim flew into the mist and vanished, only to reappear in a gliding arc as he skimmed the walkway of the bridge.

I stopped a few yards from the stone pillars and turned in a circle. "Ellius!" I yelled, letting the name echo off the line of trees and into the canyon behind me. "Fellow! Kotis!" My voice was lonely, the last sound in the world.

Scrim flew from behind me and landed on the ground several paces away. He walked with the movement of a large chicken, his wings folded back and his head bobbing forward. I followed him, hoping I would see a trail of smoke drifting up from a campfire.

We made our way up the bank and stopped at the top. There was a gap in the woods ahead, and I could see the terrain changed drastically from dead scrub grass to packed earth to gray stone. Scrim called from down the bank, and I took two steps before my foot crunched on something and I stopped.

A thick layer of sickly orange flakes lay strewn in an oval shape on the ground. I stepped back and knelt to examine it. The flakes were deep amber and brown in spots, with curled edges. All the pieces were two or more inches in diameter. Cautiously I nudged one. It moved enough for me to see black tar that soaked the ground beneath the pieces.

"Rust," I said, poking at the chunks of decay again. I picked one of the pieces up to get a closer look. Several fine, black hairs grew from the scale and swayed in the breeze.

I dropped the scale in disgust and wiped my hand on my jeans, as if I'd touched a pile of noxious waste. I stood and took two more steps before encountering another pile, almost identical to the first. This time there was a smattering of blood that continued in a line toward the trees. The grass was bent and broken in several places, and when I stepped back, I realized the entire area I stood in looked as though a herd of buffalo had stampeded through. There were deep depressions in many places, and when I examined them closely, I saw the familiar tread of bare feet, much larger than a human. "Kotis," I said.

Next to the tracks were a set of dents that could only have been Fellow's. Fear wiggled a finger in the bottom of my stomach, and I crouched to stare at the forest ahead. I waited. Nothing moved, and since I was pretty much in plain sight, I assumed whoever or whatever took my friends was gone. For they had been taken, that much I was certain of. I could see the footprints of their attackers leading from the depths of the woods, their tracks long and clawed.

I walked down the bank and traced the battle that must have happened just moments after I'd fallen. I found another pile of rust, and this time I saw what looked like deflated facial features at one end. Two spots that could have been eyes gazed up at me, their sockets filled with the same black tar, and a mouth still held a round expression of surprise. Where the dead grass transitioned into dirt, I saw scuff marks raked in wide swaths. It looked like someone had made a snow angel in the earth. Two deep channels continued on from that point, and ended as the ground became solid stone.

"They dragged them away," I said, as Scrim walked to me from the edge of the woods. "Something took them." Scrim dipped his long beak once and clicked. I faced ahead and stared at distant shapes that looked like narrow spires shooting up from the ground. The drag marks led in a straight line to the pointed towers.

I let out a shaky breath and walked to the woods to look for something I could use as a weapon. All the sticks were either too short or too brittle, and after a few minutes I gave up. "Of course there's nothing," I said. Scrim hopped toward me, his head tipping back and forth. "Yeah, let's do this," I said, and we walked through the break in the trees, toward the shapes in the distance.

The stone spires shot straight up and towered over us, the tallest of them being at least two hundred feet from base to tip. They were conical in shape, but withered near their tops, and looked like jagged, broken fingers of the dead. I stopped at the border of the formations and gazed into a passage that wound away into the city of rock.

The trail left, undoubtedly, by Kotis's dragging heels, led into the city. The sun sat to my right and threw long, ungainly shadows across the path. Every so often a sharp crack would echo deep within the towers, making the back of my neck prickle.

I bent down and picked up a rock smaller than a baseball. It wasn't the best protection, but I remembered how the jagged stone cut through the tentacle wrapped around my leg and decided that it was better than nothing.

"You fly high and check things out. Come back to me if you see something wrong," I said to Scrim. He let out a short screech and leapt into the air. In a few seconds he was a dark spot against the clouds, and then nothing at all.

I was alone again. The curved bases of the towers were immense and stretched like crumbling tree trunks into the ground. The darkness between them played tricks on my eyes and shifted, moved, and danced with forms that almost took definitive shape and then melted away. Part of me wanted to turn away and run in the direction I thought my family must be, away from the shadows that spoke of death. But I couldn't forsake them. My friends. I moved out of the feeble light and into the forest of stone.

The air immediately became cooler, and I buttoned my jacket as much as I could. My fingertips were still numb, and the chilly air nipped at them, causing a dull throb beneath my fingernails. I studied the rock formations as I passed them, my heart beating harder each time I saw what resembled movement between the monoliths. The rock was cracked and striated, but otherwise smooth. It was light brown, but I could see stains of yellow and pocks of black in different places. A smell permeated the air, organic and pungent, with hints of salt, like the ocean at low tide.

The path I walked on was unbroken and level because of the tread of many feet. It had the feel of an abandoned highway, the centerline worn away with time. The sharp cracking I heard earlier came again, and I froze, waiting for one of the stalagmites to topple. When nothing approached or fell, I continued on. The trail dipped and then ran up, creating a rise before another, deeper, drop. I hesitated on the crest, listening for what I thought I heard: a yell on the wind that wound its way through the spires. It came again, this time in the deep bellow of Kotis's voice.

I ran. The massive trunks hurtled by, and the trail narrowed. I gripped the rock in my right hand, my muscles thrumming and ready to heave the rock at the first sign of danger. The path threaded hard to the left, and suddenly an opening appeared. I skidded to a halt and ducked down behind a nearby outcrop. Tentatively I peeked over the rock I hid behind.

The clearing was the size of a football stadium. The rock upthrusts ran in a curved ring, making up its boundaries. The center resembled a flattened lava field of unblemished, rolling stone. A rough channel ran around the circumference of the clearing, and I saw a short bridge made of cobblestones leading across the nearest gap.

In the center of the opening, naked and chained to the ground, lay Kotis and Fellow. From where I stood, it looked as though Kotis bled from a wound on his head and Fellow was unconscious, his face turned to the side, away from me, unmoving. Around them stood dozens of hunched figures, all skeleton thin and deep orange. Their heads were small and their arms long, some scraping the ground with their fingertips. I could make out fine, black hairs growing on the closest ones, along with scabrous breaks in their orange skin—rust.

"You know where he is," a deep, velvet voice said, and I shifted my eyes to the left. A man stood a few yards in front of Kotis—or what I at first thought was a man. When it turned in my direction, I saw that it was anything but. A long shock of deep-black hair swept back from a flattened forehead. Its skin was a sulfurous yellow, the color of a diseased tooth. Elongated eyes hugged the sides of its head in reptilian fashion, and its body was rail thin, matching its compatriots in stature. It wore a dirty black dress shirt that dangled from its lean shoulders and a pair of brown pants, which at one time might have been white. When it opened its mouth to speak, I saw rows of pointed, interlocking teeth.

"He's hidden somewhere, and you're going to tell me," the creature said.

Kotis raised his head, hawked with a scraping sound, and spit a mass of blood and phlegm at his captor. The lugi landed on the thing's shirt and drooled down the front. Before the spit could drip, the creature swiped it up and, without hesitating, licked it off its hand.

"Delightful," it said after chewing for a moment. "Now where were we?"

Kotis coughed. "I was tellin' you to get fucked, and you were about to oblige."

"Hmm, no, that's not right. I think you were about to say—"

It leapt forward with speed that made my neck muscles jerk in an attempt to follow it. There was a resounding crack as it struck Kotis on the side of the head with a pointed foot, and I knew where the sound that I heard in the passage earlier came from. Kotis's head snapped to the side, and blood flew in a shiny spray from the raw wound on his temple. I saw the giant clench his jaw and the muscles ripple beneath his dark gray skin. The chains rattled as he strained against them, but then he relaxed, his breath puffing out in another, smaller, mist of blood.

"Piss in the wind," Kotis managed after catching his breath.

"I'll piss your blood," the creature hissed, and slid to one knee, grabbing Kotis by the throat as he did. "Tell me where he is! They saw him with you across the river!"

"He fell, he's dead," Kotis croaked.

"You lie!" the thing yelled, and pounded on Kotis's face with a fury of fists. I was shocked as another set of arms sprouted from the thing's sides. The new arms were long and segmented, with sharp points at their ends. They unfurled and rose into the air above Kotis and Fellow, and hung there ready to stab downward.

"No," I yelled, and leapt from behind the rock.

Dozens of heads swiveled in my direction. The creature's spear-like appendages froze in mid-strike. I stood in the open, with no protection other than the stone in my hand, which felt silly now. After a moment I let it drop to the ground beside my foot. "Don't hurt them anymore. I'm right here," I said.

The creature hovered over Kotis for another second and then stood, its secret arms retracting out of sight. Now that it faced me fully, I could see its eyes were black with red centers, which looked like small fires as it blinked, and rows of teeth gleamed dully in the fall light when it smiled.

"So gracious of you to join us ...?" The question hung in the silence.

"Michael," I replied, glancing down at Kotis, who shook his head and jerked it in the direction I'd come from.

"Ah, Michael. Such a human name," the creature purred. Its voice carried effortlessly across the distance between us. It sounded hollow and bottomless, as if it spoke from a cave within itself. "Michael, why don't you join us and we'll have a bit of a talk."

I started to reply, but movement caught my eye to the right of the creature. Something zipped through the air, a streamlined bullet of gray and brown. Scrim dove sharply, his eyes trained on the creature with deadly awareness. At the last second he released his wings from his sides, and I saw their bladed edges flash.

The creature stepped to one side with the speed I'd witnessed earlier, and threw a halfhearted punch, knocking Scrim from the air. The bird crumpled and hit the hard rock in a rolling flurry of feathers. He somersaulted twice and then lay still, his beak pointed toward the sky.

"No!" Kotis bellowed, his voice full of pain. He made his hardest lunge against the chains yet, the cords in his neck sticking out in ropes, his eyes bulging with hatred. "You fucking prick! I'll kill you! I'll kill you!"

I stared at Scrim's unmoving form and felt despair slide over me. I waited, hoping for him to move, to shift a wing or open his beak. He remained still.

The creature inspected the long nails on its hand, ignoring Kotis's insults and threats. "Yes, yes. You'll tear me limb from limb, I'm very concerned." It looked up and motioned me to come closer. "Michael, come here before any more life is lost."

My legs trembled as I stepped onto the makeshift bridge spanning the small gap around the field. My mind searched for possible ways to get out of the situation, and I glanced in every direction, looking for something, some sort of diversion or means of defense. There was nothing. I walked past the ring of rusted beings, who stared at me with hunger, their dark eyes shifting from my feet to my head as though I were a walking banquet.

I stopped several yards away from the creature in an attempt to stay outside of its reach, but then I remembered how fast it moved and knew if it wanted to kill me, it would.

It smiled again, revealing the rows of interlocking teeth. "Michael, so very nice to meet you. I'm Dagnon of the Lonos, and these are my prodigies," Dagnon said, waving a hand at the rusted figures around us. "And, well, you know these two, I suppose," he said, jerking his head toward Kotis and Fellow. I looked at Kotis, who bared his teeth, his breath coming out in heavy puffs.

"Don't tell him anything, Michael. He's a vile disease," Kotis said, and I could see he wanted to spit again.

"Oh, can't we be civil?" Dagnon asked, his voice lightening with syrupy good humor. "This is all just a misunderstanding."

"What do you want?" I asked, finally finding my voice. I kept the question steady, even though Dagnon turned his strange eyes upon me again. The red in his irises flickered, and in that moment I knew he was mad.

"Just a simple favor. You'd do a favor to save your friends, wouldn't you?" he asked, leaning forward.

I licked my lips, weighing my words carefully. "It depends on what it is."

Dagnon smiled. "You're really not in the position to bargain."

"Maybe not, but we all would be dead if you didn't really need me for something," I said. My brain shot in multiple directions as I tried to buy more time, to figure out how to free Kotis and Fellow without getting us all murdered.

Dagnon considered my words and stroked his chin with dirty fingers. "You humans are an interesting lot, you know that? Some time ago there was a vent to Earth that showed up just a few feet from where we're standing. It appeared in your world in a man's attic, and he happened to peer in just as I did the same. He was in a stupor and stepped back before I could grab him. So I asked him his name instead, tried to lure him a little closer. He said it was Lovecraft. The vent disappeared shortly thereafter. Such a shame I couldn't bring him here for a longer stay." Dagnon shifted his reptilian eyes away, and then back to me. "I like your name much better."

He turned and walked away from me, stopping beside a short-legged table I hadn't noticed before. There were a few ornate carvings in the wood, swirls and diagrams that meant nothing to me but could have been a language. Dagnon reached down and, with one pointed fingernail, peeled up a piece of the table's top. With a quick snap of his hand, he ripped the strip of wood up and off. Blood flew into the air in a rainbow of red, and a lipless mouth opened on the end of the table and screamed. I took a reflexive step back, and flinched when Dagnon threw the piece of wood at me.

I caught it, expecting the rough feel of laminate against my palms, but instead the strip hung limp like a dead snake. It was soft and pliable, sticky with blood. When I looked closer, I realized it wasn't wood at all—it was skin. I dropped it on the ground at my feet, rubbing my hands on my jacket as my stomach pole-vaulted toward the back of my throat. The table sobbed and let out an agonized scream every few seconds until Dagnon kicked it, drawing an abrupt yelp from it that trailed off into soft crying.

"You see, Michael, I'm quite adept at changing things. I make dead things alive and alive things, well ..." He tipped his head toward the weeping table. "Let's just say I alter them. And your two friends here would make great additions to my little collection. Is that enough negotiation for you?"

My mouth was full of sand, and all I wanted was to get the smell of blood out of my nose and the feeling of it off my hands. A sound like sandpaper on concrete came from around us, and I saw the rust creatures laugh, their mouths open and their eyes hungry.

I turned back to Dagnon. "What do you need me to do?"

His smile seemed to split his face. "There is a house not far from here, where no house should be. There is something there that I want. You will know it when you see it. Bring it back to me, or your friends will end up as something too terrible to speak of, something I can torture and that will be torture just to exist as."

"Why don't you go and get it?" I asked, feeling as if I was already on thin ice and had just stepped closer to the edge.

Dagnon's face clenched in a fist of rage, and then relaxed in a blink of an eye. "Because, I will kill your friends and then kill you," he said, grinning crazily again. "Is that a good enough answer?"

I looked at Kotis, who shook his head again, pleading in his eyes, along with a heavy grief that was already etched into his blocky features. "I'll do it," I heard myself say.

Dagnon threw back his head, his long hair bouncing as he laughed. "Wonderful," he said between giggles. "Two of my helpers will escort you to the house. Be back as fast as you can. And remember, if you run, not only will your friends end up as my new favorite pastime, I'll make it my sole purpose to find you and peel out your bones one by one."

My bowels felt soupy, but my gaze didn't waver from Dagnon's. "And you'll let us go if I do this?"

Dagnon's face grew serious. "Of course. Be quick and I'll set you all free."

I knew the lie for what it was, but I nodded anyway and tried to appear satisfied. I took a couple of steps closer to Kotis. "Is that table Ellius?" I asked in a low voice.

Kotis shook his head. "He managed to get into the forest when we were ambushed." I glanced around at the rust creatures as two moved toward me on spindly legs.

"Is Fellow okay?" I asked. I hadn't seen him move since entering the clearing, and I feared the worst.

Kotis glanced to his left, then back at me. "I think so. They hit him hard on the head when they took us. He hasn't been conscious since."

"That's enough chitchat," Dagnon said behind me. "Get moving."

With no other choice, I followed one of the rusted guards, while the other fell in step behind me. We walked away from the group to another bridge. I realized the direction was the same as the one we'd been following before reaching the river. We wound our way into the maze of rocky spines. I heard the creatures breathing, and they sounded like overheated radiators, wheezing and whining with each step. I wondered briefly if I could overpower them. Kotis and Fellow had seemed to get the best of a few before being taken. I studied the guard in front of me, its skin layered like a snake's, the patches of rust overlapping to form scales that rose and shifted with its movement. I looked for a weak spot, somewhere to strike. After a few moments I gave up the idea, knowing that I had no weapons besides the Zippo in my pocket, and my fists didn't seem the best tools for the job. Kotis may have been able to smash them to pieces, but I knew I'd die if I tried the same.

We walked for approximately the same distance that I had earlier to gain view of the open area, and soon came out onto a plain of hard-packed ground. The slight wind blowing pulled a wave of dust from the ground and lifted it in a twisting cloud that rolled beautifully before us. I watched it go, and when it settled, I saw the outline of something not far away, something boxy and tall, with a peak. Its gray color did nothing to contrast it from the soil it sat upon, but its shape was distinct: a house.

"That's it," one of the creatures growled. "Come right back, or we'll find you, and the prince won't have the pleasure of his torture."

I hesitated. "You're not coming with me?"

The one who'd spoke remained stoic, but its eyes flitted between my face and the house, and I saw something in them: fear. They were afraid of the house. I didn't question them anymore, and turned away. Without glancing back, I walked toward the outline of the structure in the distance.

CHAPTER NINE

THE HOUSE OF MIRRORS

The house was old, I could tell that much. The paint that covered it at some point was gone, flaked away beneath the wind and the ever-present sun. Its wooden siding was rough and decaying, with loose fibers that twitched with the breeze. The first story was fronted by a short porch, its railing gone in some places, as well as several steps to the front door. The second level narrowed to suggest only a single room upstairs. Windows looked out at me, every pane of glass still intact. A picket fence surrounded perhaps an acre of property. A lone toy truck, its yellow paint faded to watery urine, sat half submerged in the drifting dirt of the front yard. That chilled me the most.

I glanced over my shoulder to inspect the distance I'd traveled and to make sure the rust creatures hadn't followed me.

A shadowed figure stood a hundred yards away.

I stared at it, even as my heart leapt into furious action. I dared it to fold away as it had done before, to become a mirage that faded, but it remained. I couldn't make out any features on its face, but its build and stance were familiar. Familiar because they were my own.

I turned back toward the house and watched for some sign of danger. No faces appeared at the windows, the door didn't creak open ominously. The wind rustled my hair and pushed at my coat.

Unhooking the gate, I walked through the yard to the front door. I could smell the rot of the wood, a punky, thick odor that invaded my nostrils. The door handle was worn and corroded, but when I turned it, the door opened without protest. A blast of air rushed past me, as if the house were pressurized and I'd just broken the seal. For some reason the air made me think of a drink, a cold beer, an iced whiskey. My mouth watered. Before I stepped into the house, I glanced over my shoulder again and saw that the shadow was gone.

The moment I stepped through the door, movement flashed at me from directly ahead. I ducked instinctively, expecting a blow to the head. When none came, I looked up and saw that mirrors lined both short walls flanking a central staircase that led straight up to a landing and then disappeared out of sight. I shut the door behind me and examined the mirrors. They were dusky and stained with time, their reflected images mottled and distorted. I moved toward the one on the left and stopped, my breath freezing solid in my lungs.

A little boy looked out at me from the mirror.

I blinked, waiting for the reflection to move on its own, to grow teeth and leap free of its glass prison, but it merely blinked too. I raised my hand and it did the same. Until then I hadn't really studied the boy's face, but when I saw that he wore a polo shirt with colors that chimed tones in my memory, I knew that he was me. I was seven years old in the reflection, and saw that my other hand held the lifeless body of a guinea pig. Its brown-and-white fur was barely discernable through the age of the glass, but I could still see a black eye glazed with death shining through the tangles.

"Pal," I said, speaking the name of my pet for the first time in over twenty years. I'd named him Pal after my father brought him home for my sixth birthday. His name was chosen in honor of being my self-proclaimed best friend. He had been my responsibility, my charge. Water, food, and cleaning. Simple enough to an adult, but for a kid of six it was, at times, overwhelming. I'd forgotten his water the day after my seventh birthday, the day we left for my aunt's for a week. He'd died of thirst, and it had been no one's fault but mine. I remembered coming home, wearing the shirt that the boy did in the mirror, and stepping into the house and smelling the putridity of something days dead.

I tore my gaze away from the boy in the mirror, who began to cry. I felt tears on my cheeks and wiped at them, yet I saw no matching movement in the mirror. I turned and walked to the other side of the staircase. My mind hummed with the memory of my failure. I'd caused Pal's death, and although most would scoff at such a petty loss, it still bothered me.

I studied the darkened foyer to the right of the stairway, breathing out and trying to shake off the feeling of despair. I wasn't here to wallow in my failures, I needed to focus. I needed to find what Dagnon wanted, bring it back, and think of a plan along the way to free Kotis and Fellow. I saw nothing of significance in the dim light that entered through the dirty windows. Dagnon said I would know when I saw it, and I hadn't seen it yet. I glanced toward the stairs; the upper floor my next destination. My eyes swept past the second mirror intentionally, but the urge to look was too great, and I glanced at the reflection in spite of myself.

The mirror showed me again; although this time I almost thought it was a normal mirror, because it was clearer, and the first thing I looked at was my face. The features that stared back at me were not those of a young boy, but they weren't currently mine either. There were no lines around my eyes and my face was leaner. I wore a faded Weezer T-shirt and jeans that were torn at the knees. In my right hand I saw a crumpled wad of money, and my stomach clenched.

I'd taken the cash from my best friend in college. Tom had left thirty dollars lying on a coffee table after we'd gotten drunk the prior night. He was asleep when I woke, and seeing that it was already raining outside, I took the money from the table, knowing I had none to buy the booze that would get me through the thunderstorm. I never told him or paid him back, and he never asked. He slowly separated himself from me over the following weeks, and deep down I knew why.

I staggered out of the mirror's reach and gripped the molding banister that lined the stairway. I felt ready to throw up, the guilt that coursed through my mind making my stomach foam with regret. What the hell was wrong with me? I coughed and tried to straighten. It felt as though weights hung from each of my shoulders and the top of my head. I wanted to lie down on the floor and curl up, to give in to the guilt that pressed down on me. The images of Kotis and Fellow chained floated through my mind, but they were hazy and without definition. It wasn't my problem anymore. I didn't even remember why I was here.

Jane, Sara, Jack.

My spine stiffened and my head cleared at once. My kids, my wife, that's why I was here. My gaze traveled up the stairs, and I took the first step, which groaned under my weight. As I climbed the landing came into view, and I realized that I'd been correct in assuming there was only one room on the second floor. I stopped at the last step and looked at the space before me.

The room was fairly long. A single window set high in the farthest wall shone a pale shaft of light onto the wooden floorboards. A table sat beneath the window and ran the entire width of the room. There were several objects on its surface, but what caught my eye first was the noose.

It hung from the middle of the room, the rope strung through a sturdy eyelet screwed into the middle beam of the roof. The noose was open wide, its mouth drooping like a silent scream. A dusty chair sat beneath it, its thin legs unsupported by cross-rungs of any kind.

I waited for something to happen. The quiet mimicked the dirty surfaces of the room, unmoving, stolid. I stepped onto the second floor, and something moved at the far end. I noticed a darkened mirror that ran above the long table. Without something to reflect, its surface blended into the wall. Now I stood suffused in muted light, small and indistinct in the polished glass.

Part of me cried out to flee the house, to abandon the search for whatever the demon in the clearing wanted. I could devise another plan to rescue my friends and my family. But even as the thoughts danced through my mind like ill-conceived sprites, I knew I couldn't leave. Somehow I knew the house would stop me now that I was inside its boundaries.

I centered my will on finding what I needed to free my friends, and moved forward. Wary of the noose in the middle of the room, I gave it a wide berth. But as I passed it, I couldn't help but see the maroon stains on the rope and the scuff marks on the seat of the chair.

Once at the table, I stood before it, my head anchored down, my eyes focused on the objects, unwilling to let my attention wander up to the outline in the mirror. An ancient revolver sat to my left, a thin layer of dust covering its heavy steel. I saw several places on the table where it had been moved and set down by unknown hands innumerable times. The next item to the right was a long knife; its blade curved and stained a uniform black from tip to handle. It was all but free of dust. My gaze shifted again and I stopped.

Two more objects sat in the row. The first was a clear vase almost a foot high. It was wide at the bottom, its base the size of my hand. It narrowed at its top and nearly came to a point, ending in a stopper that looked like a hand-carved cork. But the most interesting aspect was its contents. The inside of the vase was amber in color, with bits of black swirls that moved of their own accord. They corkscrewed through the viscous fluid and left wakes where they swam.

The second object was a bottle of whiskey. For a few seconds, the sight of it didn't compute and I felt nothing. The label was gone, peeled away, but I could see its outline and knew it was Jack Daniels, my favorite. The impulse to snatch the bottle from where it sat became strong. I imagined unscrewing the cap and smelling the oaky sting that would leak out. I could feel the bottle's mouth against my own, the fire that would race down my throat, and the pervasion of the alcohol as it softened everything.

I didn't realize the bottle was in my hands until I looked into the mirror and saw it there. I wanted to look away, but my image was so clear in the glass, so sharp, I was mesmerized. Again my reflection wore different clothes, but I was closer to my current age. I lifted my hand, but the other me didn't follow suit. Instead, he lifted the bottle and drained a few swallows. The bottle in the mirror had a label, and the clothes were mine. I still had them, I remembered, although now the jeans were torn and—

A hole opened up on the left knee of the jeans my reflection wore. He raised the bottle and took another swig, and sighed silently with pleasure. Blood seeped out of the hole at his knee, my knee. It coated the blue jeans and stained the material almost black. I still had the scar from tackling Sara off her bike in front of the passing car. But she never would have been in the street if I hadn't slipped off to have a drink.

Jane had taken Jack uptown and I was watching Sara, except I wasn't. I was drinking, even though there were no clouds in the sky. Somewhere behind me in the memory I heard the soft sound of a door closing, and it echoed in the house where I now stood.

My grip tightened on the bottle's neck, and I brought it closer to my face. I could smell the liquor, and looked down to see the cap was off. It smelled so good, so warm and welcoming. My hand shook and sent ripples through the brown liquid. I needed to forget how I almost let my daughter die in the street. No, almost killed her. Tears sprang to my eyes. I never told Jane that I'd had a drink that day, I couldn't bring myself to.

The guilt and the shame coalesced into something new, a feeling I encountered each time the sky darkened. I wanted to drink and hide away from the storm of my memories. I wanted to curl up on the floor, shrink until there was nothing left, cease to exist.

"You can, you know," a voice said behind me.

My impulse was to look up in the mirror to see who spoke, but I couldn't stand to look at myself anymore, so I turned to face the shadow at the head of the stairs.

It stood motionless, blending with the background of darkness that coated the far end of the room. I could see its eyes, though, cold and piercing, the same color as mine.

"What do you mean?" I asked.

"You can cease to exist. You've lived with pain and fear most of your life, and it's not your fault. There's no reason for it. Fairness doesn't even enter into this, not when you've been plagued by something you don't understand, can't understand."

The shadow's words were cool, soothing to my ears, and I realized that its voice was a version of my own, the one I used with Jane when I was trying to hide the fact that I was drunk.

"Why?" I asked, tears coming again to my eyes. It was what I wanted to know from the moment the fear began. Why me? Why did I have to suffer? What was the purpose?

"It's just how things go, how the world works. You can't question it, you just have to deal with it. No one can blame you for having a drink once in a while."

I nodded. That was what I'd told myself over and over. Each time I turned my truck into the parking lot of the liquor store. Each time I poured myself a drink, that was what I'd said. I deserved the relief, the numbness it brought.

The shadow stepped forward into the light, and it was like looking in the mirror again. Its face was an exact replica of mine in the flesh, down to the growth of beard on my cheeks. The figure wore the same wool coat, but below the belt its legs were still shrouded in roiling darkness. "Take a sip and we'll talk about it. Maybe this is what you've been waiting for," it said, gesturing to the room, and I saw its hand float upward toward the noose also. "Death is the final escape, right?"

I squinted at it, swallowed. The bottle was near my collarbone, hovering close enough to smell again. My mouth watered for a taste. I wanted to douse myself in the whiskey, to drown the fear and self-loathing that boiled beneath my skin. I wanted it to all go away.

"Yeah, I'm so tired," I said.

My likeness nodded. "I understand. Go ahead, have a drink and we'll figure things out. No one would do any different. In fact, your family might be safer without you around."

A sob escaped me, and I looked at the floor. It blurred with the tears that coursed out of my eyes and onto my cheeks. I'd almost killed my daughter with neglect, with my fear, with my addiction. When would I make a mistake again? Would it be my son this time? My wife? All three? Would I drive when I shouldn't and crash? The thought made me cringe, and I blinked, wiping away the tears with the heel of my free hand.

"Okay," I said. "You're right. I'll be saving them."

The thing that wasn't me smiled and agreed with a sympathetic nod of its head. I brought the bottle up to my chin, relishing the thought of being drunk again. It would take the edge off what I had to do next. I'll be saving them, I thought as I tipped the bottle to my lips and paused.

Saving them.

My wife and kids weren't safe. They were here, in this world somewhere. I needed to find them. That's why I was there. The clarity of the thought magnified until it consumed my mind.

The bottle dropped away from my mouth, and my likeness frowned. An invisible veil shifted, and for the first time since I stepped into the house, I became aware of its presence. It clung to me with desperation, tried to slip back over me, to cover me in doubt and old memories of failure, addiction, and weakness. Everything but the memory of why I was there. I focused on that memory. The journey I was on, my family. The veil receded more. I closed my eyes and saw them, felt them in my arms, held them close, breathed them in. They needed me; they'd always needed me. The veil fell away. I opened my eyes.

My twin had a snarl frozen on its face, and I saw that the darkness below its belt was higher than before. Shadow slid up from the floor and began to cloak it once again. "You need it," it said through clenched teeth.

I shook my head and tipped the bottle.

Whiskey poured out onto the floor and splashed in a widening puddle at my feet. "No!" it yelled from the other end of the room, and I saw darkness inch gradually up its chest.

"I don't need you anymore," I said. It screamed in response, its voice changing from my own into a deeper tone that radiated anguish. It took a halting step forward and stopped. I continued to pour the bottle out, the whiskey permeating the room with a scent that smelled much less alluring than it had moments before. I watched the thing in my clothes take another begrudging step, and saw that it was trying to hold itself back. A force pulled at it, dragging it forward with an unseen grip. Only its face remained free of shadow, a grimace of pain carved into its appearance, which broke the illusion of humanity.

"You're weak! You're broken! You're nothing," it hissed.

"I was, but not anymore," I answered. I watched in morbid awe as its face swirled into something unrecognizable before shadow swallowed it completely. Its foot stepped forward again and landed on the seat of the chair in the middle of the room. With one motion, it pulled itself up onto the rickety seat and stood, arms vibrating at its sides, before reaching up to grasp the hanging noose. The bottle in my hand glugged once as a bubble raced up to flush the remaining liquor out. The shadow pulled the noose around its neck and tightened the rope, the knot to one side of its head. I turned the bottle completely upside down, and the last dregs slipped free of the glass.

The shadow burned with licking flames of darkness at its edges. It stood completely still for one beat, and then kicked the chair from beneath its feet. Its body fell a foot and jerked to a stop at the end of the rope, its head jolted sideways, and a resounding crack filled the room as its neck broke.

I stared, transfixed by the sight of the swinging body. At any moment, I expected it to fly into life, to jerk on the rope and claw at my face for purchase. It stayed still except for the pendulum sway of death.

The last drops dripped from inside the upside-down bottle, and I lowered it. My hand hurt from gripping it, so I relaxed. The room felt different somehow, and it wasn't until I turned to face the mirror that I saw I no longer had a reflection in its depths. The noose behind me was motionless and empty, the chair below it back in place. I looked over my shoulder. Everything was just as before.

I stepped forward and peered into the vase. There were more dark streaks, and several clotted together to form a pulsing tumor that stuck to the glass. As I looked at it, I felt that I was being studied at the same time. This was what Dagnon wanted, there was no question about it—it was evil.

I picked up the tapered vase and shifted my gaze from it to my other hand, where I still held the empty Jack Daniels bottle. I breathed out. I knew what I had to do.

I walked down the short hill to where the rusted guards waited, my feet leaving the dried soil behind for the solid feel of rock beneath them. The creatures heard my approach and stood from where they sat on the ground at the mouth of the passage.

"What took you so damn long?" one of them said as I neared.

"Oh, just this," I said, tossing it the glass vase with the liquid inside.

Its black eyes shot open in surprise, and it leapt forward to catch the bottle. Without breaking my stride, I drew the curved knife from the back of my pants and thrust its tip through the chest of the other creature.

The knife drove through the rusted hide without slowing. I jammed my hand hard against the handle and felt the blade break through the other side of the creature's back. Its face was close to mine, and a small amount of satisfaction rose within me as I saw the look of disbelief on its jagged features.

The other guard bellowed, and I yanked the knife free as I spun toward it. The vase sat on the ground nearby, and the rusted figure was almost upon me, its eyes narrowed to slits, its clawed hands reaching for my throat. I stabbed at its face and felt the blade make contact. A grating sensation traveled through the knife and up my arm. The weapon lodged in its left eye socket, halfway to the hilt. The grinding I felt was the tip dragging across the inside of its crusted skull as it shifted.

I drew back my arm and pulled the blade free. The creature stood on wobbling legs for a full second before it crumbled and fell in a pile of flaking rust at my feet. When I turned to find the first guard I attacked, I saw that it too was a mere layer of sediment on the ground.

A savage triumph rolled through me as I stood over the two fallen bodies. At that moment I vibrated with energy, a rush of life pulsing through my veins with the rapid beats of my heart. The danger because of what I'd done tried to settle over me, but I shrugged it off and embraced the adrenaline that shook my hands.

I carefully tucked the knife close to my back again, hiding it as best I could beneath the jacket. I picked the bottle off the ground, and hugged it close to my side as I set off down the trail.

The high points of rock scrolled past, and in no time I saw the clearing ahead. Kotis and Fellow were still on the ground. Fellow hadn't moved from his position, but Kotis craned his neck around in my direction when he heard my footsteps on the bridge. Dagnon and the other creatures also turned toward me. I saw a flicker of uncertainty cross Dagnon's alien face when he saw that I was alone.

"Ah, Michael. You surprise and delight to no end. But where, may I ask, are your escorts?" Dagnon asked.

"They fell behind," I said.

"I'm sure they did, they can be slow animals at times." The monster's eyes left mine and slid to the glass bottle tucked beneath my arm. "Your journey was most beneficial, I'm impressed. Please bring that here, and we'll see to setting your friends free."

I stood my ground, and took a step back when a few of the rust creatures began to move forward. "You need to tell me what's so important about this bottle and what's inside before I give it to you."

"I don't have to tell you anything, human," Dagnon growled.

I casually hefted the bottle in one hand, displaying it above the solid rock we stood on. "Then I guess you won't mind me dropping this right here?"

"No!" Dagnon yelled as he took a step forward and raised a clawed hand. His features drew back, tightening his already strained countenance. His cheekbones seemed to shift before he dropped his arm to his side and pulled a smile back from his pointed teeth. "You little bastard."

"Just tell me what this is for," I said. My eyes shot to the ground behind Dagnon, and I saw that Scrim was still there, his feathers ruffling in the breeze. I squinted and tried to remember if his beak had been pointed in the same direction as now.

"Very well," Dagnon said. "As I said before, I am Dagnon, the last acolyte of Lonos, God of this world, preserver of the darkness."

"Flattened shit!" Kotis called out from where he lay. "Lonos is a fucking myth, you crazy little bird!"

Dagnon made to take a step toward the chained giant, and I shook my head and tilted the bottle above the rock. I could hear his teeth grind together as he shifted his attention back to me and continued.

"Lonos was here before the sun rotated. He shaped the land to what it is. He carved the riverbed and planted its tongue in the deepest abyss. My brothers and I served his needs and paid homage to him until he was struck down by an assassin's poison in an offering." Dagnon's eyes throbbed in his sockets with the memory. "A man, from your world. Lonos fell, but his soul was too strong to flee and meant to inhabit his murderer. But the man caught his life force in that bottle and built the house on the plain to protect it. One by one my brothers died or were driven out by creatures such as these." He motioned to Kotis and Fellow.

I glanced at my friends again and noticed something strange. Fellow's right hand was unwinding in slow, delicate movements. The vines and brush that held his wooden palm together were unlatching themselves. I saw the manacle grow loose on his wrist before my eyes shot back to Dagnon, who continued speaking.

"But I remained faithful to the order, always seeking, never resting, to find a way to reunite my master's body and soul." His snake-like eyes burned into me, and he sneered. "When my pets here saw you and your companions across the river, I knew the time had come for rebirth. I knew you would be the one to retrieve the true God's soul from the wretched prison and return it to his body."

My gaze shifted to the ground behind Dagnon, and my heart leapt as I saw that Scrim was gone. Trying to keep the tremble from my voice, I said, "If Lonos died that long ago, his body would be dust. There's nothing to reunite this too." I gestured with the bottle.

Dagnon smiled again. "Oh human, you know so little. Look around you and behold Lonos, for you stand in the center of his mouth."

I glanced to my left and right, a sick feeling growing in my stomach like a poisonous plant. The high, pointed rocks in the ring around the clearing were suddenly arranged in an order I hadn't noticed before. Their concentric rings were set in odd formations, like rows of teeth in a shark's jaw. The flat expanse we stood upon was ridged with small serrations I mistook for natural erosion. Now I could see them for what they were: petrified taste buds. The gap around the perimeter of the tongue was the space for the jaw and gum, long since decayed and solidified to stone. The enormity of the creature that owned the lower jaw we stood inside almost didn't compute in my mind, and I blinked at Dagnon, who smiled victoriously.

"You see now, don't you?" Dagnon asked.

I nodded, glancing at Kotis and Fellow before returning his gaze. "Yes, I see."

"And you know you don't have a choice but to give me that bottle."

I nodded again before I took a step and tossed the bottle. It flew to him, and he snatched it from the air, his eyes flashing in rage.

"Now set them free," I said, preparing myself.

Dagnon caressed the bottle and drew it close to his face. "Lonos, it is time," he said, grasping the cork at the top of the vase. "Kill them," he said to the creatures that smiled at one another and began to move forward.

My body tensed as I reached to my back and looked at Kotis. I grinned for a split second and winked.

"What is this?" Dagnon yelled, halting the guards in mid-step. The bottle was open a few inches beneath his nose, the yellow liquid inside sloshing back and forth.

"Oh, that?" I asked. "That's piss."

In one motion I drew the old pistol from my jacket pocket and the blade from the back of my pants. Out of the corner of my eye I saw Fellow leap to his feet, the shackles that no longer bound him flew free with a clanking sound. Without looking, I tossed the blade in his direction, hoping he would catch it. With my other hand, I brought the handgun up and centered the sight on Dagnon's astonished face. The trigger pulled the hammer back with smooth fluidity, and the gun bucked in my hand. Blood flew from Dagnon's shoulder, and he spun with a cry.

I was about to squeeze off another shot when one of the rust creatures hit me from the right. Its ragged scales tried to poke through my coat as we crashed to the ground, but none pierced my skin. I struggled to roll away from it and bring up the handgun, but the creature flattened itself on top of me and pressed its face down to mine. I smelled its fetid breath and leaned away as I pushed it back, my head turned to the side. Its jaws snapped shut inches from my cheek, and I twisted beneath it, trying to free my gun hand to get a shot. It lunged forward again, trying to reach my throat, just as a brownish blur raced by behind it. The creature froze, its eyes widening in shock as its head tipped from of its body and rolled across my chest. Its form collapsed in an array of rusted chunks, and I stood, shaking its remains off. Scrim swooped straight up into the sky, and then dive-bombed another creature, cutting it in half with his bladed wing.

Fellow yelled to my left, and I saw that he had caught the knife. It flashed in a whipping motion that cut the throat of one creature and then plunged into another's stomach. A creature dashed toward me, its hands bunched into solid fists, and I shot it between the eyes, a puff of smoke flying from its nostrils before it disintegrated.

"Michael! Free me!" Kotis yelled, and I ran the few yards to his side.

"Turn your head," I said to him, and aimed at the joint where the shackle met the thick chain. He twisted his face away, and I fired. The steel severed, and his hand sprung free, the manacle hanging from his wrist like a dangling bracelet. I was running to his other side to do the same for his other hand when he sat up, reached over, and grasped the chain. With a guttural yell, he yanked on the steel, and I heard a popping sound. The stake holding the opposite end of the chain to the rock broke in half, and Kotis rose to his full height.

His eyes widened as he looked past my shoulder. "Down!" he yelled, and whipped the chain in a sweeping motion at my head.

I bent my knees and fell to the ground, rolling over just in time to see Dagnon's pincers stab the air where I'd been. The chain attached to Kotis's wrist wrapped twice around the monster's neck.

Dagnon's eyes flared with surprise, and his hands reached to the chain. Before they could get there, Kotis whipped his left arm back, almost pulling Dagnon off his feet, and threw his massive right fist forward. His knuckles crashed into Dagnon's face with a wet explosion of tissue and bone. Blood splattered out from the circumference of Kotis's fist in a halo of gore. My eyes widened as I saw the monster's face cave inward before he flew back from the force of the blow.

Dagnon's features were a flattened mess. Blood rushed from torn flesh where jagged bones poked free. His right eye stared sightlessly at the crater where his nose used to be, and his left was a gelatinous stain that drooled down his cheek. He opened his mouth as though to say something, and a handful of pointed teeth tumbled free onto the ground, a few trailing bright red roots. Without another sound, he crumpled and lay still, his legs splayed in a V.

"That's for hitting my bird, prick!" Kotis yelled.

I stood and turned to see Fellow a short distance away as he pulled the curved blade from the back of the last rust creature. There was a tinkling as its body fell to pieces, and then silence except for the singing of the wind through the jutting teeth around us. I sagged and my legs threatened to drop me to the rock beneath my feet. Scrim swooped past me and fanned his wings before landing on Kotis's outstretched forearm. The giant's eyes shone, and I could tell he was close to tears. Scrim clicked and made the purring sound I heard before. Kotis smiled and petted the bird's head, smoothing the upraised feathers that stuck out in several directions. Scrim let out a short squawk and then clicked rapidly, sounding like an old typewriter.

Kotis smiled and shook the bird in mock anger. "I know I'm naked, you fool, give me a minute to get decent."

Fellow approached and handed Kotis his vest and pants, having donned his own clothes moments before. I was relieved that everyone was alive, and all I could do was stand with a smile plastered on my face.

Kotis noticed my expression and grinned. "Now that you've seen what a real man looks like, don't be gettin' any ideas."

"Yes, like I said, I'm married," Fellow said deadpan.

Kotis's head jerked around as he tried to break the shackle at his ankle, and he lost his balance and fell to his back with a grunt. Scrim hopped free and flapped above his supine form, screeching what sounded like laughter. I chuckled, and soon my stomach ached with convulsions.

"Bollocks on all of you!" Kotis yelled as he broke his ankles free of their chains. This only made Fellow and I laugh harder, and when the giant finally struggled to his feet, I saw a smile stretching across his hard features.

Once Kotis put on his clothes, we moved out of the mouth of Lonos and left his last acolyte lying where he fell. As we walked I related what I'd seen in the house and how my shadow had followed me inside. Both Kotis and Fellow grew silent as I told them about my worst memories and the suicidal hold the house possessed on anyone who entered. When I reached the portion concerning Lonos's soul trapped in the glass container, Kotis stopped and tilted his head to one side.

"So where's that thing's soul now?" he asked.

"Tucked safely inside a Jack Daniels bottle in the second story of the house," I said. Both Fellow and Kotis stared at me, their jaws hanging open. "I got the idea when I emptied the whiskey onto the floor," I explained. "The whiskey bottle's top fit perfectly inside the mouth of the vase. I just poured it in and capped it."

"Then you pissed in the vase?" Kotis asked.

I nodded.

"Oh, I've heard it all now," Kotis said, putting a hand against his forehead. He laughed again as we resumed walking.

"What I want to know is, why Ellius let you both get captured while he ran away," I said after a time.

"He thought you were dead, Michael, we all did. None of us expected you to survive after you fell," Fellow said. "When Dagnon and the others sprung out and took us by surprise, Ellius tried to call the roots up from the ground like he did outside of the bone field. But Dagnon saw him do it and attacked him. Ellius had no choice but to flee into the safety of the forest."

"He's right, mate. He did what any of us would've done," Kotis said.

"But you were brilliant!" Fellow exclaimed. "That was an amazing plan, Michael. It worked perfectly!"

I shrugged. "I wouldn't say it was brilliant. Maybe crazy and reckless."

"But it worked," Kotis said, jabbing me in the shoulder with a finger. "You kept us all alive when you could've left us to die."

"I would never do that," I said.

"Then you're a shining beacon of what's good from your side, even if you are an ugly wanker," Kotis said with a wry smile.

We emerged from the outer teeth of Lonos's mouth and headed to the right of the house in the distance. I wanted to swing wide around it, even though I knew it would hold no more horrors for me if I stepped inside. The hard-packed earth provided an easy walking surface, and we trudged on, the exhaustion of battle slowing our steps with each one we took. Fellow led us, his head erect and watchful, never deviating from a line that only he could see. After an hour of walking, trees became visible on the horizon, a welcome sight. We made camp at their edge, and fire had never felt better on my chilled hands and face. Kotis handed around the last of his dried meat, and Fellow offered to go hunting for something in the woods. But we agreed tomorrow would be soon enough. We were all tired and sore, fatigue pressing upon us with irresistible fingers, and soon after eating we bedded down in a semicircle around the fire.

"The stars you spoke of," Fellow said, breaking the silence I'd mistook for sleep. "Do they have names?"

"Some do. There's billions upon billions of them, so most only have numbers or areas assigned to them. But some have names."

"Like what?" Kotis asked.

I blinked, trying to will the gray-tinged clouds above us to part so that Kotis and Fellow could see something of my world, a common ground of beauty and wonder that still held sway in anyone's mind if one wasn't oversaturated with everyday life. Before I spoke, I wondered when I'd last taken time to look at the stars.

"Most times there are a few stars grouped together, forming a picture, and they're named for really old heroes or gods. There's Aries and Taurus, Aquarius, the Big and Little Dippers, Orion the hunter, things like that."

"What a thing, to be immortalized forever in the sky for a deed," Kotis said.

"Nothing's forever," I said, closing my eyes. "Even the brightest stars burn out and disappear."

"But you'll remember them when they're gone, won't you?" Fellow asked.

I thought about the nights I'd spent with Sara and Jack looking up at the speckled sky. Their questions so full of childish simplicity, so direct and honest that they deserved an equally honest answer. I remembered telling them the names of the stars and how I hoped someday they would tell their own children.

"Yes, there's always someone to remember," I said, as a tear slipped free of my eye and trailed down the side of my face.

A stick snapped in the darkness of the trees nearby, and we sat up as one, our eyes trained on the spot the noise came from. My hand found the pistol in my pocket, and I mentally counted how many shots I fired earlier. Three, only three. I had three shots left. With a scraping sound, Fellow drew the long blade from his belt. He'd offered it back to me on the walk to the camp, and I declined, seeing that he'd taken a shine to the weapon after experiencing its usefulness. Kotis stood and balled his fists, his shoulders hunched with anticipation. Scrim tensed on Kotis's shoulder and shrugged his wings. My grip tightened on the ancient handle of the revolver as I scanned the edge of the trees. The twilight condensed to pure darkness between their trunks, but after endless seconds of staring, I caught movement a few steps in.

"There," I said, pointing the pistol.

Fellow moved closer beside me, the wicked blade he held waving back and forth. "Who's there?" he called. We heard a few scuffling footsteps coming in our direction, and a shadow formed an outline I recognized at once.

"Never a sight was better seen by eyes alive or dead," Ellius said as he hobbled out of the trees and into the camp. His wrinkled features were warm with a gracious smile as he made a straight line toward me and hugged me close. I hugged him back, glad that our group was whole again. He pushed me to arm's length and examined me, perhaps to make sure I had all of my appendages. "Unbelievable," he whispered. "I thought we'd lost you."

"Not yet," I said.

Ellius turned and greeted both Fellow and Kotis and patted Scrim on the head as the bird issued an appreciative screech. Without preamble, Ellius asked us to relate what had transpired during his absence. I told him of my trip down the river, of nearly freezing solid, of the escape from the river's tongue, and of the rescue and subsequent battle we'd fought. He listened raptly, nodding and exclaiming at times. When I finished, his face became solemn and he looked at each of us before speaking.

"I failed you all, and I'm very sorry for that. I searched for you, Michael, after Fellow and Kotis were taken, but I must have passed you by more than once. After that I canvassed the woods and found a group of chitnas—"

"What are chitnas?" I asked.

"Forest imps. Nasty little bastards. Don't care for anything but acorns and nuts," Kotis said.

Ellius nodded. "They wouldn't help me, even though their numbers were enough for rescue. So, instead, I wandered the woods looking for help in any other form, but found none. I was about to double back when I saw the fire and hoped against hope ..." He stopped and bowed his head. "Forgive me for failing you all."

"There's nothing to forgive," I said. "You tried your best, and it's only by chance that we were able to fight our way free."

"He's right. You did what had to be done, no harm in that," Kotis said.

"We're just glad you're back," Fellow added.

Ellius smiled, the bark on his cheeks crinkling. "Thank you."

"Ellius, how much farther?" I asked.

His eyes brightened, and he put a gentle hand on my shoulder. "I think we'll be close tomorrow."

Elation and longing surged within me, and I nodded. Tomorrow I would find my family. Tomorrow I would face whatever took them, an evil without name, without age. I wanted to force everyone to move on right then, but I resisted the impulse. It would be foolish and reckless to continue when we were so exhausted. I would make a mistake that I couldn't afford, not now, not with how far I'd come. Instead, I sat and tried to make a plan of how to save my family from a threat I knew nothing about.

We talked for a while longer before sleep pulled me to the ground. The last thing I heard were the comforting murmurs of my friends before closing my eyes.

CHAPTER TEN

THE NAMELESS CRATER

I woke before anyone else. My head felt leaden, and my stomach growled with clawing hunger and anticipation. I would see my family today. I would hold them and tell them everything would be okay, or I would die with them.

Fellow, Kotis, and Ellius lay around the fire, each snoring at a different volume. Scrim sat beside Kotis's shoulder, his wing pulled tight over his tucked head. The fire burned low, and I threw several pieces of wood on the flames.

I stood and stretched, pulling my coat around my shoulders to stop the chill creeping up my back. My body felt like I'd fallen down several flights of stairs after running a marathon. Every muscle was sore to the touch, and my head throbbed in strobe-like pulses. Drinking some water from Kotis's water pouch, I turned to look at the sun. It hung just above the horizon behind us, its light bloody and running across the clouds, streaking them crimson.

"Red sky at night, sailor's delight, red sky in morning, sailor's warning," I said to the light breeze. Unease flowed across my skin, giving me of goose bumps. No matter how many years I watched the Weather Channel to try to plan my day, the very best indicator of a storm was always the sunrise.

"Not thinkin' dark thoughts, are ya?"

Kotis stepped up beside me, and I jerked at the sound of his voice. I hadn't heard him rise, and for his size he moved with considerable stealth.

"No," I said. "Just thinking."

He turned his head to study me before facing the sun again. "I can't imagine how you must feel, being away from them so long. I miss my own sorely, and I've only been gone a few days."

"Yeah, it's something I never thought I'd have to deal with. It's not that I took them for granted, but ..." I searched for what I wanted to say, finally letting my breath fizzle out between my teeth.

"You've come this far for them, mate. They're special to you and you to them. Enough to risk it all, am I right?"

I nodded, thinking of their smiles. "Yes, you are."

Kotis grunted, satisfied. "Then we find them today and bring them back. Do or die, mate."

"You're goddamn right."

We set off after a meager breakfast of mush Ellius provided from his satchel. The stand of trees we camped by swung out and to our left, and we followed its border for hours. The trees became sparse after a time, and soon there were only a scattered few, scabbing the ground with their long shadows. The soil went from dry and cracked to rocky again. The rocks were dark and sharp, strewn haphazardly everywhere, ranging from baseball size to a towering twenty feet. At one point we rested, and I examined a nearby boulder, placing a hand against its side, and felt the small flakes of rock biting into my skin. When I pulled my hand away, I saw that it bled freely from multiple slices. The minute incisions were not deep, but they covered my entire palm. I made a mental note not to fall against any of the stones if I could possibly help it.

The day wore on and our pace slowed. Ellius led the way, with Fellow behind him. I was next, and Kotis took up the rear. Scrim flew ahead every so often and reported back, saying that there was no obvious danger in our immediate future. The ground began to rise, slowly at first and then in a more obvious grade. My legs burned from the exertion, and my breath came in short bursts.

After almost an hour of climbing, I was about to ask Ellius how much farther it was when he halted the group with a raised hand. We stopped, listening for the sound of footsteps or approach of any kind. Nothing met my ears, and I gazed around, taking in our immediate vicinity.

The slew of rock we treaded through had diminished, and now only a few small stones lay on the ground in close groupings, as if piled by an unseen hand. A beaten trail ran beneath our feet and led away, onto a flattened area and then into what appeared to be foothills of a sheer mountain. The mountain was black, matching the rock that lay around it, making it look like a crusted sore. Its height ended abruptly in a flattened top, a rough irregularity that suggested an unnatural formation.

"It's a crater," I said, staring at the huge cone thrust upward from the rest of the flatland. I took a few steps so that I stood even with Ellius. "That's an impact crater."

Ellius nodded. "It gouged the ground and rock free, making a burrow of unfathomable proportions."

I turned toward him, understanding dawning in my mind. "That's where it lives, that's where it's keeping them."

"Yes. This place is nameless, just as its master. There is no life but what it provides here, and that is monstrous creation, unfit for light and horrible to behold."

"It stinks," Kotis said.

I agreed. There was a taint to the air that hadn't been noticeable before when we stepped onto the plateau. It was musky and thick, pungent in a way that made you feel as if you were breathing liquid. It held a tinge of decay, but mostly it smelled of unwashed life, something neglected and unclean.

I gazed at the crater's wall, looking for a way up, and saw a few promising routes. The path we stood on looked like it had been trod for millennia, the dirt and sand compressed into a smooth pack that shone as it wound up the side of the rise and vanished in an outcrop of rock.

"So what's the plan?" Kotis asked, folding his arms over his chest.

"We need to get off this path," Ellius said. "This is its hunting trail. We'll eat and rest before we attempt to climb the pass. All we can hope is that it is not present and remains absent while we're inside."

"What?" I asked. "We need to go now, we've wasted too much time."

"Michael, we've been walking all day. Everyone is weary and dull-witted. We must rest and form a plan for success. Everything balances upon our actions. If we make one misstep and it kills your family, we are all doomed."

"What if they're hurt or dying? I can't just sit here while they need me. We have to go now." My voice nudged the edge of hysteria, but I didn't care. I was within a mile of my family, and I couldn't wait anymore. The thoughts that had plagued me over the past days returned and painted the walls of my mind with murals of my children's mutilations, my wife's tortured death. Their cries of pain echoed in my ears until it was all I could hear.

"Michael, he's right. We need to form a plan of some sort," Fellow said as he laid a hand on my arm. "Without contingency, we might as well accept defeat. It is wily and older than all of us, it will have the upper hand when we enter."

I was about to protest again when Kotis stepped forward. "I understand what yer saying, mate, I really do. I would probably sprint that hill and take on all of hell if it were mine in there. But a few hours of sleep and planning might make the difference between success and the end of all things."

I opened my mouth to say something, but then I remembered that there was more on the line than my family's lives. There was the world I stood in, Earth, and somewhere else, a place of pure beauty and goodness, all of which relied upon our choices. If I made the wrong one, I would doom innocents to death and tear worlds from moorings I didn't fully understand.

"Sometimes all you can do is wait," Fellow said.

I sighed, my shoulders slumping in defeat. Ellius stepped forward and squeezed my arm, his brown eyes kind and reflective of the pain that burned within me. "Please, Michael, we've come this far."

I nodded, feeling something break inside me. "Let's get off the path before we're spotted."

Ellius gave me an encouraging look, and headed into a patch of bushes and brush that grew from the unforgiving rock. I threw another look at the crater's rim, then followed my friends to make camp.

The pungent air tousled my hair and whispered in the bushes around us. I studied my companions in their various states of sleep. Ellius lay on his back, his lips parted just enough to breathe through. Fellow was beside him, propped against an angled rock that jutted from the ground, his eyes shut tight. Kotis and Scrim lay curled together, closest to me, the giant's hand resting on the bird's back. I'd volunteered for the first watch, since we all agreed it would be smart to sleep in shifts.

I stood, gradually easing myself up, taking care that my feet didn't scrape across the ground and my coat didn't brush against one of the outstretched branches of the scrub that concealed our camp. With a cautious step, I moved out of the lightless ring and ducked low to avoid another tangle of dead bushes. If one of the others woke, I would use the excuse of going to the bathroom.

No voices floated after me as I made my retreat, and I heard no sounds of movement, wakeful or otherwise. In a few minutes I was back on the trail, standing just where we had an hour before. The rim of the crater stood in contrast to the horizon, its dark mouth open to the vast sky. My heart pounded harder as I took a step toward the waiting aperture. I looked to the right one last time, at the spot I knew housed my friends, and said a silent goodbye to them. I knew when they awoke they would be alarmed and angered by my absence, but it was the only way. I couldn't ask them to venture any farther on my behalf. Each of them had almost died at least once, and I couldn't risk their lives again. Besides, the knowledge that my family was so close wouldn't let me rest. The burgeoning questions of their safety prodded me until action was the only possible answer.

I walked down the path with light steps, my feet barely making a sound. My head felt like it was on a swivel, my ears pricked to the noises of a few aberrant leaves skittering across the uneven ground, far from any trees that could have produced them. I identified with them. My home so distant it seemed like an imagined thought, a story I'd created in my mind to keep it from tilting over, so top-heavy from the madness I'd seen.

A line of darkness edged closer as I walked, and when I looked up I saw what caused it. The sun was directly behind the crater, throwing its ragged shadow toward me on the ground, but something else caught my eye and sent a lancing jolt of fear through my stomach.

Above the crater, storm clouds gathered.

There was no mistaking what they were, their heavy bellies bulging with rain, tumorous with barely restrained power. They hung in the sky, unrelenting in their oppressive churning darkness. I stood, paralyzed on the beaten path, staring at them, terror building in my veins. I watched the storm, hoping that it wasn't on the course it seemed to be on. I pulled my head down as a low growl built from the corners of the sky and continued to heighten, until the air was filled with thunder. It concussed the ground until the rock beneath my shoes thrummed with its energy. A forked tongue of neon lightning ricocheted through the clouds, then shot downward and out of my sight, while the last peals of thunder drained away, leaving a vacuum of silence.

My legs shook with the effort of holding me up, and at that moment I had to restrain myself from running for cover. This was the root of my addiction; it suspended itself from the heavens and laughed in a voice of anger and violence. This was what robbed me of happiness and stole what little solace I sought from the help of alcohol. Fury blossomed in a fiery veil that coated my mind. I wouldn't fail my family again.

Bracing myself against a large boulder, I ignored the small cuts it reopened on my hand and focused on the pain it brought. I took two deep breaths and then began to walk once more, my head down until I knew I was well within the shadow of the crater. When I glanced up again, relief washed over me upon seeing that the buttressed wall blocked the sight of the storm.

The ground rose, evenly at first and then in sharper jags that jumped in stair-like columns, sometimes five to ten feet high. I climbed up without looking back, and held tight to the rock when blasts of thunder reached over the top of the crater to slap at my ears. The pass rose higher and higher, switchbacking for hundreds of yards at a time; all of my energy became centered on the next step. Sweat broke out beneath my coat, and I patted the pocket with the pistol inside, its heft little reassurance but better than none.

After what seemed like hours of climbing, the path leveled and turned in a sharp corner. I stood facing a hallway of sorts. The crater's edge was still hundreds of feet above me, but a crude archway cut through the rock, creating a tunnel that held oily patches of darkness before relenting to the stained light of the storm on the other side.

I stepped back, concealing myself from the passage. The tunnel was at least fifty feet across and a hundred feet deep, opening up to the vastness of the depression. I strained my eyes to see inside, and tried to spot any abnormal shapes in the waiting darkness. I remained still for five minutes before I drew the pistol and moved onto the path again.

My footsteps came back to me in short crunches that echoed off the tunnel's sides as I walked beneath the archway. I saw long striations carved from the rock in several places, as if the hole had been scraped open, but by what I couldn't fathom. The shadows deepened around me, and I swung the pistol to either side, a feeling of eyes watching my progress from all sides growing on the skin of my neck. The sensation agitated a sixth sense on the basest level and told me to flee, but if something was there, I couldn't see it, no matter how hard I searched.

Just as I was about to take another step, I became aware of something else. It was as feeling so preposterous that I almost dismissed it immediately. I watched the darkness churn in the tunnel, and let the déjà vu wash over me in waves, each one pulling on a string of memory that faded when I tried to bring it to light. I looked up and to either side, trying to jump-start another bout of familiarity, but the feeling only came when I looked ahead at the pitch black. A flash of lightning lit the tunnel in flickering strobes that revealed nothing impeding my way, chasing the déjà vu from my mind. For the first time I was thankful for a storm's light. I let out a held breath, then emerged from the overhang, walked to the edge of the tunnel, and looked down.

The sight stole any semblance of sequenced thought from me and robbed me of movement. It thrust itself into my eyes, raping my senses as it went deeper and deeper, furrowing a gaping wound on my consciousness.

The crater's interior writhed with movement.

A black, pulsing musculature veined with twitching tendons coated the entire depression. Enormous internal organs pumped fluids through semitransparent arteries, their varicose glaze feeding into various orifices that belched and sucked at the air. A coating of yellow bile ran steadily from an open sore on the opposite wall of the crater and multiple lesions bled freely, creating a pool of gore at the lowest point. Digestive bubbles expanded and burst on the surface of the burgundy slick.

I tried to breath and gasped at the hot smell that assaulted my nostrils. Until then, it had been the same stench that pervaded the air outside the crater; but within, it was noxious and insurmountable, physically hindering as it pushed against me. I felt the meager mush Ellius made earlier froth behind my tongue, and I choked, my eyes watering as I doubled over. The vomit flew from my mouth, and even as I coughed and tried to regain my balance, my mind registered the last detail I glimpsed before being sick.

On the glistening, exposed muscle of the crater floor lay three forms, two small and one larger.

I swiped at my watering eyes and cleared them enough to stare down at the spot where my family lay. Even across the distance, I knew their shapes. Jack lay closest, his small legs curled tight to his chest with his arms laced around them. He slept that way sometimes in his bed at home, especially on nights after a nightmare stampeded through his young mind. I would comfort him the best I could, stroking his hair and telling him a story of a bright day. Sara was beside him, her body only a thin line stretched out straight beside her brother, her arm wrapped protectively over his shoulders. Her hair twitched with the exhalations of a giant, toothless mouth embedded in the nearby wall. Jane was next to Sara, her knees drawn beneath her and her hand on Sara's arm. Her head tilted forward so that her hair obscured her face. None of them moved.

I almost called out to them but cut the yell short. The thing that took them from me could be anywhere. Scanning the pit's pulsing interior, I saw nothing besides the conglomeration of bowels and flow of unnamable fluids.

I ran from the lip of the tunnel, down a ramp made of corded ligaments. My feet sank sickeningly into them, and I nearly slipped twice on my way down. All the while I kept my eyes on my family. I couldn't get to them fast enough, and the need to hold them was all encompassing. I wound my way around a pile of excrement that boiled from the crater's floor, and glanced in different directions to make sure we were still alone. The gun felt heavy in my hand, but I kept it pointed in front of me, my finger hovering on the trigger. Skirting movement flashed to my left, and I spun, the gun outstretched and the hammer almost all the way back. Nothing leapt at me or shot in my direction. I slid the sights of the pistol 180 degrees and then lowered the weapon, releasing the tension on the trigger.

Something was here with us.

I was sure of it. The urgency to be gone from the crater howled inside of me, a warning siren only I could hear. Sweat poured down my back, and I flinched when a fractured rod of lightning split the air above me. I turned and ran toward my family, not bothering to look back to see if anything followed. Either it would be there or it wouldn't, but it didn't matter because I was intent on holding my children and my wife again, even if it was the last thing I did.

Rounding a curled pillar of exposed nerves, I found myself in the open area. The taut muscle beneath my feet was sticky and flexed in metronome timing. It made me feel as though I stood below deck on a ship at sea, unaware of how the floor would move next. The air stunk of blood, and I felt my nostrils filling with the odor, until I was sure I would never smell anything else. But all the assaults on my senses dulled in comparison to the surge of relief and love I felt at the sight of my family.

Jane saw me first, and I realized why she sat the way she did. She stayed upright to watch over Jack and Sara. When I stepped into view, her head jerked up as though she'd been dozing, but from the deep bags beneath her eyes I could tell that sleep hadn't visited her in some time. Her mouth opened in an O of surprise, and I didn't know if it was the sudden movement or the sight of me standing there that elicited the response. I smiled, and tears flowed from my eyes, spilling down my cheeks.

"Honey," I said in a choked voice.

Jack and Sara sat up, and my heart ached at how thin their faces looked. Their skin was white and drawn, tightened by hunger and fear. Their hair was dirty, and I saw smudges of gore on their bare arms.

"Dad?" Jack asked. His small voice in the midst of the alien setting was almost too much for me.

"Dad!" Sara cried and jumped to her feet.

Three steps and then they were in my arms. I pulled them tight to me, Jack in my left arm, Sara in my right, Jane pressed in behind them. Their skin and hair against me, Jane's lips seeking mine, frantic to know it was me. All the while she whispered, "You came, you came, you came," like somehow she'd expected me at any moment. I soaked them in, every ounce of the love that poured out of their hugs and tears. The landscape around us faded and we were one again, a family, unbroken and whole.

I knelt with Jack and Sara still in my arms. Jack nearly choked me with his embrace, but I didn't mind. Sara just cried on my shoulder. Jane leaned her head against mine as I told my daughter it would be okay.

"How?" Jane asked, her voice hoarse.

"I found a way," I said.

Her face crumpled as more tears rolled from her eyes. "I knew you would, I knew you would."

As much as I wanted to stay that way forever, the awareness of where we sat was too much to contend with. I rose, setting my children on their feet. "We have to go now. We need to be quiet and fast, can you guys do that?" I asked.

Sara seemed shell-shocked, but Jack's eyes were wide and alert. "Dad, they haven't been here for a long time, they'll be here soon."

"Who? Who's going to be here?" I asked him. I looked up to Jane for more explanation, but her face was a mask of pain.

"I tried to stop them, Michael. I tried, but there was so many. They bit them, drew blood. I'm sorry ..." Her voice trailed off in a soft sob, and she leaned against me for support.

"Stop what?" I asked.

Jack raised both of his arms and held them out for examination. "The heads bite and talk," he said. I squinted, and realized that I'd been wrong in thinking the streaks of blood and crusted scabs were from the bare muscle below us. Within the clots I saw spots, punctures, and scrapes.

Teeth marks.

I heard a sound over the gesticulation of organs and bubbling fluid. At first I thought it was raining, but then the sound changed and took on other nuances not associated with the pattering of water. I listened for another second, then recognized it for what it was: the scrabble and tapping of movement all around us. I spun and stepped forward, shielding my family from whatever approached. The handgun trembled in my grip, as a blast of thunder detonated and shook the mass beneath us. The storm was so close I could taste it, an atmospheric tang of burned air and cold rain. The fear of what moved toward us was nearly overridden by the clashing power above, and I felt my right knee unhinge, trying to drop me to a crouch on the ground. I wanted to huddle with my family for comfort, but instead I took a step forward and peered around the bundle of nerves.

There were hundreds of them. Their chitinous bodies articulated toward us, emerging from every nook and hole in the organic crater. Long, segmented legs skittered, some brown, some black, all covered with spiny fur. Swollen abdomens swung with their movement, and teeth gnashed with hunger—human teeth.

The spiders were roughly the size of small dogs, and were biologically similar to most I'd seen on Earth, except for their heads. Their heads were human. The faces of men, women, and a few children glared at me with fury and excitement as they made their way over the bulbous landscape. Their skin was unblemished and fully human from the neck up, their eyes flashing in the flickering light of the storm.

"Oh, he's come to rescue them. Ain't it sweet," a woman's voice said from my left. The spider that spoke had a head that belonged to a pretty woman with full blond hair and green eyes the color of the Caribbean Sea. "We've been tasting your kids and wife for a while, honey. Took you long enough to join us."

I staggered back with shock, unprepared for seeing what moved toward us. I raised the pistol at the woman's face, and she grinned.

"This is what we've been waiting for?" a man's voice asked, and I turned to see another spider approach from the right. Its face was a middle-aged man with dark stubble growing from his cheeks, matching the spider fur on the rest of its body. "I've been holding back for days because of this? Oh, I can't wait to feed on your little ones, and now I can finally give your wife this." The spider reared back on its four hind legs to show me a throbbing human erection hanging obscenely from its abdomen. "She's been eyeing it up. I bet she can't wait to su—"

The man's face exploded in a spray of bone and brain matter. His jaw hung slack, and blood fountained down into his open mouth from where the bullet had done its work. The long legs holding up his body seizured and then gave out, dumping his bulk onto the ground, where it lay still.

The pistol barrel smoked as I pointed it at the female spider. Again the sight above the muzzle jittered, but this time my muscles were full of rage, not fear. These things had bitten my children and wife. They'd tried to prey on them while I wasn't there. My finger tensed on the trigger.

"Get back!" I yelled and took a step forward. I motioned for Jane and the kids to follow me.

"You're not going anywhere, darlin'," the blond spider said. I fired again, and she mewled in pain, her distended hindquarters spewing ichor in black gouts.

"Get the fuck out of my way!" I yelled.

I pointed the gun back and forth at the upturned faces that cursed and spit at us as we edged toward the distant tunnel. A spider bearing the face of an elderly woman with ringlets of gray hair lunged forward. I swung a kick at her and felt her jaw tear free beneath the sole of my shoe. Teeth dripped to the ground, and her tongue dangled and swung in the open air.

"Get back!" I yelled again.

The knowledge of the last shot in the gun pounded in my brain. Sara cried out from behind me, and I turned, swinging the gun at a spider with a black man's face.

"You can't get out," a spider hissed in a boy's voice.

"Can't get out," came the echoes from dozens of other mouths. I felt them ringing us in on all sides, their legs tapping closer and closer.

"Michael ...?" Jane's voice wavered and broke. I felt her hug me from behind, both of the kids between us. I reached back and held out my hand, taking Sara's and then Jack's fingers in my own, intertwining, holding on tight.

"I love you guys so much," I said.

A massive spider approached from directly in front of me, its grinning face that of a crew-cut young man. I aimed the pistol at him just as the rain began to fall in freezing drops. Lightning raced across the sky, splintering the dark clouds above. I hadn't envisioned my death like this, and definitely not my family's. The depression of knowing that I'd failed them in the worst possible way crushed inward, as if I were a thousand feet underwater. Thunder broke overhead again, and I cringed, hating myself as I did so, hating my fear and weakness.

"Daddy?" came Sara's voice, high and frightened. Jane sobbed, and Jack's hand clutched my own.

"It's okay," I said. "Everything's going to be okay." My finger began to squeeze the trigger as the spider neared, and I held on to the small solace that I would take as many with me as possible.

"Stop!" The command rang out over the storm and resounded across the interior of the crater. The voice was deep, full of confidence, and my heart surged as I looked to where the call came from.

Ellius stood at the mouth of the tunnel, his hands held out before him.

The spiders froze, and a few turned to stare at the figure above us. As one, they moved away from us like a tide receding. Rain fell around us, each drop a silver streak that plummeted to the ground and mixed with the blood in the crater. Ellius kept his hands out before him as he moved down the ramp toward us. One by one the spiders retreated, their legs skittering, slipping at times, as they made their way back to the holes and folds of flesh they'd emerged from.

I watched in awe as hope filtered through the promise of death, which moments before seemed imminent. Ellius strode with confidence through the muck and mire, his face serene as he neared us. Some of the spiders remained, but shrank far enough back to allow me to lower the gun.

"Daddy, who is that?" Jack asked.

"He's a friend," I said, stepping forward. In all of my life I had never been gladder to see another person. Ellius strode closer and stopped a few yards away, his face gentle and smiling.

"Ellius," I said.

"Michael, you went ahead without us."

"Yes, I'm sorry. I had to get to them," I said, stepping to the side to reveal my family.

Ellius nodded. "I know, Michael. I completely understand, but you risked everything by coming alone. They might've killed you before I could get here," he said, gesturing to the few remaining spiders that watched from a distance.

"You're right, I'm sorry. But I have them now, we can go." I put the pistol in my pocket, and grasped Sara's and Jack's hands before walking toward the tunnel.

We took two steps, and Ellius hit me in the chest with an open hand.

The blow caught me just above the solar plexus, and my lungs expelled all of their air in a single whoosh. I lost my grip on Sara and Jack as I flew backward, propelled by the power of the strike. My back connected with Jane, and I heard her shriek as she fell. We landed in a heap on the wet muscle.

I coughed and tried to pull in air that didn't want to come. It felt as though I'd been kicked by a horse. I shook my head and blinked, reaching out to find my kids and wife. They were there, and Jane was already on her feet, her hands cold, grasping at my wrist, trying to pull me up. I managed to prop myself on one arm, and stared at Ellius, who stood motionless with a small smile on his lips.

"No," I croaked, just above a whisper. It was a plea against the wrongness with which my mind reeled.

"I'm afraid yes, Michael," Ellius said, walking toward us. "Yes, we are finally here. Yes, you found your family. And yes, I just struck you."

"Why?" I asked, sitting up. Sara and Jack huddled close to me, their knees soaked with bloody water, their arms around my neck.

"Oh, that is the question of questions, isn't it?" Ellius said, stopping a few feet away. I looked up into his face. The worn lines in the bark that covered his cheeks no longer looked humble and wise. His cheeks were cracked and etched with age, and something else—malevolence. A keen hatred graced his features, pulling them into unkind angles. "Well, Michael, I would have to say freedom is why."

I stood, letting the pain ebb from my sternum with each breath that drug in a little more air. "Freedom from what?"

"From this," Ellius said, turning in a slow circle. "From the captivity of this crater and the forests around it. This world of twilight is too small for me. It fits like a tight coat, strangles my air and restricts my every move. I need space and free range." He stopped and looked at my hand that was in my pocket, clutching the pistol. "Go ahead, Michael, it makes no difference to me."

I pulled the handgun out and pointed it at him. "Don't come any closer. You're going to let us pass."

Ellius took a step forward, the same evil smile playing at his lips.

"Stop," I said. My finger flexed on the trigger, yet I hesitated. For even though he'd struck me and the words he spoke were anything but kind, I wondered if he was my friend, corrupted in some way I was unaware of but still my friend.

"Like I said, Michael, I'm not one of the lesser beings of this place. I won't bleed like that piteous fool Dagnon." Ellius took another step, and as a group we shrank back. "I'm not afraid of your pathetic mechanical threats. I'll see you begging for death before I'm through."

I fired the gun into his face.

The cordite smoke obscured his head for a second before he leapt through it, a black hole just above his left eye. His gnarled hands grasped my jacket, and then I was airborne, the world sideways as I flew. I landed on my shoulder and rolled, the muscle and tendon, thankfully, a relatively soft cushion.

Rain beat down on my face when I finally came to rest, and I looked up at the clouds, moisture fogging my vision. The storm swirled above the crater, and lightning walked across its folds in jerking steps. I levered myself up and raised the pistol over my head like a bludgeon. Ellius had his back to me, and seemed to be focused on my family.

"Don't you touch them!" I yelled as I walked forward. "I'll kill you if you touch them!"

Ellius turned, and he looked larger, more substantial. He smiled. "Oh Michael, it's not them I want. It's you."

It took me a moment to register what he'd said. I stopped in mid-stride and waited. My family inched back, closer to the rounded wall of the crater. Ellius sneered unwaveringly at me, his eyes narrowed to slits.

"What did you say?" I asked.

"It's you that is important, not these walking husks of flesh," Ellius said, jerking a thumb over his shoulder. "You've been the one all along."

My jaw worked up and down, but no sound came out. "What are you talking about?" I said at last.

Ellius sauntered toward me, his gait so out of character it was stunning. "Let me answer your question with a question. Did you ever wonder why storms frightened you so much?"

My blood chilled, and I blinked. "How do you know I'm afraid of storms?"

"This is a fun game, let's do it again, shall we? Did the tunnel above this nest seem familiar to you?"

The moment of déjà vu rushed back. I swallowed.

"I thought so," Ellius said, coming closer, his voice sarcastic and conspiratorial. "You remembered something, didn't you, Michael?"

My arm tensed, and I wondered if I could lash out and bash his head with the pistol, but my brain slowed involuntarily and pondered what he said. Flashes of my past flitted out of the corner of my mind's eye. Twitching shadows of memories moved forward and back, in and out of scrutiny.

"You recall that place, don't you?" Ellius said, standing even closer.

I looked up at my family as my arm lowered to my side. They huddled together, Jane standing over the kids with her hands on their shoulders. Her eyes were lances of pain and worry that begged for salvation from all this, and I wanted nothing more than to give it to her. But something held me back. Ellius knew about the fear that had plagued me all my life. He knew about my suffering, more than I did, and I was submissive to his will, against every fiber of my being.

"You remember this place, Michael, because you've been here before."

There was a beat while the words soaked into me, and despite my denial, they rang true. I clenched my eyes shut as the memories came flooding back, choking my mind with their colors and sounds.

I saw the shimmering hole hovering in the evening light, a rippling haze against the shadows beyond. My shepherd, Gunner, barked in his way to tell me not to go any farther.

"You remember, Michael," Ellius said.

I reached toward the unreflecting mirror, sure that my hand would meet emptiness, but it vanished and, before I could cry out, I fell inside. Darkness enfolded me, caressed my eyes until I thought I was blind.

"You came here by accident, and saw."

In the memory, rain pelted down on me from above, and I realized that I was at the mouth of a tunnel, standing over a depression. Thunder shook the air and rattled the hurried breath in my chest. Lightning stabbed the bloated clouds above, feigning a flickering dawn against the black. Something moved below me, something pale and huge. Its head was wide and ungainly, its legs and arms disproportionately long. My breathing stopped and I froze, unable to move as the thing turned to look up at me from where it crouched over an unrecognizable bloody carcass. Its eyes were orange flames of malice burning in the gloom, and when it opened its mouth, the smile was the same as the night my family was taken.

"You ran away, fear clawing at you, shredding you from within," Ellius whispered.

The memory sharpened as I ran through darkness, frantic to be anywhere away from whatever climbed into the tunnel and chased after me with scraping steps and strangled grunts. I tripped and fell, my heart sure of the death that would follow my stumbling. But cutting blades of grass bit my hands when I landed, and Gunner's soft fur brushed my face before he fell over me, his tongue licking my face fiercely. Terror still coursed through me, and I scrambled up, ready to run from the thing in the tunnel.

When I turned the shimmering was gone and night was complete around us. The riverbed was still and the woods were quiet. But the sound of thunder and the flash of lightning was all I could see as I ran home, a storm in my mind that wouldn't leave, roaring and consuming with a horror I couldn't name and refused to remember.

My eyes came open, and I sucked in air tinged with rain. Ellius watched me from a few paces away, his branchy head nodding, his eyes knowing. I gagged and nearly doubled over with nausea. My muscles shook with weakness.

"So glad I was able to lubricate your memory," Ellius said. "I'm sure you were curious about the origins of your fear." He raised his soaked hands to the sky. "When you mentioned storms before, I realized what had happened. You had a transference, of sorts. Instead of remembering what you'd witnessed, you focused on the lightning and thunder. Everyday occurrences that would shield you, give you a crutch to lean on, so you wouldn't have to face the true fear of what you'd seen."

My arm twitched, and I wanted to whip the pistol into his temple to silence his tongue. But deep within, I knew he spoke the truth. The flashback was a memory, true and unbiased, exactly the way I'd seen it and subsequently blocked it out.

"What do you want?" I asked.

"Oh, just all the blood in your body spilled on the sacred ground you stand on," Ellius said, and struck me in the face.

I reeled back and fell. The empty gun flew from my hand and bounced away. I rolled to my feet and rubbed my cheek, expecting a gaping wound but finding only a sore swelling of tissue. I glanced at Jane and the kids and then shifted my vision to the tunnel, pleading with them to run while they had a chance. Jane gripped the children tighter and sidled behind Ellius, guiding them with the whitened grasp she had on their shoulders.

"Why?" I said again, trying to think of something to draw his attention away from my family's escape. "Why do you need me?"

"Because you are the only human to have ever crossed the boundary and returned to Earth," Ellius spit. "So many have come and died. They lose their way, or blunder here and the vent closes behind them. They become trapped, lose sanity, and die at the hands or teeth of the things that inhabit this land. But you ..." Ellius said, circling me. "You were special. You came here, to that very tunnel, and saw this place, only to somehow find the way back to your world without so much as a scratch!" He pounded a fist against one of his legs, and spittle flew from his brown lips. "No one has ever done that, Michael. No one."

I edged backward and to the right, trying to keep Ellius's back to my family, who moved toward the ramp in the distance. "So what?" I asked. "I came here and saw it, what does it want me for?"

Ellius stopped and stood stock-still. His brown eyes roamed over me, as if examining a feast. "You brought something back with you that night, a part of this world, breathed into your lungs and clinging to your skin. You took the essence of evil along with you when you escaped."

My stomach roiled, and I resisted the urge to glance at my family's progress. "You're lying."

Ellius laughed, a callus and cruel scraping sound. "Oh no, Michael, but you'll wish I were soon enough. You see, the energy inside you was trapped like a splinter encapsulated by a cocoon of flesh. It festered and grew, slowly gaining power without your knowledge. Your fear of storms only fed it and encouraged its black malignance to expand further." He gazed at me coldly. "That's why your blood's so precious in this world. Human blood is a rare commodity, used for many things, but yours ... yours is powerful beyond measure."

Anger flared inside me. "You were in league with it all along. The horrible evil you preached to me about, you were its servant while you led me here to be slaughtered. And for what? What was the price you sold your soul for? Freedom? From traveling only in the forest? Is that it?" Pure rage consumed me, and I stepped forward in spite of the power Ellius possessed.

He lowered his head and nodded, his arms clasped inside of his shawl. "I am bound to the trees in this form, a cruel construct of having destroyed the thickest forest when I fell here. Unable to change, unable to expand my reach, I am bound." His eyes met mine, and they were full of anticipation. "But I knew when you came here that someday I would find you. I knew the power your blood would hold. It was only a matter of time before a vent opened close enough to see you, the beacon of darkness that you are." Ellius grinned.

I stepped back, the implications of what he'd just said wreaking havoc inside me. "No," I breathed.

"Oh yes, Michael," Ellius said, except his voice was different. Deeper and without life, a corpse voice spoken with a living tongue.

His arms began to lengthen, the bark and wood cracking and flying free. His eyes expanded, and the branches on top of his head formed curved, leathery fins that ended in sharp points. The shawl he wore split as his body grew, and his skin became pale, roughened sandpaper. His legs thickened with muscle, striated with black veins. A vibrating roar erupted from his mouth, which was ringed in an orange glow, as he threw back his arms in terrible glory. His eyes found me, flames burning in both slits.

Pure evil incarnate stood before me.

I found my family, cowered at the edge of the clearing near the totem of tangled nerves. They were awestruck, staring, open-mouthed, at the creature that had brought them here.

"RUN!" I screamed.

Jane snapped out of her trance and yanked the kids away. I saw a flash of Jack reaching for me before they disappeared from sight.

"They'll not get far," it said, taking a step toward me. The change in Ellius's voice was complete. It spoke in tones of sepulcher bass. "My minions will attend to it."

Even as the words left its mouth, I saw movement at the corner of my eye. I watched as Jane and the kids backpedaled into view, a dozen spiders herding them with snapping teeth and shouts of delight.

"Just take me," I said. "Kill me and let them go."

It laughed. "I will kill you, Michael. It's the only way for my life force to grow." It widened its arms and gestured to the growth that covered the crater floor. "I will be free of the curse of the forest, and my realm will cover this world. And perhaps I will find a way to spread it to Earth."

I looked around me. There was nowhere to run or hide. An immense heart beat just below a layer of translucent fat to my left, and a sheet of white bone was to my right. The thing without a name approached, its slanted eyes studying me with hunger. My back met the crater wall, and only then did I realize I'd been retreating the whole time.

"I've waited patiently, and now the moment is here," it rumbled. "I'll savor every ounce of your blood."

My heart hammered against my chest, as thunder racked the clouds. I heard cries from the spiders above the storm, and sobbed. I'd failed them for the last time. There would be no other chances at redemption. The freedom from addiction was too late and too little; it made no difference now. I only hoped that it would kill me before I saw what the spider's teeth had done to my wife and children.

It raised a giant hand studded with razor claws, their tips catching the flash of lightning just before the hand fell like an executioner's ax. I closed my eyes and waited for the ripping of my flesh.

It didn't come.

"Not so fucking fast, you pale bastard."

My eyes snapped open at the deep, grumbling voice that sounded like it was straight out of Sydney.

The creature's hand hung suspended at its apex, but now gray fingers encircled its wrist, holding it from dealing the killing blow.

Kotis stepped out from behind the thing and swung a fist at its surprised face. The wet smack of knuckles connecting with bone was the most beautiful sound I'd ever heard. The thing's head rocked back, and it snarled with pain. Kotis swung again, bashing his fist into the same spot. His third strike stopped short as the thing that had been Ellius caught his fist in an oversized palm. It pushed Kotis back, creating space between them before thrusting a kick into his midsection. Kotis flew back and landed beside me. His eyes fluttered, but when he opened them, they were clear.

He shot a quick grin at me. "Hiya, mate."

The thing ran forward and slammed a fist into the soft skin of the crater as Kotis rolled out of the way. I sidestepped the two battling behemoths and ran toward my family, hoping I wasn't too late.

Black ichor and fresh blood covered the floor. I knew then that I was wrong. The cries from the spiders hadn't been exultations, but ones of fear.

Fellow jumped and weaved through their midst, his knife swinging in whipping arcs. Gouts of blood mixed with the spiders' fluid sprayed the air and mingled with the falling rain. Dozens of dead spiders lay prone, their legs broken and lifeless. There were several that continued attacking Fellow, and more came out of the holes in the depression's floor, but he seemed to be holding his own. The speed at which he moved and fought was graceful, poetic, and sure. Scrim flew in darting dives and cut through several spiders' legs with a wingtip before soaring away into the stormy sky.

I turned my head, still expecting the worst, but my heart flooded with joy as I saw Jane huddling with the kids outside of the ring of dead spiders. I ran to them and slid to my knees, hugging them close.

"Dad!" Jack cried. His face was a mess of tears and smudged gore, but he smiled at me. Sara gripped my hand.

"Hide over there," I said, jerking my head toward a nodule of flesh at least four feet high.

Jane nodded and pulled the kids up. "Come on, guys, let's go."

I pivoted to see Kotis spin and snap an elbow into the side of the thing's head. It staggered and shook its skull.

"Come on, you fucking chump, you've got nothing on me, you traitor!" Kotis yelled.

The thing opened its mouth and bellowed loud enough to make my eardrums flutter. It swung its claws at Kotis, and the giant dodged the swipe with a returned cry.

Turning to Fellow, I watched as he dispatched two spiders at once, cutting their heads from their bodies with an upward swipe of his blade. Three spiders emerged from a scabrous hole behind Fellow and rushed toward him.

I sprinted at them and yelled a warning. Fellow spun and stabbed one through the face just as it reared to bite him, his blade sinking into the bridge of its nose. I jumped into the air as another spider latched on to Fellow's slender leg. My feet came down on the back end of its bulbous body. It felt as if I were balancing on a basketball, and then there was a sickening tear and my feet sank into the stinking warmth of its guts. Its head was of a middle-aged man with a goatee, and it screamed obscenities until I pulled a sneaker free of its fluids and drove the ball of my foot into the side of its head. It flailed and twitched for a few more seconds, and then lay still.

Looking up I saw Fellow hack at the last spider's face until it was a bloody mass of skin and bone, dripping chunks of meat to the ground. It cried out one last time before I kicked it in the throat, silencing it for good.

"Thank ... you," Fellow said between heaving breaths.

I nodded. We looked at where Kotis and the Ellius thing battled just in time to see Kotis throw a left hook that was caught in midair. The thing twisted Kotis's fist until it opened, and then continued to turn it at an odd angle. Kotis's lips peeled back from his teeth in a grimace of determination and pain. A loud crack made my stomach clench. Kotis cried out, and I saw his hand hanging backward at the end of his arm, with a white glint of bone exposed at the wrist.

"No!" I yelled, and sprinted toward them with Fellow behind me, his feet pounding the slick muscle.

Scrim appeared above the two sparring giants and dove at Ellius's skull, pinning his wings back as he flew straight down. With a casual swipe, the monster slapped the bird aside. Scrim flipped over once and landed with his feathers knotted in a pile. Kotis yelled a primal scream of rage and jabbed at the demon's face with his other fist. In horror I watched its mouth open and snap shut.

Kotis screamed again, this time in pain, and drew back his arm, which spewed blood from the stump of his missing hand. He dropped to his knees, as the thing stood above him, chewing and grinding the bones and flesh before swallowing. Ellius brought his foot up and jabbed a clawed foot into Kotis's midsection, then kicked downward.

Kotis's stomach unzipped, and his intestines rolled into view. Ellius grinned over Kotis's shoulder at us before picking the giant up as though he weighed nothing, and threw him in a straight line at the hard wall of bone.

Kotis landed on his back, and I heard his spine break. His eyes flashed open before he slid to the ground, his mouth agape with agony.

"No! You fucking bastard!" I yelled, and jumped into the air, trying to aim a kick at the thing's chest.

It batted its hand at me and knocked me askew, so that I landed on my side, the wind blasting from my chest. I rolled over to see Fellow lunge toward the thing and try to stab it in the thigh. The knife hit the pale skin and glanced off, as if it were made of granite. With speed so fast its hand blurred in the rain, it snatched Fellow by the arm and swung him around in a circle. The knife flew free of Fellow's grasp and landed on the tissue beside me a few feet away.

There was a snapping sound, like dry brush breaking, and Fellow flew free of its grip. He landed opposite me, his legs splayed out and his face upturned into the pouring rain. He didn't move.

The thing turned to me, holding something in its hand that, at first, I didn't recognize, but then it became clear: Fellow's arm. It had broken from his body just below the shoulder, and an amber sap dripped from the splintered end. The Ellius thing tossed it aside and shifted toward me, its eyes lanterns of red in the gloom.

"Your friends died for you, Michael. So comforting, isn't it?"

"They were your friends too," I said, scrambling to my feet. I inched closer to the knife on the ground and stooped to pick it up, my eyes never leaving the pale demon before me.

It laughed. "I have no friends, I am timeless. I used them to acquire what I needed. I planned ahead, gaining their trust, until the moment was right and I was able to find you. The tale about every world ending was a nice touch to entice them and make sure you reached this place safely."

I pointed the knife at its face. "You could have left my family out of this! You could have just taken me!"

It shook its head and took a step closer. "You could only be brought here willingly. The power in your blood would have destroyed this world if you had been taken. Your family was the decoy to get you here."

I swallowed and tasted blood. Fellow hadn't moved and I couldn't bring myself to look at where Kotis lay. Movement to the creature's left drew my attention, and I glanced, not absorbing what I saw until I looked back at its leering face.

The sap from Fellow's disembodied arm was eating through the tissue below the creature.

A million thoughts sped through my mind at once, and the thing nearly caught me as it jumped forward, its splayed hand outstretched. But I rolled away and dodged another swipe of a fist as it swept through the air at my back. Squinting through the rain, I looked past the hulking figure, and was rewarded with a strobe of lightning just when I needed it. Kotis lay on his back, his mouth opening and closing, his blood pooling in a rough crescent around him. The muscle of the crater receded from the blood like an army of ants from a flame.

"So small the whims of man compared with those of gods, don't you think?" it rumbled.

I unbuttoned my coat and let it fall to the bloody ground. "You're no god."

"But I am, Michael, just an unfamiliar one. Soon all will know me, fear me, die for me."

"It's funny you bring that up," I said, flipping the knife around so that I held it by its wide blade. "Let me be the first."

I gouged the tip of the knife into the inside of my forearm, just below the elbow. It slid through without effort, and I yelled at the sensation of my skin parting under the blade.

"NO!" the thing screamed and ran forward as the cut crossed the finish line of my wrist. Bright blood spurted from the wound and ran off my fingertips in streams. The waterlogged muscle at my feet remained whole for a beat, and then exploded with motion as it tore away from my blood in sizzling layers.

The monster slid to a stop a few steps away and threw its hand back to cut me in two. I raised my head and dropped the knife on the ground, hearing more sinew snap and hiss. Without pausing, I whipped my bleeding hand in the creature's direction and saw crimson drops land on its face.

The effect was immediate. It fell back, hands flying to the burns on its face. A high screeching filled the air, capped with a hammering of thunder. The scorching heat of the cut on my arm became a numbing cold, and I was grateful for it. Stepping forward, I threw another handful of blood at the staggering abomination. The blood spattered its legs, and a howl of pain erupted from its mouth as deep gashes opened up, revealing striations of muscle beneath. I swung my hand again, and felt my vision flash with lightning behind my eyes. I stumbled but caught myself before I fell, a bout of dizziness clouding my vision before easing away. The creature's skin looked leprous in the low light. Oily patches disintegrated, peeling away to expose flesh, and then dark bone.

It keened the high freight-train sound again and reached out to crush me. I punched its open palm with my bleeding fist, my knuckles penetrating skin and sinking deep before the thing jerked away.

"How?" it screamed, stepping back. It held its melting hand as even more gray flesh flayed from its body.

"Sacrifice," I said, though the word sounded slurry and indistinct. Squeezing my eyes shut, I tried to remember if I'd breathed recently. I sucked air in and shivered from the lance of cold steel that seemed buried in my chest; it radiated arctic breakers until I was filled with a sea of ice. I'd lived in Minnesota all my life, but realized I'd never truly been cold before.

I took a step forward, and the ground felt strangely solid. Looking down, I saw that only rock and bits of sand rested beneath my shoes. The path of the demon's retreat was marked with a swath through the tissue covering the bowl's surface. Organs and muscles continued to dissolve in bubbling masses, and the air was full of the sounds of snapping tendons and shredding nerves.

Its fiery gaze caught and held mine through the rain. Although pain brimmed on their edges, there was still hatred in its eyes, a loathing so deep it surpassed the wish of my death. Its look burned with domination and extinction, slavery and defilement. It wanted utter destruction and chaos, because that was what ran through its veins.

"You'll die!" it screamed. "You'll die and leave your family alone, just as they were before!"

I steeled myself, tensing my muscles and rallying the last bit of energy I had. "They were never alone."

I ran and flung my hand forward, sending more blood at the monster's face. It howled again and stepped back to retreat, but I was already airborne. I landed on its chest, my feet catching on disintegrating thighs, my left hand wrapping over its cold shoulder. The thing immediately tried to fling me off, but I plunged my bleeding fingers into the center of its chest, feeling them drill through skin and bone like they were butter. It attempted to bellow, but lost its breath as I shoved harder, my blood opening up a dinner plate–sized wound in the center of its breastbone. I reached farther, and felt gravity pull us down as it lost its balance. It landed on its back, and again tried to pry me off. But the motions were powerless, and the massive clawed hands barely scraped my side.

My fingers slid inward. Fluids leaked around my arm and tissue squirted away. Then I felt it, the vast pulsation and movement under my palm. I strained harder, and dissolved bone bit into my bicep. The heart sac ripped apart, and then heat bloomed so hot I almost yanked my hand back from its touch. Its heart rippled in frantic beats for a moment, and then I shoved my arm in up to the shoulder.

I squeezed the pulsating muscle, and it burst, deep in the creature's chest.

Blood flowed up in a fountain and covered me, soaked me in warmth. The thing spasmed, bucking its hips up before settling back down. The glow in its eyes searched the sky for a few seconds, and then dimmed, eventually fading out completely. Rainwater began to fill up the sockets, and steam escaped in small jets.

I pulled my arm from the corpse's chest and stood up. The rain felt like small hammers on my scalp, and suddenly the world tipped. I watched in wonder as the crater turned on its side and the ground came up to meet me. The rock was soft, down feathers and cotton on my skin. I tried to swallow, but my mouth ached with dryness. I let my jaw go slack, and the rain pattered past my teeth, coating my tongue with moisture. So sweet and good. A heavy fatigue pushed my eyelids down with gentle fingers that weighed tons.

A face appeared over me, a woman. She was beautiful but angry. No, she was sad. Tears rained on me from her eyes, and she struggled with something. She yelled over her shoulder at someone, and I wanted to tell her she was the most beautiful thing I'd ever seen, but couldn't form the words. I was warm and couldn't keep my eyes open. The world slipped away in silence.

"Dad?"

The word reverberated in my mind. It meant something, but I couldn't place it. It sounded like a name. It pulled at me and made me want to open my eyes, but they were glued shut and sleep tugged in the opposite direction. I slid backward, rolled away from the word, fell down.

"Dad?"

A rope in my chest yanked me up, drew me forward toward light. There was pain where the voice wanted me to go, and I tried to retreat, even though something told me not to. Resisting, I tried to descend but was unable.

"Honey, please wake up."

Another voice, another feeling. This one of longing to hold and touch and caress. To love in a way that made life. It held hope, cupped in the words.

"Daddy, wake up."

My eyes came open.

Rain misted down from the sky, but the four forms hunched over me shielded me from it. The low light obscured their faces. An ocean rolled inside my head, and a freezing cold that was sufferable till then became unbearable. I shook. Something wrapped around me tighter, and water pressed against my lips. I drank, and tried to breathe deeply. My body felt like an open wound, blistered and enflamed.

"He's awake!" one of the smaller forms cried, and hugged me before being pulled away by a larger one.

"Jack." The word croaked from my mouth, my tongue rusty.

"Daddy, you're okay!"

"Sara, hi, honey," I managed, quieter this time.

Jane bent forward and kissed me hard on the lips. I tried to kiss her back, but didn't know if I did. She leaned away, her eyes full of tears. "We thought we lost you."

"Not a chance."

She laughed, wiping away the tears. Memory came rushing back, and I nearly sat bolt upright despite the leaden fatigue. "Fellow? Kotis?" I asked.

Fellow stepped closer, a smile gracing his gentle features. "I'm here, Michael."

"Your arm ..." I started.

He turned to the side to show me the stump clotted with sap. "I am okay. It will heal, and possibly grow back."

"Kotis."

He blinked and looked down, shook his head.

I sat up, pushing off my coat, and nearly vomited. The crater titled and tried to spin away into darkness, but I gritted my teeth and willed it to still. After nearly a minute, it did. "Help me stand."

"Honey, no. You lost a lot of blood, and Fellow just got the bleeding stopped." Jane motioned to my arm.

I looked down at the ragged wound I'd carved and saw that it was tightly wrapped in scraps of clothing and bound with pieces of intertwined vines that I recognized at once.

"This is part of your arm," I said.

Fellow nodded. "It will hold temporarily, until it dries out and loosens. Then we must find another way to bind the cut."

"Help me stand," I repeated.

Fellow glanced at Jane, who sighed and dipped her head once. With their help, I regained my feet and battled another dizzying bout of vertigo. When it receded, I looked around.

The crater was barren except for a few gathering puddles in its lowest cracks and divots. No organs or muscle remained, and only a scorched outline marked the place where the thing that had been Ellius had expired. I tried to get my bearings, and turned slowly, searching.

Kotis lay where he had fallen.

I stumbled the few yards to him, Fellow gripping my right bicep while Jane held my left hand. I sank to my knees at his side and felt warmth soak into my pants. Blood pooled around him in a dark corona. His skin, once a deep gray, looked sapped of life, and was as pale as the moon. The opening in his stomach was raw and glistened with blood and rainwater. His remaining hand pressed against his abdomen, even though it faced in the wrong direction. His face was stoic, eyes closed, brow smooth. I put a hand on his shoulder and felt cold, hardening skin.

Tears flooded my eyes. Swallowing, I tried to force them back, but it did no good. My head tipped forward to let them spill out. I cursed under my breath, hating Ellius, or what had hidden beneath his façade, so much I almost wished he were alive again just so I could kill him once more.

"Cryin' like a woman."

My head snapped up at the sound of the voice. Kotis's eyes were open a half inch, studying me.

"Kotis! You're alive!"

He smiled weakly. "Barely, mate, barely."

I sniffed and rubbed my eyes. "We're gonna get you out of here. You're going to be okay."

He shook his head, barely perceptible. "Not goin' anywhere, mate. My time's almost up."

My throat tightened and tried to cut off my words as I shook my head. "No, we're gonna help you."

Again the smile as he closed his eyes. "I wouldn't make it out of this shit bowl."

I heard a scratching sound and turned to see Scrim waddle past. One wing stuck out from his body like a folded playing card, and he limped each time his right foot came down. He stopped at the giant's side and tapped Kotis's arm gently one time with his beak.

Kotis opened one eye and smiled again. "Shit-feathers." Scrim clicked once and laid his head on Kotis's chest.

Fellow stooped beside me and put a wooden hand against Kotis's forehead.

Kotis smiled briefly. "Didn't know what we were gettin' ourselves into, huh, mate?"

"No, I guess not," Fellow said.

"It worked out good though, we made it." Kotis opened his eyes and squinted at me. "How did you do it? How did you know?"

"You both showed me," I said, motioning to the blood on the ground. "When you stepped in to save me, your blood destroyed the tissue where it fell. Sacrifice, it's the opposite of evil. I figured if what he said about my blood being powerful was true, it would have an even greater effect."

Kotis coughed, and grimaced as blood speckled his lips. "You were right." His voice sounded weaker and distant. He must have heard it himself, because he shook his head and gritted his teeth against what longed to pull him away. His eyes were clear when he looked at us again. "Fellow, will you watch over Shila and Fin for me?"

"Of course, my friend. They will be safe, do not worry."

"And give Scrim to Fin, he's his problem now." Scrim clicked once, and Kotis chuckled as more blood bubbled to his lips.

His eyes searched for a moment, and then found me and focused. "You were right," he repeated, and I figured he was fading, perhaps recalling how I'd killed Ellius. But then he looked past me, his vision locked on something beyond my face. I thought he might have passed then, but he inhaled a stuttering breath. "They were there ... the whole time."

I lifted my head and followed his line of sight. There were stars in the sky.

I hadn't noticed until then that the rain had stopped completely. A hole in the storm hung above us. The sun was still blotted out on all sides, but the view within the break was breathtaking. A billion points of flickering light dotted the ashen sky. They coated it in a shimmering blanket that seemed to move like some cosmic tide. I held my breath and gazed up at stars that I'd never seen before, and wondered what their names were. Fellow's hand gripped my arm gently, and I looked back down.

Kotis's eyes were closed. He was gone.

CHAPTER ELEVEN

GOODBYES

We walked. For days we retraced the steps I'd taken. At first I was apprehensive, but then I noticed that there was an absence other than Kotis. It was the lack of dread. For nearly a week I'd been in constant fear, pushed to thresholds in my mind, sick with worry about a family I thought I would never see again. But now they were by my side. What would come would come, and we would meet it together.

Fellow carried Scrim, who still wasn't able to fly but seemed to improve as the days wore on. His wing gradually straightened, until it looked almost normal. But his eyes had changed, and it wasn't until I looked at them closely that I realized the gold was gone from them. Perhaps it would return someday, the passage of time healing whatever pain resided within his heart just as it did his wing.

We made our way over the landmarks of my journey. There was the house of mirrors in the distance, the teeth of Lonos, and the deep river with its water barely discernable nearly a mile beneath the bridge. We rested always with a fire, and Fellow found us as much food as we could eat within the nearby woods. Jack and Sara were quiet and withdrawn for a full day before their personalities began to come back, their smiles shafts of sunlight breaking through heavy clouds.

Jane and I made love one evening when everyone else had fallen asleep. We went far enough away so our furtive sounds wouldn't wake anyone in the group. It was tender and longing in a way I'd never felt before. The passion of our intertwining rigid and soft at the same time. Jane wept when it was through, and I held her, knowing the exaltation that gripped her because it did me as well. It was a rejoining that might have never occurred, and held the power of frantic love that wished never to be separated again.

The bone field was empty when we trudged through, the house silent and still. The trepidation at seeing the path clear of Ellius's roots that had blocked it vanished when we strode from the other side unharmed. I realized then that Ellius's death had done something, if only temporary, to the land. It was as if everything evil had fled from the expended power in fear or wonder, and I was thankful for the lack of hindrances. I mentioned my theory to Fellow, and he nodded.

"They'll come back, they always do," he said, and I knew he was right.

When we reached the Field of Lies, it was quiet. Its foggy interior still held the ominous presence, but nothing approached us. Ignoring Jane's proclamations that she could help, I carried both the kids until we reached the other side.

A warm buzzing grew in the base of my stomach as we came into view of the clearing in the hollow. It felt like years had passed since the day we had left, and the concern that hung in the back of my mind vanished the moment I spied the decrepit roller coaster.

"Cool!" Jack exclaimed, and ran ahead, with Sara a few paces behind. They stopped a short distance from the ride and looked back over their shoulders.

Their spirits were resilient, and I knew then that they would recover faster than Jane or I ever would, at least on the surface. The realm had left a mark on all of us, and I worried that at some time in the future Jack or Sara would begin to show how it had affected them. Would they have nightmares? I was sure of it. Would they have unconscious fears spring like well water from time to time? I guessed they might. Would they survive and live the lives I hoped they would? I had to believe it.

"This is it, huh?" Jane asked, lacing her fingers in mine.

"Yeah, this is how I got here. I think it was less frightening than how you came."

She squeezed my hand. "We're going home, Michael."

"I know."

We stopped a few feet behind the kids, and I turned to Fellow and Scrim. Scrim sat serenely on Fellow's shoulder, his now-dark eyes half lidded. I stepped up to them and put out a hand. Scrim bowed and nibbled at my fingers, and I brushed his head.

"Thank you. You helped save us all," I said. Scrim squawked once, affectionately pinched my fingers with his beak, and looked away.

"Michael," Fellow said. His face was soft but brightened by the small smile that graced it.

"My friend," I said, stepping close and hugging him. He returned the embrace with his remaining arm around my back.

"Take good care of your family, and may we never meet again."

I held him at arm's length and blinked back the moisture gathering in my eyes. "I'll see you again someday, in some other place far from here. He'll be waiting for us."

Fellow smiled and nodded. "Yes, he will."

I turned away before I broke down completely, and gathered up Jane's hand again. "Are you ready, kids?" I asked.

"Yeah!" they exclaimed in unison, and climbed into one of the dilapidated seats. Dust swirled into the afternoon air as they settled, and I pulled the bar down over their laps.

"Keep your hands inside the car at all times." They both giggled, music to my ears. "After you, honey," I said, gesturing to the car behind Sara and Jack. Jane stepped past me, holding my hand as she climbed in.

The moment she sat down, the air tightened around us. It was a subtle shift, like a summer day turning humid before a storm, but I noticed it. I looked ahead of the coaster and saw the tracks shining through the overgrown grass, and then the dirt that covered them sifted away in two furrows. The hill the tracks led into first vibrated, then shimmered as the dead grass and leaves twisted, becoming insubstantial. The hill's center faded, and darkness ate at its middle as the tunnel opened. The cars trembled and quaked like a jet engine powering up. I threw a last look over my shoulder at Fellow and Scrim before climbing aboard to take my seat beside my wife.

Everything stopped.

The hill became solid, and the cars halted their movement. Confused, I stood and gazed past the lead car, seeing that grass and leaves covering the tracks as before. It seemed that everything had reverted to its former state. I scrunched up my brow and turned to Fellow.

"What's going—" I stopped in mid-sentence.

Fellow was crestfallen, and his mouth hung open a little. He stared at the coaster, as if it were saying something to him that only he could hear. His jaw slowly closed, and he looked up at me, his gaze sending a spike of panic through my guts.

"What?" I asked.

"Michael, I'm sorry," he began and stepped closer.

"What's wrong?" Jane asked.

Fellow said something so quiet I couldn't hear it.

My voice rose in volume from anger and helplessness, but I didn't attempt to control it. "What did you say?" I asked, hoping that I hadn't heard him right.

"Only blood can take blood out," he said loud enough for me to hear.

The words buffeted my mind like bombs, spraying the poisonous gas of their meaning and enveloping my senses. My jaw trembled, and I felt my grip slide as I sat down, unable to hold myself up.

Jane grabbed my shoulder, pulled me so that I faced her. "What? What does he mean?" Her face was as panicked as I felt.

I shook my head, not at her but at what Fellow said. I turned to him and saw the same forlorn look that I knew graced my own features.

"But how did you and ..." I said.

"His power," Fellow said. "I didn't know what he was then. His power allowed us to travel together."

"Dad, what's wrong? Why are you crying?" Sara asked. She and Jack shifted in their seats so that just their eyes peeked over the back of their car.

I swallowed, and felt my soul tear just a little. "I'm okay," I managed, and looked at Fellow again. "Is there any other way?"

He paused, searching the ground as though the answer lay at his feet. "Besides a vent, nothing that I know of. And they are constantly moving."

"What are you talking about?" Jane said.

"I can't come back with you," I said.

"What? What do you mean, Michael?"

I turned and fully looked her in the eyes. "It won't take you guys back with me onboard. Only blood can take blood back, and since we're not related, it won't move."

She shook her head. "No, no, that's not right. You are coming home with us. We're not leaving without you."

"You have to," I said, even though every fiber of my being resisted. "You have to go and take the kids home."

"No, we'll stay here if you can't go. We'll stay here and live together."

I reached out and put my hand on her cheek. "They can't stay here, and you know it. I won't risk you all living here. The danger is too much. We were lucky this time, this one time. I won't endanger you or them. That's not what I came here for."

Jane made as if to slap my hand away from her face, but instead she grasped it and squeezed, tears spilling from her eyes. Her head tilted, and I knew that she understood. I felt something crumple inside of me, and I leaned close to her, our foreheads touching. The air from her mouth and nose brushed my face. Memories of us sleeping almost the same way came to me—our bed warm around us, breathing each other's air, so close we felt conjoined. Without the other, a raw wound would open, an amputation would occur. But it would heal ... enough to survive.

"I love you so much. Remember us. I'll look for a way to come through. I won't stop searching until I find it."

My breath shuddered, and my vision swam with tears. I felt her hand on my neck, pulling me forward. I kissed my wife for the last time. I poured every ounce of love I had for her into the meeting of our lips, and she did the same.

Our kiss ended after what seemed like an eternity and a heartbeat, and we pulled away. I stood and stepped down from the car, but kept my hand on its side. The coaster remained motionless as I walked to where my children sat. Their eyes stared up at me, searching my face for the reassurance they expected and needed. I smiled and wiped my eyes.

"Daddy, why are you crying?" Jack asked.

"Because I can't go with you guys on this trip, I have to wait for the next one."

Sara sat bolt upright, and I knew she was old enough to see through my subterfuge. "No, Dad. You have to come with us. This place is creepy."

I swallowed back an upsurge of grief and tried to keep my voice steady. "I know, and I want to come, but I have to wait just a little longer. The ride won't move while I'm on it. I must be too heavy." Jack's brow crinkled, but the joke made him smile just a little. Sara didn't falter.

"No, Dad, you have to get in. Try again, it'll move, I promise." She began to cry, and I reached out to wipe the tears away.

"I want you both to know I love you very much. You're the best things to ever happen to me. I'm so proud of how brave you both are." I steeled myself and called upon the cold place inside me that every person possesses for the moment they need it. "I want you to look after your mom for me for a while, just until I get back, okay?" Their heads nodded, and I opened my right arm wide to accommodate them both as they crowded against me. Their warm bodies and tears soaked into me. I savored the moment, committed it to memory, and cried into their soft hair. When I pried my arm away from them, it was the hardest thing I'd ever done in my life.

I let go.

The coaster came to life at once. The tracks shrugged themselves from the soil, and a humming filled the air. My throat was all but closed and refused any more words, so I just put up one hand and waved to them. Jane leaned toward me, and after a moment so did the kids. My legs moved of their own volition, and then I was holding their hands, Jane's in my left and both Sara's and Jack's in my right.

The coaster began to move. I walked with it as it picked up speed. Smells came to me: fried food, cotton candy, the heavy scent of animals. They drifted from the mouth of the tunnel—the fair was running on the other side. I could hear the sounds of laughter and delighted yells, the clacking of rides as they spun around and around. Our world, our home, waited for them.

"I love you," Jane said.

"I love you all," I said, and ran with the cars, keeping their pace until the ground rose up and there was no more room. Our fingers slid away from one another, Jane crying, Sara holding Jack, and Jack waving.

Then they were gone.

CHAPTER TWELVE

WAITING

I waited. The hope that the coaster would return and that there would be some way for me to leave kept me at the clearing for days. It was a slim hope, but it was all I had. Fellow and Scrim waited with me. I urged Fellow to return home to his wife, but he insisted on staying, even when something so large passed by it shook the ground and tall trees were ground to splinters beneath its heels.

When I didn't sleep, I thought of my family, and when I slept, I dreamed of them. I selected memories that were pure and full of light, with no thoughts of despair or sadness tainting their colors. I didn't think about the days after their return home. I couldn't bear to think of them in our house without me, mourning my absence while I yearned only for their presence.

We left the little clearing upon waking one morning. I'd taken to calling these times mornings, but it was all relative. Time became insubstantial and surreal, an endless loop that was always the same with the rotating of the sun. We made our way along a trail that led through the thickest part of the forest surrounding the tracks. Fellow walked assuredly, his footsteps falling familiarly on ground he'd no doubt known all his life. As we traveled I could feel his excitement growing, and I'm ashamed to say I hated him a little for it. He was going home to his family in his own world, no matter how threatening or dangerous it might be. When we stopped to rest, I wondered if I'd made a mistake by not agreeing to what Jane suggested. I imagined our life in this evil place, and knew I'd made the right decision. Anything else would have been deluding concepts clouded by selfish reasoning.

The next day we reached Fellow's home. The forest around us became more dense and then abruptly opened into a wide swath of field. A modest home built of massive logs sat at its center, its thatched roof surrounding a stone chimney that sent up tendrils of smoke into the cool air. Fellow's wife met us at the doorway. She much resembled Fellow, as I predicted she might. The same stalks and wood lined her arms while her face was fair and smooth. Flowing vines the color of wet sand grew from her head and rolled down her back in waves. Fellow ran to her, and she threw herself into his chest. Scrim sat on my shoulder and covered his head with one wing when the couple kissed. After they'd celebrated their reunion, Fellow introduced me. His wife's name was Adrin, and although she welcomed me into their home, I could tell she harbored some resentment toward me for taking Fellow along on a quest that had almost stolen his life. Fellow's arm had healed and was already sprouting growth a few inches long. He assured me that it would grow back and be as good as new, even as Adrin scowled at me from the corner of the room.

We departed from the house the following day and threaded our way along another trail in the woods, this one twice the size of the one that brought us to the field. We headed in the direction of a mountain that I'd glimpsed in the distance the day before. It rose out of the ground in a formation of stone that towered above the forest and disappeared into the gray clouds that obscured its peak. I tried to guess at its size, but was dumbfounded as we neared its base, for it dwarfed any comparison I could bring to mind.

We arrived at a stone house late in the day, the shadow of the mountain covering us in a thick blanket of gloom. The house was made from bulky slabs of rock propped end to end, and covered with an overhang that had been hewed from the mountainside itself. A figure sat on the steps watching our approach, and when it stood and came to meet us, I had to stare for quite some time before my heart calmed.

In all respects Kotis's son was his copy. The jutting jaw was prominent, as were the wide shoulders. Even his dark eyes were set in the same way, leaving no room for mistaking who his father was. He frowned when he looked past us and did not see Kotis, his eyes questioning Fellow. Before Fellow could say a word, the door to the house opened and a husky woman came from within. Her skin was the same shade as Kotis's, and her dark hair was tied back tightly, revealing a short forehead. Her eyes were a deep green that reminded me of moss that grew on the shadiest part of a tree. They softened for a moment when she sought Kotis's form and saw nothing. Then they hardened into something like steel and met my own. Fellow began to speak, and his voice lulled me with the details of our journey. I shrank in the presence of such loss, realizing the vacancy that would inhabit the home. When Fellow finished by telling them about the edge of the expansive field where we'd buried him, there was a vacuum in the midst of us. I stepped forward, my brow broken and ten pounds of sorrow hanging from my neck. Scrim sat on my forearm, and I offered him to Fin, who stood, straight backed, beside his mother, with tears shining on the surface of his eyes. I waited for them to spill over, but none did. He was his father's son.

Fin held out his arm, and Scrim made the small leap between us before nipping at my hand once. I waited, my arms at my sides, and finally Shila came forward, her height matching my own.

"You took him from us," she said after a pause. I nodded, unwilling to break her stare. "And your family is safe?"

"Yes," I rasped.

She lifted her chin once, and then dropped it slowly. "But you are here, cursed without them." The silence stretched, and then broke as she spoke once more before turning away. "Then there is no greater loss I can inflict on you."

Fin watched me for several seconds before his mother beckoned him to follow, his face a war of emotions. He hadn't mastered them yet, but he would. I knew he would.

When the door closed behind them, Fellow and I turned away to follow the winding road down into the trees draped in the mountain's shade.

So as I write this, five years have passed. Five long years. Five years without the sight of them, the sounds of their voices, their touch.

For two and a half years I searched for a vent tirelessly. I traveled farther and longer than any human before me, and perhaps even more than some of the creatures that call this place home. I saw things unnamable and atrocities unspeakable as well as sights of dark beauty, alien to anything I knew before. My love for them kept me searching until, at last, I stumbled upon a vent.

It hung in the air over a desolate field of stone, its shimmering catching my eye immediately. I ran like I'd never run before to it, and saw my world on the other side. Trees as well as a road lined with cars came into view, and I pelted on, hope growing to an inferno that fueled my muscles and quickened my pace. An automated sign blinked a message that I barely had time to read before the edges of the opening stitched itself shut and became merely air.

That day I quit looking for a vent, and returned to the forest where Fellow and Adrin lived. By then there was a toddler wobbling around their house, his small wooden feet tapping on the floor as he explored the world around him.

Fellow helped me build a small cabin in a clearing not far from his own. When it was finished, I settled in and resigned myself to the thought of never leaving this place. For, you see, something had bothered me the day that my family vanished through the tunnel and back into our world. It was the fair. Its presence didn't make any sense. I had left our home in early June, and two weeks passed before Jane and the kids returned. The county fair that visited our town each year didn't open until late August. More than two months went by while we were here. I ignored this fact like an irritating fly, batting it away whenever it floated to the forefront of my mind while I searched for a vent. Only when I saw the sign through the portal did I finally give in to the doubts that plagued me. I can still see the words blinking with their jubilant letters of neon and high-wattage LEDs.

It read, *Good luck, Saints! Bring home the rings in 2093!*

Eighty years had passed in my absence. I tried to tell myself that it was a joke, a malfunction of the sign. But whenever I did, the smells and sounds of the fair would return to me, forcing away the lies I told myself with the unyielding truth. It seems that Ellius was right, time here does move differently than on Earth. It may not be exponential, but it is something like it. In the hours that I lay awake when I should be sleeping, I wonder what year it is there. Five years here, a hundred on Earth? Two hundred? But those wanderings of the imagination are dangerous, and lead to other thoughts, thoughts of darkness and brooding contemplation of escapes not from this world but from everything.

Most days I spend beside my cabin in a chair I built, listening to the constant wind whistling tunelessly through the branches. I think about them then. I envision their lives, the story of how they grew. I see Sara walking down an aisle flanked by rows of watching eyes, all of them standing as she passes by. Murmurs of how beautiful she looks in the swishing white fabric, her steps in time to music I can still hear. I can feel her arm in mine, almost like her tiny form when she was hours old, held in the crook of my elbow. And just as I reluctantly gave her away to a waiting nurse, she leaves me with shared tears to join the man waiting for her at the altar. Yes, I can see it.

I see Jack pushing a small boy who has hair that matches his own on a swing set, the sun laying golden layers of light on them both. Jack pushes, his hand always there when the boy comes back, always guiding, always helping. I feel the boy's warm skin beneath his thin T-shirt as I hug him, and laugh as Jack says something funny. We both laugh, my grandson and I, and I wonder what his name is.

I see Jane, her hands around a cup of steaming tea in her favorite mug, the one with the flowers and cardinals on it. She's older, as am I, but still beautiful. There are wisps of gray in her hair that speak of struggles that years can't inflict, and I ache to hold her hand, to feel her face against mine. To breathe her air. I used to make her tea, and I see myself doing it again, sorry that I've been away so long. Her smile flashes and I sit down beside her to while away the afternoon together in a glow broken only by kisses and tender words.

Deep down inside I realize what the sign I saw means. I know that eighty years is a lifetime, but I'm only concerned with three lives. I hope the years were good to them. I hope they had happiness and laughter. I hope that Jane found someone to love, someone who loved her back and tried to make things better. Of course I don't know, because the world is an ocean and has its own way. We are just small grains of sand, moved with the tide of time, unable to stop its passage, and in the worst cases unaware of it.

So I wait. I wait for time to pull me along at its own pace. I wait for the day when death takes my hand and leads me away to somewhere else, and I think about that too. Because I know that if this place is evil, and it is, there is another place that is good, and that they're waiting for me there. I see it sometimes when I dream, fields of emerald and skies cobalt. Sugared winds and warm seas that don't end at a horizon, but go on forever in endless waves of gentle peace. I imagine that time passes quickly there, and perhaps it is only a long afternoon to them until we're reunited.

But until that day comes, I will wait, because sometimes that's all a man can do.

AUTHOR'S NOTE

Thanks again for reading, I really hope you enjoyed the journey. I normally write a little note at the end of my books to give some insight as to where the story came from, so here we go.

EverFall came from a walk my family and I went on around our neighborhood last fall. I started looking at the bare trees and the dead leaves on the ground, and smelled the smells of fall we all know so well. The idea hit me as we walked, and when I got home I jotted down some notes, knowing full well that this would be my next novel. *EverFall* was a different project for me, in that I had never written a dark story set in a fantastic world. Technically *EverFall* is in the category of dark fantasy, but as always, I had to get enough horror in there to satisfy my muse. It was definitely an emotional project, in the sense that losing those closest to you is something that scares me a lot. In fact, it scares me more than I want to get into here. So as I wrote *EverFall*, I had to go to some dark places, and ultimately I came to the conclusion that sacrifice is the ultimate sign of love. Though the story ended sadly, I have a profound respect for Michael, as he sits and waits for death to lead him to his family.

Once again, dear Reader, I thank you from the bottom of my heart. You make the trips we take so much fun. I hope you'll keep coming back to take more rides, because I don't think I'll ever get tired of this.

EXCERPT FROM *SINGULARITY*

CHAPTER 2

The guard house was empty.

Sullivan cupped his hands to the glass and looked into the small space, then reached out and pressed the red button mounted beside a battered-looking speaker. The button elicited no response, and he wondered how long they would have to wait outside in the rain before someone noticed them standing here. He pressed the button again, beginning to lose his patience, and squinted through the rain at the front doors, willing one of them to open.

"This sucks," Stevens said, as he turned in a slow circle, taking in their surroundings.

Sullivan muttered his agreement and punched the button again. "And what's up with the sheriff not coming to the crime scene? I know he's been up all night, but come on. You don't just toss this kind of shit off to someone else."

Barry shook his head, equally agitated. "Let's just get up there and take a look at the dead guy and get out of the weather. I'm getting fucking soaked through this plastic."

Sullivan was about to press the button a fourth time when both men heard a sound and looked up to see a covered Rhino speeding toward the gate; a lone occupant sat in the driver's seat. The agents watched as the figure tapped in a code on a control box next to the gate and the chainlink began to roll to the side. After a few seconds, the ATV sped down to them. Once he arrived, the driver stared at them from beneath the plastic canopy.

The man looked to be in his early thirties and had narrowed eyes, which Sullivan doubted had ever fully opened, and a large nose, which sat obtrusively on his thin face. He wore a dark blue guard uniform that consisted of a button-up long-sleeve shirt, matching cargo pants, and a baseball hat that had the words *SINGLETON PENITENTIARY* outlined in bold white letters.

Sullivan stepped forward and offered the man his hand. "Hi. Special Agent Sullivan Shale, and this is Senior Special Agent Barry Stevens." The man looked down at Sullivan's hand for a moment before returning his narrow stare back to the agent's face.

"Everett Mooring. Your people are already in the cell."

Sullivan dropped his outstretched hand when he realized that there would be no reciprocation, and glanced over his shoulder at Stevens. Barry rubbed his forehead, and then walked around Sullivan, sitting down in the rear seat of the vehicle. Sullivan followed suit and sat next to Mooring.

The prison guard spun the Rhino around and accelerated up the wet drive toward the still-open gate. Sullivan studied the prison's exterior again. The dull brick walls were reminiscent of several schoolhouses he attended as a child. A small but intricate arch of stone sat atop the building just above the entrance, the prison's name carved deeply into the rock. Two paved pathways led to either side of the building. To the left sat a forlorn basketball court, its hoops devoid of nets and its floor covered with standing water. The path to the right disappeared into a thick grove of trees. Mooring pulled the Rhino under the awning that covered the entrance of the building and stopped a few feet from the doors.

Without bothering to look at either agent, he said, "The desk attendant will direct you to your friends."

Sullivan saw Stevens lick his lips and then begin to say something, but Sullivan cut the other man's words off before they began. "Thank you, Officer Mooring."

Without a glance back, Sullivan stood from the vehicle and relished the feeling of being out of the insistent patter of rain. He heard Barry exit the Rhino, and then watched as Mooring drove from under the awning and disappeared around the side of the building.

"What a fucking ass," Barry said. "I'll have to send a special thanks to Hacking for this one."

Sullivan turned and looked at him from beneath his still-dripping hood. "That guy's not just an ass. He's not happy we're here."

Stevens nodded in agreement, and both agents turned to the swinging double doors and made their way inside the prison.

The lobby wasn't very deep, but it ran the width of the building, and with a ceiling that opened into the second story, it gave the impression of a large space. To the left a door led off into an area encased in reinforced Plexiglas, with several rooms containing simple desks and chairs. To the right was an unmarked oak door with a brass handle. A nameplate sat at eye level, but Sullivan was too far away to read the name etched there. A wooden desk shaped like the prow of a ship sat directly in front of the two agents, and their wet footsteps clacked and echoed off the poly-coated concrete floor and slate walls as they approached it.

A heavyset black woman in a uniform that matched Mooring's sat behind the desk typing on an aged keyboard, and only looked up from the screen before her when Sullivan placed his hand upon the desk and leaned forward.

"Yes?" she said, looking surprised to see them standing there.

"Special Agents Shale and Stevens from the BCA. We're looking for the rest of our crime-scene team."

"Identification?" she asked. Sullivan and Barry both pulled out their wallets and opened them to their photo cards that confirmed who they were. The woman studied both IDs, then nodded and turned in her seat. "See that door there?" she said, pointing to a solid steel door set into the back wall of the room. "I'll buzz you through in a moment. An officer is positioned on the other side. He'll direct you to the rest of your team."

"Thank you," Sullivan said before stepping around the desk and heading for the door. A moment later a loud buzzing sound filled the lobby and Sullivan grasped the cold handle and pulled the heavy door open with a resounding clack.

Behind the steel door the prison expanded into an impressive two-story block of cells that ran away from the men in an almost illusionary impression of infinity. Two steel staircases shot up from the floor on opposite sides of the enormous room and ended on the second level. Doorway after doorway encased with chunky bars of iron lined both the first and second stories. The white paint that covered the cells no longer remained intact and chunks were missing here and there, giving the rows a speckled, shabby look. Several sets of disembodied hands could be seen poking out from the mouths of the cells, but other than the sound of the door slamming solidly shut behind them, the holding area was silent.

A young prison officer sat behind a wooden desk to their immediate left, and he shot up out of his seat as the two agents stepped through the doorway.

"Are you BCA agents?" the officer asked in a voice that cracked with what could have been something bordering on panic.

Sullivan nodded and opened his billfold again, revealing his ID. "Special Agent Shale, and this is—"

The young prison guard moved around the desk and began walking down the long first-floor corridor, his footsteps snapping like gunshots off the concrete. Sullivan looked at Stevens, and the other man merely shrugged.

"You have a more intimidating name anyway," Barry said and brushed past Sullivan, with a smirk on his face.

The prison stretched out before them like an indoor runway. Sullivan looked back and forth from one side of the walkway to the other. Inmates of all ethnicities, wearing orange jumpsuits, stared back at him. Most sat on their beds and their heads turned as the guard and two agents passed by—new scenery in an otherwise drab and routine-enforced world. A few prisoners stood at the doors to their cells, but their eyes did not meet Sullivan's as he looked at them. Instead, they stared either at the floor or to the side, the direction in which the group headed.

As they walked, Sullivan realized that the prison's shape was that of a T. At the very end of the corridor, the building shot outward in either direction and ended in a solid brick wall. Two more staircases accessed the upper level of the rear wall, and he could see a few more sets of eyes peering out at him from both the first and second floors. Their footsteps were the loudest noise in the airy space, and soon Sullivan realized why he felt the edges of unease grating against him: there were no yells of anger or defiance from the cells. No catcalls or agitated mutterings filtered out to them.

The prisoners were quiet.

Sullivan looked around again, searching for a jeering face or a middle finger being raised behind the bars, but saw only darkness and silhouettes.

The guard swung left at the far end of the vaulted hall and proceeded toward a set of steps that turned 180 degrees on a wide landing and descended into an eerie yellow glow. Stevens threw a look over his shoulder and Sullivan followed.

The stairway dropped down two levels and emptied out into a narrow passage, the floor they walked on earlier closing over their heads like a cave. The right side of the hall was poured concrete, unpainted and stained from things Sullivan didn't want to guess at. The left held five doors made of solid steel and resembled the entry into the holding area. All of the doors were shut tight and had small portholes at head height roughly the size of a softball and reinforced with wire mesh. A thin slot only a few inches wide and a foot long had been cut in the middle of each door. The entire area felt like being in a submarine—the bolted bulkheads, the painted doors, and the close ceiling.

Sullivan gazed past the shoulders of Stevens and the guard. The last door in the line was wide-open. Sour light cast a pale urine-colored wedge onto the floor of the hall. He could see one of the forensic specialists standing outside the swath of the door. Sullivan recognized the man as Don Anderson, a veteran and the technical head of the crime-scene unit. Unshakeable, Don was easily the most calm and collected man on the team. At the moment he had both hands shoved deeply into the wide pockets of the white smock over his street clothes; elastic booties encased both of his feet. His graying and partially bald head drooped toward his chest.

The guard leading them suddenly stopped several yards from the open doorway and leaned back against the wall opposite the doors. Barry and Sullivan stopped before him and eyed the young officer, who seemed to want nothing more than to melt into the surface behind him.

"Are you okay?" Stevens asked the guard.

The young man nodded tightly and Sullivan saw his jaw clench, the muscles beneath his cheek going taunt. "I'm going to go back up. If you need me, I'll be at my desk."

The guard tried to slip by Sullivan, but he reached out and snagged the younger man's uniformed wrist, stopping him in his tracks.

Sullivan leaned closer. "Are you the one that found the victim?"

The guard's eyelids fluttered, and then he nodded in a jerky motion, his head snapping up and down.

"Are you okay?" Sullivan repeated Stevens's inquiry, studying the pale unlined face of the officer.

The man roughly pulled his sleeve out of Sullivan's grasp, and without looking back, hurried away from the two agents and disappeared back up the stairway.

Sullivan glanced at Stevens. "Shaken up."

"Hacking said he's fresh here. Probably the first body the poor kid ever saw," Barry said.

Anderson turned toward the agents as they approached, and his eyebrows rose in surprise at the sight of Sullivan alongside Barry. "Wow, that's not much of a mandatory leave," the forensic specialist said.

Sullivan shrugged. "I guess Hacking just loves me that much." Don huffed laughter as both men stepped into the mouth of the doorway.

Sullivan was about to ask what had been done so far, when he looked into the interior of the cell and blanched.

The room was small, about half the size of the other cells on the level above them. A single incandescent bulb jutted from the ceiling, encased in a steel cover that leaked light through the gaps. A bed extended from the left wall, just wide enough for a man to lie on. A stainless toilet-and-sink combo sat against the far wall.

Blood. Everywhere.

Gore splashed each wall like a paint mixer had exploded within the room. Chunks of what could only be flesh and bone were speckled here and there among the stains. Something dark and misshapen protruded from a small heating-cooling vent in the floor. Two other members of the forensics team stood in the only bare patches of concrete within the room. Their eyes found Sullivan's, and he registered the same thing he felt at the moment—revulsion. The room smelled like a slaughterhouse, coppery with a hint of decay at the edges.

"What—in—the—fuck?" Barry said in a low voice.

Anderson shuffled closer to the doorway and leaned into the threshold. "Yeah, my sentiments exactly. We were just beginning our layout, but I'll tell you what we've got so far, and this is mainly from the file we were given by the sheriff when we arrived. Victim is male, Mexican descent, age thirty-four. As you can see, there's not much left of the body."

"Not much left?" Sullivan asked as he stepped into the doorway, keeping the tips of his shoes a few inches away from the nearest pool of blood. "I don't see anything."

Anderson motioned the closest forensic tech out of the room, and pointed to the spot he'd been standing in. "Step in there and look at the vent."

Sullivan moved carefully over a stream of blood and took the vacated position on the island of bare concrete. He bent at the knees, drawing closer to the vent in the corner of the room. It was three to four inches in diameter and circular in shape. A thick grate cover matching the vent's width sat on the floor; the headless bolts securing it were snapped in the middle and lay strewn in the blood.

The dark shape growing from the vent's mouth looked like a squashed mushroom. The top was flattened and broken in places, and its sides were crushed and disappeared into the floor. It took Sullivan a moment to realize the dark top of the object had strands that were matted together, giving the illusion of a solid piece.

Hair. He was looking at the top of a head.

Sullivan sucked in a breath and leaned back, horrified at the state of the remains. Slowly, mangled features began to take shape on the decapitated head. A flattened nose here, two smashed orbital sockets there, fractured bone stained black with blood poking through flayed cheeks.

Sullivan pivoted on the dry spot and looked at Anderson and Stevens, who still stood in the doorway. "They jammed his fucking head into the air vent?"

Don nodded. "It appears so. Severe blunt-force trauma to the top of the skull. The jaw was fractured as it was forced into the vent, but it looks like the zygomatic bones were too bulky, along with the rest of the skull's rigid structure, to be pushed farther in."

Sullivan turned back to look at what was left of Victor Alvarez as he heard Barry curse under his breath. He ran through what he was looking at again, beginning the process of categorizing and committing the facts to memory. Head cut off, shoved chin-first into the narrow vent. Skull crushed.

Skull crushed, blood arcing out in a halo around her body.

Sullivan closed his eyes and shook his head. He blinked as the room swayed and then steadied. Not now. He had too much to think about. Not now.

"So where is the rest of him?" Sullivan heard Barry ask behind him. Sullivan stood and faced the two men in the entry.

Anderson rubbed his balding pate. "Off the top of my head?"

"That's not funny," Barry said, grimacing at the forensic specialist. Sullivan smiled grimly.

"I would say whoever did this dismembered the victim systematically, then shoved the pieces down the vent. I guess we'll know for sure once we extract the remains from the floor and see for ourselves," Anderson said.

Sullivan turned in a circle and extended his arm, pointing at a large splash of blood on the wall above the bed. "Am I wrong, or does it look like he was bashed into the walls?"

"It appears so. I think that's the contact point for the first blow," Anderson said, motioning to the spot Sullivan pointed out. "Then the wall behind you, and then perhaps off the floor several times."

"So you're saying he was beaten to death against the walls? How strong would you have to be to do something like that?" Barry asked.

"Or, how many guys would you need?" Sullivan said.

"We won't know for sure until we examine the tissue samples and extrapolate velocity, angle, that sort of thing," Anderson replied. "We also might come up with an idea of a murder weapon that's not currently obvious."

"Were you the first ones in, or was it open before you got here?" Sullivan asked.

"From what the sheriff said, he took one look through the window and called the office, he wanted nothing to do with this. Other than him, no one's said they went in before us," Don replied.

Sullivan looked down at the remains poking from the vent. "Why would they shove him down the vent in the first place? Why not just beat him to death and leave him here?"

Both Anderson and Barry shrugged and stared at the blood coated floor.

Footsteps echoed down the hallway outside of the room, and Sullivan stepped out of the cell and let the technician return to his position.

Two men strode down the corridor toward the group. The man in the lead wore a charcoal suit and appeared to be in his late fifties or early sixties. He was well over six feet tall and wisp thin. Feathery gray hair that might have been blonde at one time was combed neatly to one side of the man's head. His face was slightly horse-like, with large but even teeth that already were beginning to poke from beneath a pair of narrow lips in a polite smile. The second man, who strode a few paces behind, was a glowering Everett Mooring.

The older man extended a hand to Stevens as he neared, the smile spreading warmly across his features. "Agents Stevens and Shale, I presume?" the man said.

Barry shook the man's hand. "Yes, sir. I'm Barry Stevens, and this is Sullivan Shale and our forensic pathologist, Don Anderson."

"David Andrews, I'm the warden. I believe you've already met my chief officer?" Andrews said, motioning over his shoulder at the impassive guard behind him.

"He was kind enough to give us a lift earlier this morning," Sullivan said congenially, hoping to crack Mooring's stony façade. The guard only stared at him as if he were part of the wall.

The warden nodded and smiled again. "Yes, I'm sorry that you've been called here on such grim circumstances, and with the current uncooperative weather conditions. I was just telling Everett that a possible evacuation might be needed if the rain doesn't let up soon."

Silence fell over the group of men and Sullivan glanced at Barry before addressing the warden. "We were hoping we could have a word with you. Go over some basic information before we begin the investigation?"

The warden closed his eyes and nodded. "Of course, gentlemen. Any help my staff and I can provide. We are at your service."

"Thank you," Barry said, and turned back to Anderson, who placed a set of safety glasses on his round face and began pulling on a pair of latex gloves. "Don, you'll let us know when you're done and if you find anything significant?"

"We'll be right here for a while," the team leader said.

The warden motioned to the stairs leading back up to the main holding area. "Follow me, gentlemen."

OTHER BOOKS BY JOE HART

Midnight Paths: A Collection of Dark Horror
Lineage
Singularity
The Edge of Life: A Short Horror Story
Outpost: A Short Horror Story

All interior artwork created by Wil E. Lee. See more of Wil's work on Twitter @NameBrandArtist

Made in United States
North Haven, CT
19 December 2021

13260273R00104